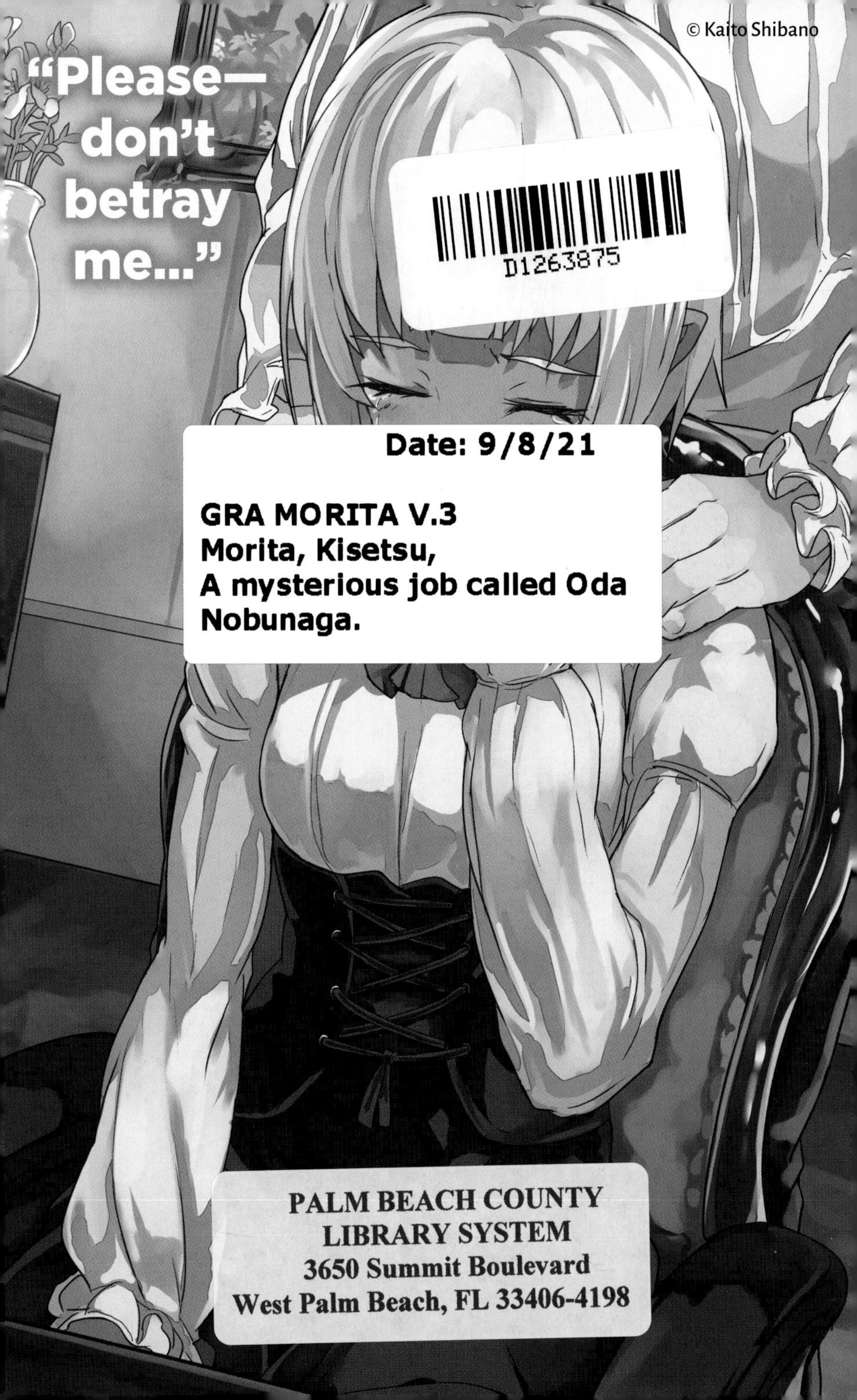
© Kaito Shibano
"Please—
don't
betray
me..."

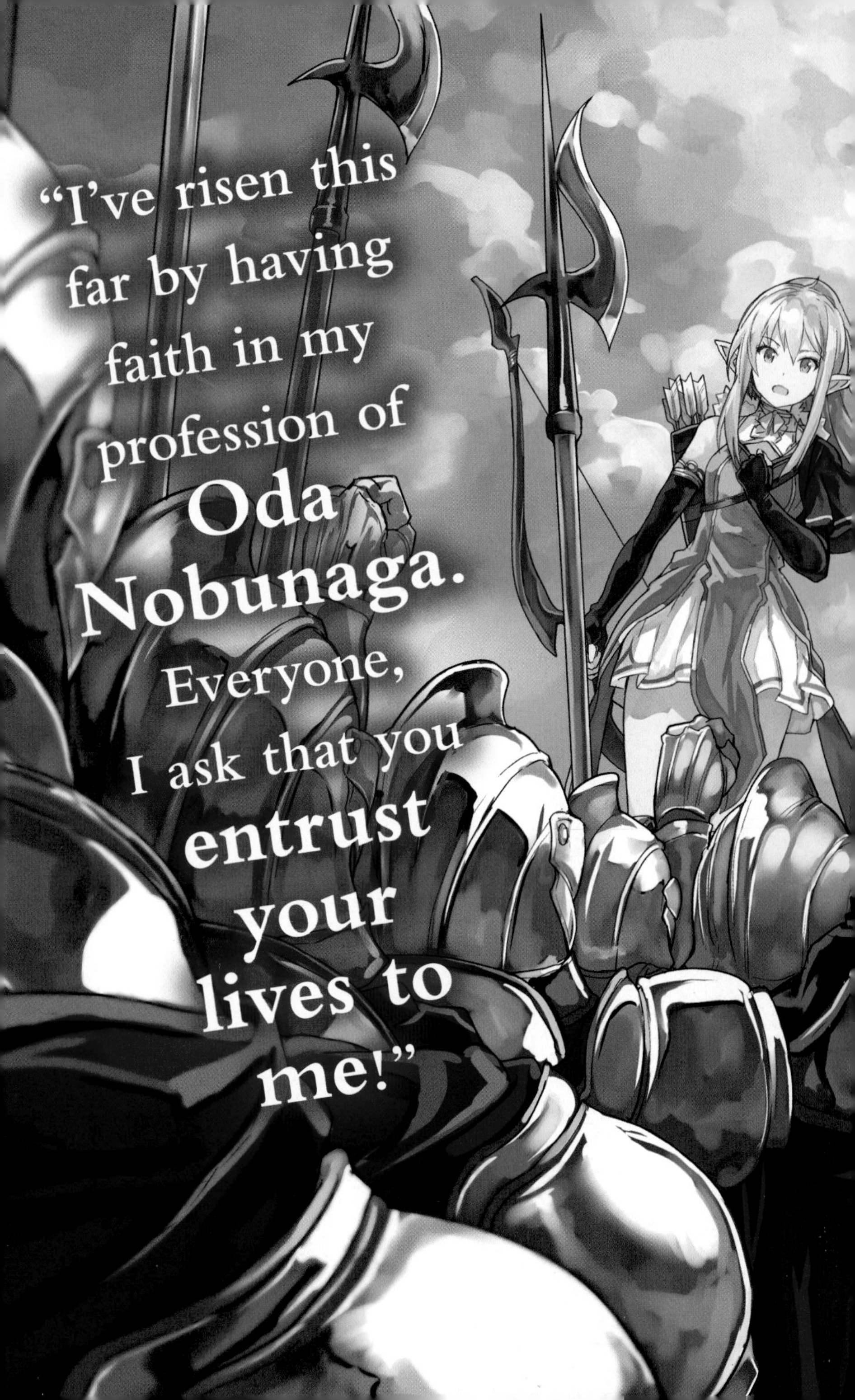
"I've risen this far by having faith in my profession of Oda Nobunaga. Everyone, I ask that you entrust your lives to me!"

© Kaito Shibano

"I received a revelation—that I would be blessed with a child today...
...A child descended from you and royalty."
© Kaito Shibano

A MYSTERIOUS JOB CALLED ODA NOBUNAGA

3

Kisetsu Morita

Illustration by Kaito Shibano

NEW YORK

A Mysterious Job Called
Oda Nobunaga, Vol. 3
Kisetsu Morita

Translation by Noboru Akimoto
Cover art by Kaito Shibano

ODA NOBUNAGA TOIU NAZONO SHOKUGYO GA MAHO KENSHI YORI CHEAT DATTANODE, OUKOKU WO TSUKURU KOTONI SHIMASHITA volume 3

Original Japanese edition published in 2018 by SB Creative Corp.

This English edition is published by arrangement with SB Creative Corp., Tokyo in care of Tuttle-Mori Agency, Inc., Tokyo.

Yen On
150 West 30th Street, 19th Floor
New York, NY 10001

Visit us at yenpress.com
facebook.com/yenpress
twitter.com/yenpress
yenpress.tumblr.com
instagram.com/yenpress

First Yen On Edition: April 2021

Yen On is an imprint of Yen Press, LLC.
The Yen On name and logo are trademarks of Yen Press, LLC.

Library of Congress Control Number: 2019942581

ISBNs: 978-1-9753-0560-4 (paperback)
978-1-9753-0561-1 (ebook)

10 9 8 7 6 5 4 3 2 1

LSC-C

Printed in the United States of America

A MYSTERIOUS JOB CALLED ODA NOBUNAGA

3

01 Misroux Prefecture
02 Machaal Prefecture
03 Brantaar Prefecture
04 Nagurry Prefecture
05 Siala Prefecture
06 Fordoneria Prefecture
07 Olbia Prefecture
08 Icht Prefecture
09 Melya Prefecture
10 Sinju Prefecture
11 Fortwest Prefecture
12 Fortsouth Prefecture
13 Royal Capital
14 Yargurtz Prefecture
15 Nargust Prefecture
16 Schweren Prefecture
17 Mixaffus Prefecture
18 Bilgund Prefecture
19 Orba Prefecture
20 Inner Doorn Prefecture
21 Central Doorn Prefecture
22 Doorn Prefecture
23 Samuur Prefecture
24 Sereya Prefecture
25 Mireya Prefecture
16
15
18
14
21
22
20
23
25
24
Great Isle Region

01
02
03
04
05
06
07
08
09
10
11
12
13
17
19
Complete Map of the
Kingdom of Therwil
© Kaito Shibano

A MYSTERIOUS JOB CALLED ODA NOBUNAGA

CHARACTER PROFILES

Alsrod Nayvil

Second son of the small Nayvil clan in Fordoneria Prefecture. After succeeding as clan head at the age of eighteen, he quickly expanded his territory and backed Hasse in conquering the Royal Capital, thereby seizing further authority as regent.

Illustration by Kaito Shibano

Oda Nobunaga

Mysterious entity and Alsrod's "profession," who often speaks to Alsrod. Is really Oda Nobunaga, a conqueror from another world.

Laviala Aweyu

Alsrod's half-elven childhood friend and lover. A well-rounded, good-natured young lady skilled in combat and strategy.

Seraphina Caltis

Daughter of Ayles Caltis and one of Alsrod's official wives. Has the highly rare profession of Saint.

Lumie

Younger sister of King Hasse and Alsrod's primary official wife.

Kelara Hilara

A military officer with the profession Akechi Mitsuhide. Alsrod was instantly charmed by her and made her one of his concubines.

Altia Nayvil

Alsrod's younger sister. Married to Brando Naaham, a minor lord of Olbia Prefecture.

Hasse

The current monarch of the Kingdom of Therwil, who recaptured the throne from his cousin with Alsrod's support. A mere figurehead under Alsrod's control.

Ayles Caltis

Ruthless leader of Brantaar Prefecture and ally of Alsrod. Feels threatened by Alsrod's rapid rise to power and stages a mutiny in response—however…

A MYSTERIOUS JOB CALLED ODA NOBUNAGA

CONTENTS

It was the day after I made an ally of Talsha Machaal, the Margrave of Machaal's younger sister.

I gathered my generals and notified them of the rebellion of Ayles Caltis of Brantaar Prefecture and Brando Naaham of Olbia Prefecture.

Ayles, the father of my wife Seraphina, and Brando, the husband of my little sister, Altia—in other words, my father-in-law and my brother-in-law—had betrayed me simultaneously. It was a truly unfortunate turn of events.

Nevertheless, hardly anyone expressed surprise. Everyone had known something like this would happen sooner or later.

"I'm still investigating the details, but there may be a fair number of lords who sided against us," I said. "Many of them must not have enjoyed being under my thumb."

This was a dire situation, even if I had expected it. All of my generals looked solemn—a single mistake could cost us our lives.

"What sort of strategy do you have in mind then, Lord Alsrod?" Laviala, my half-elf milk sister, was the first to ask me a question.

"Wait a second, I have to think."

Not so much think as discuss. *Oda Nobunaga, if you have a plan, let me hear it.*

——Indeed. Ayles Caltis will likely invade Fordoneria Prefecture's Nayvil County from Mineria. Capturing your homeland is one way

he can assert his side's superiority. Next, they will likely attack your stronghold, Maust Castle, so that you have nowhere to return.

And give the impression that I'm losing... My father-in-law Ayles would do a thing like that.

——Fortunately, however, our forces are stronger. The expedition to Machaal itself succeeded. Certainly, most people will consider it tactical relocation, not retreat. If nothing gets in your way, you have the strength to invade your enemies' main strongholds, and you left enough troops to execute a defense as well.

Yes—I entrusted Maust Castle to someone dependable for that very reason.

This war would be an offensive one, not a defensive one. It would be an operation to eradicate those who thought ill of my expanding power.

I looked over to my generals.

"Listen, everyone."

They all watched me with bated breath.

"This didn't exactly happen out of the blue. In fact, we've been waiting for this opportunity. Brando Naaham's faction, and especially Ayles Caltis, have been holding a grudge against me. Therefore, all the necessary preparations are already in order. The only difference now is the question of where to strike them."

This was all a prelude. The important part was to come.

"Let us return to Maust Castle with haste! If they take it, the entire realm will think Your Excellency has fallen!" yelled one general. Indeed, returning to my main stronghold would be the obvious choice.

However, and perhaps fortunately, I didn't need to go out of my way to play things by the book this time.

"I am not the least bit worried about Maust Castle," I replied. "The battle-hardened veteran Kivik is defending it, after all. That old dog's legs aren't as strong as they used to be, but he's just as good a leader as ever."

He might well have been excited that it was his turn to shine. He was probably even more thrilled that Fanneria's schemes had apparently caused betrayals in the castle vicinity as well. Kivik was the sort of man who couldn't get fired up if he knew he was going to win a battle.

The financial officer Fanneria must have been disgruntled that I'd favored other officials after taking the royal capital, even though I'd simply selected people who'd taken the exam, and many of them were outstanding individuals, such as Yanhaan. Compared to someone like her, who had been a merchant in the economic center that is the royal capital area, Fanneria was, I'm sorry to say, a provincial merchant, always one step behind.

"With a concubine from the Nistonia clan, I have bolstered my defensive position. The royal capital has a large enough garrison, too, so they're not in immediate danger. That means we can attack my father-in-law."

"Where do you intend to fight the enemy, Lord Alsrod? Will you go all the way to Ayles's capital in Mineria?"

Laviala was also wondering about that, naturally.

Laughing, I replied, "In Fordoneria's Nayvil County, where I was born and raised."

Judging by everyone's face, that was apparently quite the unexpected suggestion.

They voiced concerns, like "Why don't we head for the enemy's capital, then?" and "Wouldn't returning to Maust Castle be safer?"

"I know well the power of Ayles the Terrible," I explained confidently. "The enemy's stronghold will undoubtedly be formidable. Nayvil County, however, I know like the back of my hand. And I know it isn't well suited for defense. Nayvil Castle is no fortress. If the enemy takes it, they won't be able to stop our forces. Their seizure of it would be a dream come true."

"Wha...? But won't they ransack the castle...?"

"Nayvil may be my hometown, Laviala, but I also have Maust Castle and the royal capital. Even if the enemy burns the castle down, we can always rebuild."

This conflict was a clash between the old and the new.

If the old were to push us back now, that would be the end of me.

"I'm sure some will obstruct our return to Nayvil County, but I want you to crush all who do. Anyone who tries to cast their lot with the winning side is worth nothing!"

The regiment's spirits finally rose at my words.

One among them came directly before me, not listening to those nearby who tried to stop her.

It was Talsha, the younger sister of Machaal's Margrave Seitred.

"I would like to join this battle." Talsha stared at me with the same powerful eyes as when she'd faced me on the battlefield. "Worry not, for I have no intention of siding with the enemy."

"Very well. So what do you want if you win?"

Surely she was not so admirable as to say such a thing without wanting something. You could tell by looking at her face she was not so pure-hearted.

"I will take my brother's place as the Margrave of Machaal. That would be the best way to preserve my house."

My profession was laughing, saying, *"She really is Takeda Shingen. She's not satisfied unless she's exiling her own blood."* I also felt like laughing at this woman's display of spirit.

It would be boring if my generals weren't like this.

"Understood. I will lend you some dependable men. I expect great things from you."

"Of course."

"However, I have an important job for you before battle. I need you to determine if the Margrave of Machaal has indeed withdrawn his troops."

There was a risk the margrave would join the war because of Ayles and Brando's uprising. If I couldn't make sure he was incapable of pursuit, I couldn't advance.

Talsha nodded.

"Even if my brother attacks, should you lend me a thousand-strong rear guard, I'll defeat him."

◇

As we advanced the troops back the way we'd come, news continually came in, such as that Altia's husband, Brando Naaham, had approached Maust Castle and was in battle with our lords, and that the turncoat financial officer Fanneria was going around scheming to bolster the numbers on his side.

As far as the reports were concerned, at least, it seemed the enemy wasn't yet ready, either.

"If the enemy's rebellion fails, the existence of their clans will be in jeopardy, after all. Until the situation becomes clear, I think most lords will keep sitting on the fence," Kelara explained calmly as we made our way to the battlefield. "If this were a conflict between lords in times past, when betrayal was extremely commonplace, the enemy would typically be forgiven if they submitted. However, Your Excellency has not forgiven any betrayers. The lords must be afraid of that."

"Of course I haven't. I am only leading kingdom troops, not my personal ones. I will make any who draw a bow against His Majesty get what they deserve."

I had given a chance to surrender to those who had been my enemies from the beginning, but I never forgave allies who betrayed me.

I had thought there would be more resistance as we moved our troops onward, but Kelara must have been right about the fence-sitting, as most lords weren't simply friendly but tried to treat me graciously. It would be absolutely meaningless for them to do something careless here. They chose well.

Thanks to that, we were able to approach Nayvil County with almost no fighting. Maust Castle, under Kivik's command, was still holding strong, too.

The lord of Olbia Prefecture, Brando Naaham, must have originally wanted to fully suppress Olbia and then seize Maust Castle if he could. With so many resisting forces, however, he'd lost the chance as he struggled to handle them.

Or rather, he'd never had the chance to begin with. If an enemy is prepared for you, a surprise attack is worthless. Even if Brando didn't like me, he should never have joined a war he wasn't sure he could win.

Brando Naaham avoided Maust Castle and took a defensive position against me in northern Fordoneria Prefecture.

Such a position would prove problematic if he was attacked from behind, but since the indecisive lords were unable to attack, it didn't seem to be an issue.

Brando's greatest weakness must've been that he had so much ambition, as well as the power to back it up. He seemed to fancy himself something of a hero holding multiple prefectures.

However, if I created a new political order after becoming regent, he wouldn't be able to do away with the lords around him, who bore the same allegiance as he. As a tenacious young lord, he felt suffocated.

What you did, though, was a mistake.

I rallied the soldiers of lords who wanted to side with me, and I confronted Brando with fifteen thousand men.

While Brando must have also had reinforcements from Ayles's camp, he had only about seven thousand.

——You know, there was a man called Azai Nagamasa, and he, too, had bad luck in so many ways. He opposed me, which led to his death. When a warrior has raised troops, however, they must take responsibility.

Oda Nobunaga had clearly seen many examples of that. I had a good idea of it, too. If Brando had been born ten years or so before me, our positions probably would have been a bit different.

Judging from his numbers, Brando was probably not thinking about winning here, either. Linking up with Ayles and engaging me in battle at my home, Nayvil County—he likely meant this as a prelude to an attack on Maust.

I would therefore use this as an opportunity to test what my forces were capable of.

I summoned Talsha to my prebattle lodging—which was essentially a small hut.

"You really called me without any personal guards? What would you do if I tried to kill you?"

"I would draw my sword. Besides, it was you who said you had no intent of siding with the enemy. I will be the one to decide if I can believe the words of my allies," I replied nonchalantly.

"*Sigh*... If only my husband had had such backbone, he would still be alive."

"If you have need of a man, I'm here."

Lewd jokes were common on the battlefield. Talsha and I had killed each other's troops before, so at this point there was no need to mince words.

"Even if I were in the mood, I would release that exhilaration on the battlefield."

"I will lend you soldiers if you stand on the front line, but being on the plains it will be hard to plan anything like a surprise attack."

"No need," Talsha said flatly. "If I am in command, I can break the enemy easily. I will smash them to pieces."

What a stubborn woman. Is that part of her profession, too? No, it's the other way around. She has a personality like Takeda Shingen, and that's why she got that profession. Professions come from the individual's personality.

Exactly as she'd said, Talsha, leading two thousand men, really did have her way with Brando, crushing the soldiers on his front lines.

The enemy's morale had probably not been high to begin with, but they were routed in no time.

——She may be a woman, but she has Takeda Shingen as her profession, after all. An enemy so weak stood no chance.

Oda Nobunaga acted as if he had been reunited with an old rival. I knew how he felt. Only the greats understand the greats.

I praised her when I was conferring awards, too, but I summoned Talsha to my lodgings that day.

"Well done. I didn't see your achievements for myself, but I heard many compliments about you."

"It's nothing. I make a decision as quickly as the wind, attack as violently as flame, and move as swiftly as lightning. So long as I stick to those tactics, I can easily overwhelm weak soldiers. Those are simply the basics of war."

Talsha was totally relaxed, not even bragging. It was the first time I'd ever seen a woman so thoroughly masterful as a warrior. Laviala was an outstanding warrior in her own right, but she was more of an individual archer than she was a commander.

"I'm sure you could display such ability on your own, but it should've been far harder this time. After all, the soldiers you led weren't your personal troops or anything."

Continually overwhelming enemy forces using borrowed troops alone was much more difficult than fighting alongside long-known comrades.

"In other words, whether you recognized your men's capabilities immediately or made them entirely into your own troops within such a short time, either way that is some formidable talent."

"Ah, that...," Talsha said a bit hesitantly. "Look, you know that professions have special abilities... For me, it was The People Are Your Castle, I think... It has a slightly longer name, but I forgot the rest... That's why the abilities of the soldiers under my command are supposed to double..."

"Just as I thought, special professions have the most incredible abilities."

That explained her great victory.

"There's also something called Wind, Forest, Fire, Mountain, which raises your own strength, but...anyway, thanks to it, I've almost never lost... You might say it's like cheating..."

"It's nothing to be embarrassed about. What's wrong with fighting using the power you have? I use my profession's special abilities all the time."

"But I feel like it makes victory a given."

"You lost to me, though. That's what a contest is—you never know the outcome."

At my words, Talsha sullenly glared my way.

Apparently she got mad if I said it, even though she disparaged herself—although I couldn't help but feel like she wasn't just angry, but was being somehow bashful as well.

"Actually…I tried to relieve my excitement on the battlefield, but the enemy was such a pushover… It wasn't much of a relief…"

"So you want me to relieve it for you?"

Talsha was silent for a bit, but then she spoke with hesitance.

"Actually, I'm a bit on the lusty side… If you wish, I won't stop you from taking me to bed…"

"A regent can't take back what he's said, after all. If you wish it, then I don't mind, either."

I approached Talsha and put a hand on her back.

I didn't have to do more. Talsha offered her lips of her own accord.

In any case, she'd probably guessed what I was after when I'd called her to my quarters.

She'd called herself lusty, and she sure did come wanting. Even I felt like I might get tired.

It was just as well, as some things you can't talk about except in bed. After we had calmed down, I discussed with Talsha the policy for the Northlands.

"Talsha, is it possible your brother would hand over his title as Margrave of Machaal to you on his own?"

"Frankly, I think that's impossible. He is most eminent, having greatly elevated the position of margrave. He's hungry for power, too. He wouldn't listen to his younger sister. I'm not even his rightful successor anyway."

"Then gather some troops and drive him out. The land I reward you with will depend on how much you take. I'll lend you my soldiers."

Still in bed, Talsha looked dubious.

"Supposing I can, what would you do if I became independent?"

"Talsha, you're smart, so I'm sure you know—there are limits to the power you can have far away from the royal capital. Your own preference for being a margrave proves that."

Talsha had never had a desire for supreme power to begin with. That would be far more difficult to achieve for someone from her region than for someone from my own homeland. Talsha's end goal was to be a margrave.

"Besides, I realized I can trust you. I have a better eye for women than most. And I don't recall ever being wrong about a woman before," I said, drawing her body close once more.

"You really are a better man than my husband ever was."

◇

The situation thereafter went just as I'd expected.

Ayles and Brando placed regiments near the Nayvil clan's graves and seized Nayvil Castle. It was a clear act of spite toward me.

With that as their stronghold, they lay in wait for me. Their men numbered roughly twenty thousand, about the same as mine, which had also gradually grown more numerous.

On the other hand, Ayles made his own son a general and sent five thousand men to prevent a sally out of Maust Castle, keeping my numbers stagnant.

Good old Ayles. Though he had gathered troops from other lords, it was impressive that he had been able to get such numbers together.

Setting your eyes on Nayvil County will be your downfall, though.

Capturing my main stronghold of Maust Castle would have been far more important. If he had wanted to show himself as overwhelmingly superior to me, that's what he should have done. This was no time to be appointing a son to attack Maust.

After all, my men, who had fought many pitched battles, couldn't possibly lose in my home of Nayvil County.

In fact, Laviala was clearly more lively than usual.

"I'm not sure why, but I feel so very excited, like I might enjoy the battle despite how important it is."

"It's sort of like a homecoming, after all. Laviala, I want you to lure away one of Ayles's regiments—take them into the forest and obliterate them. Can you do it?"

By first delivering a blow to Ayles, I would get him to leave the area. My victory would then be mostly secure.

"Yes—there are many paths only the elves know of! Even if I live somewhere else now, I'll never forget them!"

Leading the vanguard of Ayles Caltis's forces was a top vassal, a man called Motai.

He had long worked together with Ayles in Brantaar Prefecture, also known as the domain of Mineria, and outside it.

Thus, he also knew they absolutely had to win this war.

I positioned about a third of my forces in Aweyu Forest, Laviala's birthplace. I had the word spread that I, commanding general and regent, was there as well.

I embellished the story, while I was at it, as follows:

Having lost Nayvil Castle, Regent Alsrod Nayvil will make camp in front of the forest, where his milk sister Laviala was raised, and here, together with his faithful elven vassals, he intends to take his own life.

In his childhood, Alsrod always lamented his obscurity within his clan. The only ones he could trust were his milk sister's elven relatives. He must have finally embraced his fate.

Turncoats are already appearing on Alsrod's side, and they have not the strength to make a full-on attack on Caltis and Brando's men. Thus, Alsrod has taken two thousand of his fourteen thousand total troops and headed to the forest.

...That summed it up.

It was all lies, of course. I had no intention of dying here, nor was my men's morale low. I also had about the same number of troops as they did—twenty thousand, not fourteen thousand.

The important thing was making it look like I'd done all this because I thought we had no hope of winning.

——Going out of your way to scheme like this is just like you.

Oda Nobunaga seemed a bit surprised.

——I always fought with enough numbers to overwhelm the enemy, if I could afford them. Sometimes smaller forces win, but larger ones naturally have the advantage. There is no meaning in going out of your way to gamble.

Well, it would be different if I had fifty thousand men to use, but unfortunately, not so much in this battle. When the time comes that I can field fifty thousand, my opponents will probably be on better behavior.

Also, casualties increased when similarly numbered forces clashed.

If given the choice, I'd rather win gloriously with few sacrifices. I still had conquering to do, so if I could create a mythology that I was powerful, then I should do just that.

——Very well, very well. Do as you please. I believe your troops can overwhelm them with Conqueror's Guidance anyway.

Even then, it's risky. The forest is safer.

While I took up position before the forest, Laviala and her clan schemed away inside it.

Laviala's last name happened to be Aweyu, after all. For a long time I had only called her Laviala, so I'd almost forgotten her last name.

Finally, she returned, looking giddy.

"We are ready! All preparations are complete!"

"Great. Well done, Laviala. Give me your all in the actual battle, too."

These days, Laviala seemed the most excited of anyone.

"Yes, sir! I feel running through the forest like this is what I'm best suited for, after all. Both the royal capital and Maust Castle are too stuffy for me. When I work in the forest, the trees speak to me."

"Look at you getting so poetic on me on the eve of battle."

"It's not poetry. The trees really do speak to the elves. The flowers and wind all speak to us. If we do as they say, we cannot lose."

"I'll take your word for it. It's my big sister talking, after all."

Laviala was just a little bit older than me, so I grew up watching her.

I had made her my concubine, so perhaps it was fate that we would stay together forever.

"I have always trusted in you as well, Lord Alsrod. I will do what I can in this battle. I'm going to let loose!"

Behind her, the other elves' and archers' faces were full of lively determination.

Now we only had to wait for the enemy to come.

Motai, on Ayles Caltis's side, confronted us with five thousand troops. He must have decided that was enough to take us down in one stroke.

As a matter of formality, I sent an envoy to the enemy camp to see if we could make peace with Seraphina as arbiter.

My demands were flatly rejected—even going through a daughter of the Caltis clan would not work. Of course, I'd had no intention of keeping any promises if they had accepted. It was only an act to pretend that I was afraid.

Besides, though Seraphina was a daughter of the Caltis clan, she was also my wife. I had already made up my mind to crush the Caltis clan.

The enemy would surely come try to kill me with all their might. Since it would be a pain for them if I fled into the forest, they probably at least wanted to capture me as soon as possible.

Before noon, Motai's troops began a charge.

Just as planned, I had my men back up slowly.

This was only to show that the enemy was pushing us back.

I heard enemy troops yelling things like, "Push, push!" and "It's just a little forest! Don't worry if they make it in!"

Sure, Aweyu Forest wasn't horribly big, stretching to who knows where.

But it would have been a problem for us otherwise. If the forest were too deep, the enemy would be on guard, and an obvious trap like this would be meaningless.

Any general like Ayles Caltis would probably think they had nothing to fear—that even supposing we fled into the forest, we didn't have the time to lay a trap, and if they forced a push, they should be able to crush us without trouble.

Well then, come get us.

"To the forest, everyone!"

Laviala guided the troops into the woods. I went along as well.

The enemy was in hot pursuit.

"Shall we set fire to it?"

"Fool! Our comrades ahead of us won't be able to get back!"

Such were the voices I heard. If they came in with us, they couldn't burn the forest down.

Once the opposition's troops had entered far enough into the woods, we began our counterattack.

Our foes fell noisily as arrows flew in out of nowhere.

"Shit! It's the enemy!"

"Where are they?"

The soldiers stopped in their tracks, looking for where the arrows had come from, but to no avail.

To be honest, even I didn't know where they were coming from.

We were surrounded by countless trees, with absolutely nowhere that had an open field of view.

However, Laviala and her unit could still fire their arrows in spite of those obstacles.

—Laviala's Archer profession.

—The home terrain advantage.

—Their being elves, a race that excelled at the use of bows.

Here more than anywhere else in the world, Laviala and her elves shone.

The traps were well set, too.

Enemy soldiers who ran into the forest fell into holes. I knew because I could hear their screams.

Pitfalls had been made everywhere in the forest. Elves were also good at inner-forest engineering.

The holes were shallow, but their depth made no difference. Once a person had lost their balance and fallen in, they would be shot with an arrow and killed.

Everything's going well so far. Guess I'll link up with Laviala.

Laviala was standing atop one of the taller trees.

At a glance, it looked impossible to climb, but it was placed so you could get there relatively easily by using the trunks of the surrounding trees.

I gave it a go. It was a bit treacherous here and there, but I wasn't particularly heavy, so I made it to the top.

"Ah, you came all the way here? Don't fall, okay?"

"My body remembers more than I'd thought. I climbed up here a long time ago, didn't I?"

Aweyu Forest was my old stomping grounds. Nayvil Castle was extremely uncomfortable, and I was sent to outlying villages like Hardt, so when I was feeling down, Laviala had taken me into the forest.

I managed to get a vague idea of how the battle was going from atop the tree.

I could hear the confused voices of the opposition's troops. Little by little, we seemed to be whittling away at their numbers. They were getting totally lost, as we'd planned.

"Elves really are good at what they do," I observed. "The enemy is already unable to command their troops."

"Charging headlong into an elven forest is the height of foolishness. I don't think the elves of Aweyu Forest are particularly outstanding, but I suppose we can handle any number of people who don't know how to fight in the woods."

Our soldiers are many, so if we push with these numbers, it'll work out—that must have been the naive assumption of the enemy.

Besides, they must've thought it'd be a pain for them if they let the regent get away. As rebels, they had to seize victory quickly. There was the wandering former king, but these people weren't allied with him. It would be far from a justification.

"Some enemies are attacking Aweyu Forest from behind—is that going well, too?"

"Yes, we cut off the rear entrance, turning it into an artificial cliff, so a breakthrough is impossible. They ought to be having an awful time, getting shot from high up."

If Ayles's troops had been more careful, they wouldn't have tried to attack the forest.

However, they'd had no choice.

Leaning on their hopeful expectation that they could make it work, they'd attacked me.

- **I had already given up winning.**
- **The forest made no difference since they outnumbered us.**
- **I hadn't had enough time to prepare.**

Based on those conveniently provided pieces of information, they'd thought they could win.

That was the biggest trap of all.

"I wonder where Motai is, then. Of course, if he plays it safe, he'll stay out of the forest," I said.

"He's here. Killing the regent would be the exploit of a lifetime. Risky or not, he would surely want to stick his neck out."

"Right. I agree, Laviala."

Fweet, fweet, a whistle echoed out finally.

"Sounds like they found the enemy commander—although it's probably not Motai," I noted.

"Ah, that person there must be Motai," Laviala said, but I couldn't spot him at all.

"Really? I can tell that soldiers are moving, but..."

"Ah, it might be a bit too far to see well. I have no doubt, though."

Laviala then swiftly readied her bow.

Just by being next to her, I felt an aura from her that seemed to give off heat.

"Now then—please die!"

There was so much power that she gave the illusion of firing a gun.

The arrow flew, threading the needle through the tiny spaces between the trees.

It stuck without fail into someone far away.

Another shot, then yet another.

The arrows were never stopped by tree trunks, but pierced the flesh of something again and again.

Finally, a grief-stricken voice cried out, "Viscount Motai has been shot dead!"

"See? He really was there, wasn't he, Lord Alsrod?"

Laviala smiled mischievously.

"You really are a genius with a bow."

Laviala must've been the only one who'd mastered the Archer profession this well.

"I wouldn't do something like that in an unfamiliar forest. This place is special, though. I have many memories with you here, Lord Alsrod."

Laviala's expression was close to that of the big sister I'd chased in my young days.

The fact that a different sentiment was nevertheless mixed in must have been proof I had become an adult.

It might not have been appropriate for a battlefield, but I gently locked lips with her.

"I want to have another child with you."

"Elves have a fairly hard time getting pregnant, but I'll do my best."

With Motai dead, the enemy troops finally fell into disarray, resulting in many casualties.

Being part of a defeated army in an elven forest would be a living hell. All stragglers would be killed.

I gathered my men and announced, "We've taken the wind out of

their sails. Now we return to the main battlefield. I need to reward the ones who stayed behind!"

◇

At the main battlefield, Little Kivik and Kelara's regiments defended the center, and from the flanks, Noen Rowd and Meissel Wouge were set up to attack as a flying column.

When Laviala and I returned, one of the rappas came to apprise us of the situation. They looked no different from simple hunting dogs. The werewolf rappas really were quick-witted.

"We're currently at a stalemate—nay, I do not believe we have yet had a real fight."

"As I thought. I didn't think the enemy'd be able to deliver any kind of crushing blow."

I chuckled. It looked like things would work in our favor.

"Tell Little Kivik, Kelara, and the others I'll be there right away. Now in one stroke we'll take Nayvil Castle back from the enemy's hand!"

"As you wish."

The werewolf rappa swiftly vanished.

"Lord Alsrod, why did you think the battle would drag on? The enemy holds Nayvil Castle, so I thought they would be getting impatient."

"Laviala, has Nayvil Castle ever been attacked?"

"Since you and I were born, at least, this is the first time."

In other words, Nayvil Castle had never once been under siege.

"Well, Nayvil Castle's defenses are strong for a lord of one and a half counties. It's good enough for driving away a small enemy force. However, when a petty lord holes up in a castle, it's usually when they're only thinking about holding out."

"True. You hole up in a castle to avoid getting wiped out."

Then the answer was clear.

"If you put your main force in there, it becomes overwhelmingly difficult to attack. Our forces are on a distant hill themselves, so attacking first makes it easier to cause lots of damage in the beginning."

"Ah, I see! Nayvil Castle isn't adequate as an attacking position!"

Laviala must've been thinking of Nayvil County's topography right then.

"That's right. Ayles and Brando must've taken Nayvil Castle because they thought they could show themselves as superior. However, they must've felt it was bad to use as a base—that they couldn't move if they wanted to."

A petty lord's goal was not to take supreme power, but to protect their own land.

Nayvil Castle may have been suited for defense, but it was absolutely ill-suited for offense. That was one of the reasons I had moved my capital to Maust.

——I see. So you sacrificed your hometown. Good idea. I could not have holed up in Owari indefinitely, either, though. I suppose I can empathize somewhat.

Oda Nobunaga, sacrifice *is a bad way to put it. I'm merely going to take back my hometown from the enemy.*

——It would seem many of the petty lords who sided with this Ayles Caltis followed him because they had no choice, rather than promising loyalty unto death. It looks like that prevented him from making a resolute offense as well. And when you moved separately from your main force, he tried to see if they could kill you off by attacking the forest.

That was it. The minor lords near Ayles hadn't wanted him to destroy them, so they had gone along with his demands. However, their goal was to protect their own clans, not to kill me.

Thus, the tide would turn when I arrived.

...However, just as I returned, the enemy troops were making their attack.

"It's Brando Naaham's troops!"

"Shit! It's the hicks from Olbia Prefecture!"

Such voices I heard from the direction of my allies.

I see. So thinking things can't go on as they are, Brando is making his bold assault.

He also was a young man of ambition. He knew when he had to fight.

Little Kivik was commanding flawlessly, but the fierce enemy attack looked like it would push him back. This sort of thing would be rather difficult with his fortitude alone.

I needed to put my allies into a sort of drunken state—that is, get them to ride out this wave.

The eyes of the men who realized I had arrived gradually lit up. Under the effects of Conqueror's Guidance, a soldier's ability went up a level.

"Sorry to keep you waiting, Little Kivik."

"Ah, Your Excellency! I am glad to see you!"

In the middle of his ongoing defense, Little Kivik breathed a sigh of relief. I could see Kelara behind him.

"From here on, it's our time to shine. We make for Nayvil Castle!"

"You're taking the castle?"

"No one would be foolish enough to put all their troops into such a tiny fortification. Once the castle vicinity is attacked, they will pull out."

First, we would drive back Brando.

I might even be able to confront him.

"Everyone, the regent is back from destroying the rebels! Next, we drive Brando back to the southern mountains! Who's with me?!"

"""Hoorah!""" echoed their booming voices.

Special ability Conqueror's Presence activated.
Takes effect when recognized as a conqueror by many at once. All abilities are tripled from the usual.
Additionally, all who lay eyes on you experience either awe or fear.

All right, no problem. I'll show my brother-in-law the difference in our power.

Now under my command, the troops charged into Brando's, which had been on the attack.

Brando's men then lost their momentum. Because we outnumbered them, it would be simple to drive them back.

"Nobody retreat! If we don't defeat this traitor who calls himself regent, the Kingdom of Therwil will be his!"

Brando was shouting gallantly from atop his horse. He had attacked too much from the front for someone whose profession was Thief.

"What a thing for you to say, brother-in-law!" I cried as I confronted Brando.

"A-Alsrod..."

I thought he seemed to have aged since I'd first met him, but Brando's eyes still had the glint of youth. Actually, maybe I was the odd one because of the slowed aging effect from my profession.

"I didn't send my sister to marry a traitor, Brando."

"You're the traitor here! I, Brando Naaham, do not recall ever saying I would be your vassal!"

——I knew it—this is no different from the time with Azai, after all.

Oda Nobunaga sounded a bit sad.

——I do understand how he feels. However, only those who accept becoming my vassal can live. One cannot become a conqueror when he has peers.

"You are not my vassal; you are the king's. Don't misunderstand."

"Shut it! I can see through your schemes!"

The power of the Thief profession, perhaps. Brando approached, running swiftly through the crowd.

In his hand was a short sword. It seemed he meant to stab me.

But you see, I am on a different level from you.

You're not at the level where you can be a hero. Your limit is ruling one prefecture, at most.

I slashed once with my sword.

Brando's short sword flew away.

"This is what a difference in level looks like, Brando."

He was momentarily shocked, but he wasn't foolish enough to stay there in a daze. He immediately backed away.

Thanks to Oda Nobunaga, my physical abilities on the battlefield were second to none. A clumsy little approach wouldn't stop me.

Now that Brando had backed off, the enemy troops were starting to retreat.

Just then, a thunderous noise rang out.

Those who fled were getting pelted with gunfire.

The situation had turned completely our way. Now I only had to hunt the enemy down.

Still, it was impossible to completely eliminate them here. I had to be content with having just taken back Nayvil County. Destroying the enemy detachment attacking my castle at Maust would have to come first.

"Are you hurt?"

Kelara dashed over to my side.

"I'm fine. More importantly, I'm going to keep up the attack, so get your unit ready. I know exactly where to strike."

"The way you say it, it's like it's a place you meant to destroy long ago, not your own territory, whose weaknesses you know."

Kelara seemed to be surprised at the total confidence of my words.

"Exactly. I've captured Nayvil Castle once before, after all."

I had known there would come a day when I would have to fight my elder brother, and I had prepared myself accordingly. To make a long story short, my brother dug his own grave, invited me in, and was killed by my hand.

"This land has memories. But those memories are of no use to me if they cause my sword to dull. My foes will be defeated."

My troops pursued Brando's retreating men.

Of course, my goal was not to eradicate them.

I had studied everything about where to attack to get behind the enemy, as well as how to break further through their defenses. I gradually forced them to retreat even more.

I decided to send a secret messenger to the minor lords fence-sitting in Brando's stronghold of Olbia Prefecture and ask them to side with me. Specifically, I wrote that they should take military action within Brando's domain.

In the letter, I was clear that Ayles Caltis and Brando Naaham's plan had failed. The lords would likely at least position themselves to attack Brando's domain. That was enough. Brando would have to withdraw into the mountains of Olbia.

That night I stayed in a village in the county. The enemy's fall was already guaranteed. Apparently, several petty lords were starting to abandon the other side, and some had even made an appearance before me.

I was making plans in one of the rooms of my lodging.

I seemed to be alone, but Oda Nobunaga spoke to me for some reason. Or, more accurately, he was using me as someone to talk to rather than joining in the strategizing.

——What choice do I have? You are the only person I can speak with. I wonder if I could have made one or two of my former attendants part of your profession, too.

You being my profession is enough of a miracle—there's no way that could happen. If you're not going to help me out, then just be quiet…

I felt like the air had changed slightly.

Yadoriggy, representing the rappas, entered my chambers.

"Ayles Caltis's and Brando Naaham's units have each withdrawn to their main stronghold."

"What happened to Nayvil Castle, Yadoriggy?"

"Their strategy seems to be to leave the castle in capable hands and flee in the meantime."

A sacrifice. Those poor men.

"I guess I'll have Little Kivik surround Nayvil Castle with three thousand. The others will advance east and head for Maust Castle. Some of my vassals have betrayed me, after all. I shall put them to death, no matter what. Do you have a list of these traitors?"

Yadoriggy listed them off by title and name.

There were a lot of officials. It seemed the people with fewer opportunities to prove themselves under my expanded territory, such as Fanneria, had been taken in by naive talk.

"Looks like they realize how incapable they are. Tell the elder Kivik, protecting Maust Castle, we're going to do a pincer attack."

"Understood."

"Also...another thing I wanted to mention..."

What came after was a bit embarrassing, so my voice naturally got softer.

"Call Talsha to my chambers. Then after one hour, call Kelara, and Laviala another hour after that."

My body became awfully hot after a hard day of fighting.

Talsha had said she sought company whenever she couldn't relieve her excitement on the battlefield.

I rather felt the opposite—I got excited because I went to battle.

"I think you ought not to overwork yourself so much."

"The hardest part is over, in my opinion, at least."

"I agree. Well then, I shall do as you have bid me."

I stared into Yadoriggy's eyes a moment.

"If you have the time, why don't you keep me company, too? It really was a hard day. I don't think I'll be able to get any sleep like this."

That night was unusual, even for me.

Yadoriggy nodded, expressionless.

"I don't mind, but it will be harder to notice intruders, so please do not make much noise."

Even I could tell how greedy I had been that day. I was still thinking about how I'd acted when crossing blades with Brando.

Although in theory I was fighting to unite the realm—and to bring peace to it—I was too eager for battle. That was where I felt at home.

Afterward, Laviala scolded me, saying I "smelled of women."

◇

The next day, I sent troops toward Kinaseh County, where Maust Castle lay.

Of course, I had no intention of going into the castle right away, nor did I think I could. The forsaken enemy troops were in between.

As for why they had been forsaken, this lot was a collection of officials who had worked around Maust and former lords on welfare. Thus, Ayles Caltis must have decided they didn't matter.

The commander himself was Ayles's son Dakkar, but it didn't seem Ayles had thought he could capture Maust Castle with that detachment. Its purpose was only ever to impede us, so Ayles must have meant to strike together with his main force.

By the time I set up my position, I got word that Dakkar and his attendants had already fled. Everyone who had been made to join had apparently been abandoned.

"All right, we're moving out. Anyone who doesn't move should quit being a soldier."

I immediately gave the order to attack.

"Also, I'm sending a secret messenger to Maust Castle. I will have him tell Kivik to make a sortie from the castle. Although I suppose Kivik would know when to strike."

The enemy troops had fallen into disarray before we fought. With my attack on top of that, they were destroyed spectacularly.

What's more, at the same time, Kivik made a sortie from his defensive position in Maust Castle and pincered them. Many enemy leaders lost their lives in front of the entrance to the town of Maust.

——Joining a rebellion for no reason, without thinking for oneself, and then dying for no reason—is that any way for a man to live? What say you, Alsrod?

Oda Nobunaga asked me the question as I entered Maust Castle after the victory in battle.

That's how it goes. People vowing to build their own country, like me, are by far in the minority.

——Indeed. Otherwise, I would never have become your profession.

Oda Nobunaga was in quite the good mood. Any warrior would be pleased after winning a battle.

Among the enemies were those who had surrendered, along with some prisoners. They were the first to be to be marched out when I entered Maust Castle.

Fanneria, the financial officer, was among them. He looked gaunt, far from the prosperous merchant he had once been.

"I didn't expect you to take part in this," I said. "I didn't think I'd treated you that badly."

"It felt as though you'd forgotten about me once you went to the royal capital…," Fanneria replied, slumping his shoulders.

"If that's true, then it's only due to your lack of ability."

"Seems my fate was sealed when I handed you the rappas. If I had kept them at hand, things would have been different."

Fanneria laughed as though in resignation. He was probably right.

"Merchants go broke when they misjudge the moment. It's a fitting end for you."

Fanneria and the remaining enemies were beheaded in front of Maust Castle.

——It seems people betray you as often as they did me. But this, too, is part of the trials of becoming a conqueror. The stronger your authority, the more you'll be feared.

I understood what Oda Nobunaga wanted to say. I'd already accounted for resistance to my rise in power.

At Maust Castle I rewarded Kivik, who had defended the castle, in front of the other generals.

"It's because you held out that I was able to return to this castle. You really did well."

"You're too kind. I merely did my best in what will be the last great work of my life."

True, he was at an age when his grandson could very well take over the family. No doubt it would soon be time for the veteran general to retire.

"I'll leave it to you to decide, but do you plan to keep fighting? Or are you going to retire?"

"Well, if I may be so selfish, I would like to continue working enough to stay out of your way. After all, I wouldn't know what to do with myself in retirement."

Kivik chuckled and scratched his balding pate.

"A man like you will probably live longer on the battlefield," I told him. "Very well. I'll welcome you in a way worthy of a god of war. Now, as to your reward—Laviala, the certificate."

Laviala handed Kivik the document. Kivik's jaw went slack in surprise when he read it.

"Wha—?! Tacti and Naaham Counties in Olbia Prefecture? Are those not the territories of Brando Naaham…?"

"Yes, that's correct. I plan to put an end to him. At the very least, he intends to take me down. I will be setting out with troops soon. There are things I need to take back from him."

I would definitely get my sister Altia back—and Altia's children, too. Fortunately, she only had daughters, so I wouldn't need to kill them.

That day, I sent a letter to Brando. It wasn't an ultimatum.

It was a demand for Altia's return given that he was going to war with his wife's family. It's an old tradition invoked whenever a bride's new country becomes an enemy. There's nothing outrageous about it.

Laviala wrote a letter of her own directly addressed to Altia to send with mine.

My letter assured Altia that there would be nothing to worry about if she came to the regent's side, and that although it was tragic that the two clans were now at war, she should not consider dying along with the Naaham clan.

Those were essentially my thoughts on the matter. A regent wasn't allowed to be overly sentimental.

I looked over the letter Laviala presented to me and approved it.

"Lord Alsrod, you could have at least put down your feelings."

"I'll tell Altia in person the next time I see her."

I didn't enjoy knowing that I might be altering my sister's fate. The path of the conqueror was a hard one.

But if I could become king in exchange for Altia's life, I would probably choose that path.

Once the kingdom was unified, it would make the world much safer. It would save countless lives—or so I told myself.

There was no answer to the letter, even a week after I sent it.

In the meantime, I prepared to invade Olbia Prefecture.

It seemed Brando had brushed off my demand, although I'd anticipated as much. He wasn't a fool. No doubt he understood there was nothing left but a direct confrontation.

I moved an army of twenty thousand into Brando's territory, the mountainous Olbia Prefecture.

Brando, I am going to strike you down. Your path to glory ends here.

Olbia Prefecture's minor lords quickly announced they would side with us. They even had the bluster to say they'd help defeat the rebellious Brando for having the temerity to rebel against the king and the regent.

It wasn't a meaningless gesture. I didn't know Olbia Prefecture very well, so it was fortunate to have locals to guide us.

Brando resisted by converting several mountain passes into forts. I was impressed with his tenacity. Brando had yet to give up. He still believed that there would be an opportunity for him to defeat me.

I couldn't let up, either. I was going to take him down with everything at my disposal.

I attacked the forts from multiple directions and made sure to capture them.

Sieges were a type of waiting game. The one who buckled first would lose. Losing by itself was fine, but in this case, it could mean death.

My generals had all grown into their roles by this point, which was why I needed only to leave most of the forts to my subordinates to win.

Thanks to them, it took surprisingly little time to reach the enemy headquarters.

Several buildings were arrayed upon a mountain that took nearly an hour to climb. It was a classic mountain castle—the sort built to serve not as a political capital but as a defensive center.

It wouldn't be an easy castle to bring down. The Naaham clan had survived for so long because this fortification had never been captured.

But I was going to bring down this castle.

I placed a strict cordon around the mountain Brando's castle was built on.

——Oh? Rather rare for you to take your time on a siege. I didn't do much of that myself.

Oda Nobunaga had generally specialized in quick, preemptive attacks in his castle sieges. I wasn't much different in that regard. I had almost never played the waiting game.

But this time, I was changing up my tactics.

Or, more precisely, I was forced to change my tactics.

Brando's castle was on a steep ledge.

We'd already obtained a map of its defenses from a number of those who'd surrendered. Brando was originally an ally, so I had my fair share of information on him to begin with.

But based on that knowledge, I knew just how tough this castle was. Even if some of his forces had surrendered, it wasn't enough to meaningfully degrade its defenses.

From the surface, it looked impregnable.

That was why I started by cordoning it off.

If you don't know where the hole is in a vessel, you need only immerse it in water to find out. It was the same idea.

By sending scattered attacks from various directions, I probed for weaknesses.

And on the fifth day, we found our answer.

It was neither the front nor the postern of the castle.

We went after the flank.

We found locations that were climbable. This would let us attack with several hundred.

I could end it by commanding the attacking forces.

Of course, when I brought that up at the war council, I was told several hundred was too small a force.

"Lord Alsrod, no matter how confident you are, there are still three thousand enemy troops."

Laviala evidently was adamantly opposed to the current plan.

The other generals wouldn't accept it, either. Many insisted we maintain a blockade.

It was true that this was a more challenging opponent than the boring enemies we'd taken down until now, and there wasn't much need to force the issue of a direct assault. Maintaining the cordon would be the standard tactic here.

Noen Rowd and Meissel Wouge contended that because the castle hadn't been designed to be defended with an army of several thousand, the enemy would eventually deal with food shortages and starvation, and that we needed only to wait until then. They had a point.

But I didn't want to take that path.

"If I take too much time with Brando, others might think of rebelling against me as well. Furthermore—and this is the real reason—I don't want to prolong Altia's suffering."

Perhaps because I mentioned my sister's name, my generals had trouble arguing with me.

I shouldn't have done that. My bringing up a family member made it harder for them to voice their concerns.

"Regardless," I continued, "I understand what you're all trying to say. Then let me offer an improved proposal."

I already had several plans in mind.

"We'll stage an all-out assault from each direction. That way, the enemy will have to cover every approach. Then my forces will hit their weak flank. In other words, we'll massacre them together."

The moment I finished elaborating on the details, Laviala exclaimed, "Now that I approve of!"

Her haughty response ended up being decisive. She immediately apologized, saying, "Forgive me, I blurted that out...," and got a laugh out of everyone. She was talking like she had in the past, as my older sister.

"Let's go with that plan, then. Now give me a victory shout and we'll return to Maust Castle!"

The generals answered me with a "Hoorah!"

Now that we'd decided our positions, our army began its assault on the mountain fortress.

The enemy immediately noticed us, and we could tell they were steeling themselves for the siege.

But I doubted any of them thought the castle would fall quickly. Common sense indicated a castle this large wouldn't fall easily. It was no simple feat to get inside.

However, relying on common sense was just a hairbreadth away from complacency.

If that made it harder for them to recognize my attack upon their flank, so much the better.

During that lull, my elite units circled around to the flank.

"All right, open up a path into the castle! A reward for the first man who makes it inside!" I shouted.

Of course, even without the prospect of the reward, those who had followed me this far would have happily charged in.

There were still stone ramparts on the flanks, but compared to those at the front and postern, they were clearly lower—low enough for us to climb over and keep pressing forward.

The first couple of my soldiers were pincushioned by arrows and fell off the slope. The very front of the vanguard was treacherous. Anyone leading the charge needed to be prepared to die. While my troops were stronger due to my profession, they were not quite invincible.

But eventually, my soldiers got over the ramparts and entered the castle grounds.

That was when the tide of the battle changed. I could feel the enemy's panic.

The castle they'd believed to be impregnable was now falling to the enemy.

They probably hadn't made plans for when we got inside their walls.

I needed only to slowly follow my men. By the time I entered the castle proper, my soldiers had already sown confusion among Brando's troops.

"Keep going! Open the gates and let our forces in! This castle will meet its end here and now!"

That said, this mountain castle's terrain was complex. No doubt it would take more time to corner Brando.

Of course, Brando wasn't just any general.

The mood changed again—this time, it was charged with hostility.

Brando, sword in hand, approached me alone.

"Alsrod! Make your peace! I'll pay you back for last time!"

I leaped in front of him.

"Thanks for saving me the time, Brando!" I replied, pointing my sword at him.

The arquebusiers tried to take aim at Brando, but they weren't fast enough. Several shots whiffed past him. Once they missed, it took time for them to reload. When this was combined with their panic, the arquebusiers could hardly show their true strength.

"Don't bother. Brando's profession is Thief. Just assume that projectiles won't hit him."

Brando wouldn't come at us if he weren't confident.

"Alsrod, I figured you would lead the attack yourself! If I can defeat you here, this kingdom will return to the long era of battle!"

Brando had an extremely curved blade. It was the sort of weapon a warrior would consider heretical in design. Of course, there was no such thing as orthodox or heretical in this sort of age.

I took his blow with my own sword, the Stroke of Justice. Its blade was broad, which made it perfect for blocking attacks.

"You've just made it clear: You want everything to return to how it was." I hadn't thought there'd be this obvious a reactionary faction against me. "And? What do you intend to accomplish by returning the world to the past?"

I countered, and there was the sound of groaning metal. Brando had parried my blow with his sword, then quickly shifted to attack. His swordfighting style was completely self-taught, but he left no openings. It was a way of fighting worthy of a Thief. His was the swordsmanship of someone who believed in brute strength alone and used that to force his way to the top.

"It's simple," he replied. "If the world is in chaos, then there will be more opportunities for men like me to prosper. In fact, I could end up like you and become regent, ordering around all the other lords."

Brando grinned and licked his upper lip.

This man was a scoundrel in every sense of the word. A wildflower that could bloom only in the wastelands.

"However—"

Brando's expression changed, and he redoubled his attacks.

"—if a man like you rebuilds the world, I'll have no place to go! I'll have to bow my head in spite of it all!"

"Oh, is that so bad?"

I felt like I'd finally heard him speak his mind. I already knew what he thought, though.

"Of course it is. I'll become a man like you! I can't let you get there first!"

Yes, Brando wanted to become a conqueror who unified the kingdom.

But there was only one conqueror's throne for the taking. There could never be ten, twenty conquerors standing together.

Which meant the only option was to get rid of the conqueror ahead of you.

——This man's got a more lively gaze than Azai Nagamasa. He lives unfettered and does as he pleases. I rather like him.

Who cares if you like him or not?

——That said, if he resists you, then all there is to do is crush him.

Exactly!

I saw spears appear one after another from both sides.

The Tri-Jarg units had flooded into the castle now that there was a way in.

"Sorry, Brando, but I made no promise to duel you to the death. The reason I came in first was to fire up my allies."

My special ability, Conqueror's Guidance, doubled my allies' trust and concentration and further improved their attack and defense by 30 percent.

If I could draw in these troops, then victory would be mine.

Left with no choice, Brando temporarily retreated.

A spear line wasn't something that could be broken by a single combatant.

Still, he immediately came back to try to cut me down. That was the only way he could win. He didn't seem to have any illusions that he could simply hole up and wait for Ayles to come help him. Ayles would likely spend that time rebuilding his own castle. The two of them simply shared common interests and nothing more.

Brando the Thief quickly tried to circle around to my flank, just like I had flanked the castle.

Thieves had overwhelmingly high abilities when it came to playing havoc with the enemy. And it takes time for a spear unit to maneuver to face off against a single enemy in the heat of melee.

I stepped forward as well.

"Abandon your regency, Alsrod, so that I may take it for myself!"

I sensed an enormous amount of hostility. No part of him considered me Altia's older brother. I commended him for his attitude.

But it also angered me.

I took my own sword, the Stroke of Justice, and pressed it against Brando's. Just in terms of brute force, I had the advantage. I loomed closer to Brando.

Then, with my free hand, I punched him in the face.

"Bastard!"

Brando staggered from the unexpected blow. He was surely seeing stars.

But I couldn't have him collapse here. I grabbed Brando's light clothing—he was dressed for ease of movement, so I doubted his clothes could stop a spear—and hoisted him up by the collar.

Then I punched him again.

"Why did you betray me despite Altia?! I don't give a damn about your personal reasons—you ruined Altia's future, you son of a bitch!"

I gave you my sister as a bride because I believed in your potential! Even if it was a political marriage, I wanted my only flesh-and-blood sister to be happy.

At the very least, come at me with enough strength to beat me! If you're going to rebel and end up losing, then even if it's humiliating, even if it's embarrassing, stay loyal!

"For that I...apologize..."

Before Brando could finish, I grabbed him by the hair and slammed him into the ground.

"Losers have no right to speak of the conqueror's path."

That marked the end of the fight—at the very least, the fight between the two of us.

The soldiers of mine who were trying to run toward me stopped. No doubt they were going to say I'd end up killing Brando if I throttled him any further. I was in control enough to know that. I couldn't have him dying yet. That would defeat the point of punching him.

"Listen to me, Brando. Order your forces to stand down and surrender.

Also, we'll be taking Altia and your daughters into our protection, so hand them over. We'll decide your fate after."

"I understand..."

Brando voiced his acquiescence through his bloodied mouth.

The only reason I won't kill you now is that I want to guarantee Altia's safety. That's the only reason I'm taking you prisoner. There's no mercy here.

You're nothing but a loser. The history books won't think twice about your abilities and only emphasize the fact that you lost.

A conqueror needs foresight as well.

I won't ever forgive you for believing in miracles and going out and seeking danger.

"You just didn't have what it takes to be a conqueror, Brando."

◇

The war came to a close after Brando Naaham was captured. The other members of the Naaham clan ceased their hostilities and announced their surrender.

Once the tasks of checking the enemy generals and the like were completed, I visited one of the locations where command-level officers were staying.

I headed toward the room conspicuously guarded by soldiers, who saluted when they saw me.

"Good evening, men. Nothing unusual, I hope?"

"No sir! Nothing out of the ordinary!"

I could tell they were tense. It would literally be their heads if anything happened. Of course they were nervous.

That, or my expression was just that intimidating. At the very least, I wasn't smiling. But at the same time, I don't think I looked angry. Truth be told, I wasn't sure what sort of expression to have on at the moment.

When I entered the room, Laviala and Altia were having a conversation. Altia's two daughters were playing in the corner.

Altia immediately glanced over to me. She'd probably expected me to show up, but she, too, didn't seem to know what expression to have on her face.

Altia slowly stood from her chair, then carefully bowed deeply in my direction.

"Sir Regent...I give you my sincere gratitude for saving the lives of myself and my daughters."

There was nothing wrong with it as protocol. Having married into the Naaham clan, it was only right that Altia would conduct herself as a member of the Naaham clan.

But in all honesty, I wasn't exactly pleased with that.

The two daughters quietly stared at me, as though they were a bit frightened. No surprise there—I was the one who'd defeated their father, after all.

Laviala hadn't spoken, but she had placed her hand over her breast, watching as though silently praying.

"Altia, go ahead and speak to me as my sister. It's just you, me, your daughters, and Laviala."

"Yeah, you're right."

Altia raised her head. Her expression hadn't changed.

I slowly approached Altia and placed my hand on her shoulder. There was something there that she hadn't had before, a certain steel to her bearing. Perhaps that's the strength that comes from becoming a mother.

"Do you hate me? No, that's not a fair question. Whatever the reason, I'm the one who defeated your husband. Hate me as much as you want."

This situation was commonplace during the Hundred Years' Rebellion. Filicide and parricide weren't rare, and I myself had killed my own older brother.

There was a priest who'd once claimed that lords couldn't escape bloodshed within their own families as a punishment for the sin of failing to fulfill their duty to protect their subjects.

I had to agree that bloodshed within families was better than killing between lords. Of course, that wasn't to say I wanted to be a mere subject. They have plenty of their own hardships, after all.

Altia looked up at me.

She seemed to be at a loss.

"I don't know. I don't know how to interact with you, Brother. Should I be angry first or should I apologize first?"

It was an odd conversation, and although it might not be the most appropriate reaction, I was glad to be able to talk with Altia again.

The anger would be from the wife of the head of the Naaham clan, and the apology would be from the sister of Alsrod Nayvil, who'd married into the Naaham clan.

But there was no clear answer to her question, which is why political marriages have caused tragedies since time immemorial. If there were a right answer, no one would struggle. All they would have to do is behave like machines.

"I only have one order for you: Don't even think about killing yourself."

I'll protect Altia as her brother. That is my responsibility. And Altia, too—

"You have a duty to raise your daughters. So live. You can hate me as much as you want, but just follow that one command. Those two daughters of yours are my nieces. I'll protect them no matter what."

"Right. I know. Thanks."

Altia grabbed a handful of my shirt from around my midriff.

"My husband...is going to die...isn't he?" she said, trying to keep her emotions from bubbling up to the surface.

"I can't let a man who tried to kill me live," I answered matter-of-factly.

It was impossible for a lord to lose his castle of residence and continue to survive. The only question was how he would die.

"Could you not crucify him, then? If you could make it so that he's given the opportunity for an honorable death as a vassal of the regent..."

Crucifixion would be a clear sign that he was being executed as a criminal.

With suicide, on the other hand, while he would still be criticized, he wouldn't be treated as a criminal.

"I'll do that for you."

"Can I see my husband before he dies?"

"I can do that, too."

Altia seemed relieved that the two requests she had had coming into the conversation had been granted, but with that relief, the tears welled in her eyes.

Altia then buried her face in my chest, and I let her weep against me.

This is really hard, isn't it, Oda Nobunaga?

——Oh? What's gotten into you, speaking to me of your own accord like this?

I've done what I've had to do to become a conqueror. Even this time I don't think I've done anything wrong.

——That goes without saying. You must crush everyone who disobeys the regent, particularly if they go into open rebellion. If you leave them to their own devices, you'll be the one who dies.

But it means that as a brother, I can't make my sister happy. It's hard to try to be happy in every respect.

——One shouldn't aspire to be a conqueror if one isn't ready to make others miserable. Still, I understand what you're saying. This isn't an act; I truly do understand. After all, I made Oichi cry myself.

That's right. You come from a chaotic age, too.

——Have a drink by yourself some night when you have nothing planned. I'll join in. And I'll be thinking of the cup made from Azai Nagamasa's skull while I'm at it.

Whoa, whoa, you really haven't learned anything, have you?

——The sin of making my sister cry was not mine alone—it also lay with the one who betrayed me. I shall never forgive him!

For whatever reason, I felt a little better after talking with Oda Nobunaga.

After speaking with Altia and his daughters, Brando Naaham hanged himself in his cell.

The other male relatives and retainers who'd actively participated in the rebellion were executed, while those who had objected or turned informer when they saw the writing on the wall were taken aboard.

As promised, the core of Brando Naaham's territories—the counties of Tacti and Naaham in Olbia Prefecture—were given to Kivik, but it would be difficult for the aging commander to govern them directly. Kivik would place one of his retainers as a governor, who would govern while dealing with the old Naaham clan vassals.

Still, it'd probably be a while before we thought about civil governance.

This was the end of one of the rebel leaders. The only one who remained was Ayles Caltis of Mineria.

Of course, the danger had mostly passed the moment I returned to Maust Castle. By quickly taking care of Brando, I'd made the probability of some lord leisurely deciding to rebel close to nil.

Now that I had taken Yuca as a concubine, my new relatives in the Nistonia clan finished quashing various minor rebellions. Meanwhile, in the royal capital, King Hasse had raised his own army and nipped the rebellions in the bud.

I hadn't considered Hasse as having much military value, so it was an unexpected bonus. When I thought about it, it seemed that if I fell out of power, there was a good chance Hasse's authority would collapse as well. Currently, we were most definitely in this together.

Still, if the king got too used to commanding troops and strengthened his leadership abilities, he might very well become a threat to me, but right now, the priority was putting down the rebellions.

And as I prepared to face off against the isolated Ayles, I called one of my wives over from the royal capital.

◇

"Surely there's nothing left to discuss with me at this point."

The first thing Seraphina did when she saw me was let out a long, theatrical sigh.

"In the future, when I'm punishing someone from Mineria, the most effective person to petition on their behalf will be you, the regent's consort. I'd like to avoid being resented for issuing some draconian punishments when you're not around."

Having sat in a chair, Seraphina turned to the side and propped her face up with her right palm.

"We've already discussed this. I will fight for you, dear husband. I said that I wanted to see the world change as the wife of a great hero. My feelings are still the same, and if my family can't understand that, then I'm fine with them going extinct. You know I don't like that sort of sentimental nonsense."

She was unhappy because I'd brought up something we'd already discussed, and what's more, I'd put her in a position where she had to watch her family fall. It was rather like her, I suppose.

"Then let me be blunt. Whether this'll make you angry, Seraphina, or have you praising me, I honestly can't tell."

"Oh, so you actually had a point you wanted to make. All right, I'm listening."

Seraphina suddenly grew interested and turned to look at me. Her expression of displeasure had evidently also been an act.

"Can you send secret letters from you to those who can cause the most problems for the Caltis clan?" I simply laid out my objective. "If you can, they might be more effective than if they were in my name. After all, everyone in your family knows that you've got a determined spirit."

Meaning I'd be borrowing Seraphina's abilities to cultivate agents.

Cultivating traitors and weakening the enemy from within is a proper part of war.

Furthermore, my side had an enormous advantage, making this tactic particularly effective.

But even if we sent letters inviting defections in my name or those of my vassals, I didn't know how much the recipients would trust us. It would be easy enough to just execute the traitors later, claiming we knew nothing about the arrangements. Once the war was over, the Caltis clan would be gone anyway, so the traitors wouldn't have anyplace to return to.

So it would be more effective for Seraphina to go around saying that she'd do what she could to save the people in question and asking them to betray the Caltis clan.

Seraphina let out a small giggle, as though hiding it at first, then began chuckling rather amusedly.

"Well done, darling husband! That's the spirit! To completely and utterly crush an enemy that you can just squash with brute force by taking the extra steps—that's the sort of mindset you need to unify this kingdom!"

"Seems I haven't disappointed you, at least, so I'm relieved."

I was trying to use one of my concubines to destroy her own family. If she had yelled at me that I was going too far, the only thing I could've done was apologize.

But it seemed I had fretted over nothing.

"You're right. Even if my family is gone, the country isn't unified. You can't complete unifying the country until you take out the ones protecting the last king off to the west. In which case, you need to win without losing a single soldier. After all, this is only part of the process." Seraphina nodded firmly. "Leave it to me. It's my family, so I'll know how best to manipulate them."

As I watched her laugh in delight, I thought, *Thank the gods I managed to take Seraphina as a wife.*

I stepped behind Seraphina and wrapped my arms around her.

"If any historian claims you were an evil witch, I'll kill them all."

"Well, of course. After all, my profession isn't Evil Witch, it's Saint," Seraphina said proudly. I honestly had been a bit worried about talking to her about all this, but it felt ridiculous in hindsight.

Given how eager she was to help, Seraphina was a bit of an oddball.

"I remember now that Ayles had problems finding someone to wed you."

"Could be. Regardless—and perhaps this is a strange way of putting it—I really am thankful for you, dearest husband."

Seraphina took my hands into her own.

It was a bit different from her jovial mannerisms from earlier—a gentler touch.

"If my family is to end, I'd like to do it myself. It's a good way to find closure, and if I'm going to regret the family's end in the future, which is only natural, well...I'd rather not leave it to someone else to do."

Seraphina turned toward me.

She had her own inner struggles, of course. But she kept overcoming them.

We quietly exchanged a kiss.

Comforting a wife was also a husband's role.

◇

I finally sent a large army into Brantaar Prefecture, the core of the Caltis clan's Mineria domain.

It was a force that totaled thirty-five thousand. The surrounding lords had also invaded Brantaar Prefecture from their own borders. Some of the fronts had already broken out into open warfare. Given that more people would likely join our side, it wouldn't be a surprise if our numbers grew larger.

On the way, I passed by Fort Nagraad, where I'd first used the powers of the profession of Oda Nobunaga, and entered Brantaar Prefecture.

Back then, I wouldn't have even dreamed of sending soldiers here to take down the Caltis clan. That was how different the Nayvil and Caltis clans had been at the time in terms of power. After the Battle of Fort Nagraad, I had just become a baron who ruled over three villages.

Next to me, Laviala also looked as though she was reminiscing.

"Lord Alsrod, you came to save me when I was on the verge of dying at that fort."

"Fortunately, you survived that time, but don't do anything like that again... I honestly don't remember much about it because I was so desperate."

"True. It's so different from now that it feels like a dream."

"You know, we always used to chant, 'Death to Mineria!' at the Nayvil clan's drinking parties. That's about to come true."

Stating wild fantasies was allowed during festivities.

But it was no longer a dream or a fantasy.

"Laviala, there's no need for mercy. Seraphina's given her blessing. If anything, she'll yell at me if we leave things half-done. Something about thoughtless pity being pointless."

"Yes, you're probably right. Seraphina is fighting in her own way."

I'd placed Talsha, the younger sister of Seitred, the Margrave of Machaal, in command of our vanguard. I felt her bravely leading from the front would be a good morale booster.

Furthermore, the distance from Machaal made it impossible for Talsha to have any relatives here in Brantaar. All the more reason why she wouldn't hold back in battle.

Even though Nayvil and Brantaar were separate territories, this was still a time of relative peace. Our lands were neighbors. Surely I wasn't the only one who had family relationships spanning between their lands and Mineria. And in those circumstances, there'd be some hope of quarter.

I wanted to cut away those bonds.

There were multiple castles in Brantaar to await us, but few could be described as properly built fortifications. Based on the numbers, the enemy didn't expect to hold them.

The enemy was likely banking on having the decisive battle near their headquarters. They would focus on chipping away at our forces until then. They probably believed we weren't capable of sustaining a long campaign because of our numbers.

Of course, that was all based on optimistic projections. That they'd let us into their territory signaled a dangerous situation for them in itself. It meant there was too large a difference between our forces for them to have attempted to push us back earlier.

There had been a time when this sort of incursion would have led to widespread looting and pillaging of everything from livestock to people, but the regent's regular army didn't commit such acts of barbarism. The cities along the campaign route remained unmolested. Military discipline was strictly maintained.

Why? Because this wasn't like the old struggles between regional lords.

The regent's army had been appointed by the king himself, meaning we were the crown's army and the enemy were rebels. Our goal wasn't to take the enemy's wealth. Rather, this army had been formed to defeat any rebellious lords.

Our forces advanced according to plan. We should soon be able to see Brantaar Castle, the enemy headquarters.

——That reminds me. I've not seen Brantaar Castle. I should like to compare the strength of its defenses to those of Douzan's Inabayama Castle.

I have no idea what sort of place this Inabayama Castle was, but Brantaar Castle was built on an isolated mountain on the plains. It's a tough nut to crack. There's a river right behind it that functions as a moat.

——So it's something like the Nagara River, mm? Indeed, this is very similar to Inabayama Castle.

I quietly advanced my forces and approached close enough to see Brantaar Castle in the distance. If we got too close, their entire force might sally forth, causing a pitched melee that could end in disaster. I observed from afar.

From what I could tell, Brantaar Castle was a collection of towering buildings lined up along the ridge. It was on a completely different scale from Brando's castle. It would cost me dearly to take it out with a frontal assault.

Sorry, Oda Nobunaga, but I don't plan to take this castle with brute force. I'm planning something a bit smarter.

Things should pick up soon.

There had been no major movement on either side during the day. It was now nighttime.

My teeming masses had lit bonfires and arrayed their standards among them.

No doubt the enemy could see this from Brantaar Castle up on the mountain.

How will they react, I wonder?

Eventually, fires flared from the mountain's peak, within Brantaar Castle.

When my soldiers noticed the flames, murmurs of "Arson?" "The castle's on fire!" rippled through the crowd. Those who were sleeping were roused from their slumber.

And there wasn't just one source of the fires. Two, three, then another four. The fires had started in several locations on the buildings along the ridge. It was safe to see them as a series of fires lit in turn.

"Thank you, Seraphina. Looks like things are going to plan."

Seraphina had already sent secret missives to the younger generals she had been close to. If they succeeded, their holdings would be guaranteed. In a truly desperate situation, it appeared they'd clung to the hope offered by her letters.

"Now the preparations are set. Prepare to stage a night attack!"

My shout was answered by an enthusiastic cheer.

"Still," I continued, "you need not charge in this time like in our fight with Brando. They've lit the weapons caches and food caches on fire. Our goal is to add to their panic. At most, it will take them five days to surrender."

My words were prescient.

The castle didn't fall that day, but those who had received the letters had left the castle and joined my ranks.

"Brantaar Castle's supplies have been burned, their horses have fled, and they are out of arrows. They have no choice but to accept an ultimatum to surrender," one of the generals said.

"Yes. I plan to be magnanimous."

Fires continued to be lit sporadically within Brantaar Castle.

The betrayals were mounting. The enemies of Ayles Caltis were on our side.

Then, two days later, a messenger finally came down from the castle to negotiate a surrender.

The messenger was wearing white, the color of submission and death. It seemed they'd determined they had no chance of winning.

The messenger said, "My lord is willing to accept any punishment," with his head bowed.

"Then answer my question honestly, will you?" I decided to satisfy my curiosity before the negotiations.

"Yes, Sir Regent. What answer do you seek?"

"This rebellion—were Ayles and Brando the only ones involved in planning it? Or was there someone else pulling the strings?"

This was an elaborate scheme. Surely there might have been others involved.

Oda Nobunaga mentioned he'd been faced by an encirclement arranged by his enemies in the past. Was there not something similar being planned for me?

"If the unvarnished truth will bring some clemency…," the messenger started, his expression changing.

"That depends on what you have to say."

"It was Orsent Cathedral of Fortwest Prefecture, and the King of the West…"

"The King of the West" referred to the last king, Paffus VI. He had taken refuge in the western lands—the Great Isle Region.

Added to the mix was an old adversary that I had fought once before, Orsent Cathedral.

"The King of the West had originally prepared several secret letters to the various lords. In any event, the moment the regent eventually struck the North in order to put down rebellious lords there, those lords were to revolt all at once… I don't know if Seitred, the Margrave of Machaal, intended to cooperate, but it was likely that he knew of this plan."

"I see. So the plan was to rob me of a place to return to while I was on campaign."

"Regardless, the choice of whether to obey was left to the discretion of each lord. There were probably many who didn't contribute forces."

"Well, secret letters merely need to be burned to remove any evidence of their arrival. Most of the lords were probably waiting to see how it would pan out."

And yet I felt a chill through my heart.

My precautions had kept it from becoming a serious issue, but one wrong step and I would have lost my home.

Greater power wouldn't necessarily make me more secure. As my reach expanded, there would be those who would rebel.

"Very well," I said. "Now, concerning the fate of your lord, I'd like to discuss this with my vassals before coming to a decision. I ask that you wait here."

I headed to the rear of our cantonment.

I entered the council building, a particularly large, well-built structure in the city we had occupied.

That was where Seraphina had set up her temporary residence.

"Welcome back, dear husband. I think it's safe to consider this a win for our side." Seraphina smiled at me. "Congratulations."

Of course, Seraphina was on my side. Her words were genuine. But even now I felt a bit guilty about having her say it to me. I still had a heart. While I'd killed plenty of people, that didn't mean I'd stopped being human as a result.

"We're currently in the middle of negotiating terms of surrender. It seems your father knows the game is up."

"I see. Then we've won. This land will be at peace again."

"So I wanted to ask your opinion on what terms to offer."

I supposed this was a pointless feeling of mercy.

Perhaps this would just make my wife suffer more.

Either way, this was the choice I'd made. It was simply my way of doing things.

Seraphina and I spent several moments gazing at each other.

But the mood wasn't unpleasant. Seraphina smiled as though we were at the castle. Nothing in her gaze indicated any blame or struggle.

I was reminded once again that Seraphina's profession was Saint.

Seraphina had constantly supported me. She would always be my ally, even if her house was on the verge of extinction.

"What opinion is there to express, except that there's no reason to let a rebel like this live? All there is to decide is how he should die, no?"

"True, we couldn't just do a slap on the wrist like seizing half his territories, but if the enemy ran, then it's another matter entirely whether or not we should pursue them."

Seraphina probably knew the castle layout well. "Ohhh," she said softly to herself. "If you left open the castle's equivalent of a postern, no doubt he could run toward the Northlands."

"It's not plausible for all of them to escape, but I'd imagine Ayles and his escorts could get out. We could advance into the castle as it's in chaos and execute the main parties that remained within. That would bring the rebellion here in Mineria to an end, and it would save your father's life. How about it?"

I thought it wasn't a bad idea. This way, I could maintain my conqueror ambitions and avoid hurting Seraphina's feelings at the same time.

Seraphina softly wrapped my hands in hers.

"Sweet husband, you're a gentle soul. I've made you worry on my behalf." She then shook her head from side to side. "But if Ayles survives as a general, he'll be a complication down the line. It's best to kill him now."

Seraphina intentionally referred to him as Ayles to show he was the enemy.

"There's no need for any further sympathy," she added. "I've made my decision. Even if staying by your side leads us straight to hell itself." Seraphina lightly kissed my knuckles. "I'm not afraid of that if it's by your side. I say bring it on. So unify the kingdom as soon as you can."

I embraced Seraphina tightly.

I hadn't noticed the tears flowing from my eyes.

"Thank you."

"This is just part of living in chaotic times. There's nothing to thank me for."

◇

I gave the messenger my terms.

"If the family and its vassals that we name are willing to fall upon their swords, we'll spare the lives of the garrison and consider employing the others. This is merely a proposal; it's your choice whether to accept it. You're free to choose to continue the bloodshed."

The messenger must have known, but his expression clouded when he saw the list of names presented by my vassal.

"This would spell the end of the Caltis clan."

"That's the way things go in war, isn't it? Surely you know that as well as we do. If there were more who hadn't cooperated with the rebellion, I would have considered sparing more of them. But such a man is Ayles that you came together as one to try to defeat me."

"Then I will take this back to my master..."

It looked like the messenger had lost weight in this short time.

I guess it's that sort of man who clings to even the smallest bit of hope. Unfortunately, there was none this time.

The next morning, the Ayles side sent over a messenger stating that it would accept the terms. It was at that moment that, for all intents and purposes, the independent country of Mineria was doomed to end.

The main Caltis clan members and the various pro-war members slowly came down from the castle.

There were gallows erected, and there they began to hang themselves one by one.

I was able to have a conversation with Ayles before his sentence was carried out.

"No doubt my daughter insisted that I die?"

"That's right."

"I should have expected it of that hoyden...," Ayles said with a chuckle. "I will die here, but I've left plenty of seedlings. Hell, among my descendants is a child of the regent. My bloodline will prosper."

"You were a great general, but you made a wrong turn at the end of your journey."

"I regret being born in the same age as you. If not for you, I would've wiped out the Nayvil clan long ago."

Then our time was up.

Ayles, too, died upon the gallows.

Seraphina calmly witnessed the end of her clan from afar. She didn't need to be there, but she had insisted, saying she didn't want to look away from reality.

Laviala appeared sadder than Seraphina herself.

"I think Seraphina's trying to shoulder the burden of her clan's demise. Perhaps she thinks that's her fate. She really is a brave woman."

"Laviala, if she seems to be hurting, could you reach out to her? I worry that she won't show the true depths of her pain in front of me."

"Yes. After all, the people dear to you, Lord Alsrod, are dear to me as well."

After staying at the castle for about three days to deal with the handover of the castle and confirm assignments for the surviving officers, I turned back toward Maust Castle.

Kaito Shibano

With the rebellions quelled for now, I finally had some time to spend with the children.

"Grandfather was killed, yes?"

My eldest, growing up bright beyond his years thanks to education, spoke rather sadly. As a child of Seraphina, he was Ayles's grandson.

"This is what it means to live in a time of war," I told him. "I believe that this sort of thing shouldn't continue forever. Yes… By the time you have your profession-bestowal ceremony, I'll bring peace to these lands and make sure such things won't happen again."

"Thank you, Father." He nodded intently. I could still sense his fear.

I gently reached over and ruffled his hair.

"Worry not. I'll make sure my children won't suffer in that way. You'll never have to fight your brothers or sisters. I promise you, so long as I live, that'll be true."

Seraphina and I had taken on so many sins—we might as well shoulder so much that everyone else would be liberated by it.

There were several other minor rebellions in lands near the capital, but as information that I had the upper hand spread, the reality was that they fizzled out on their own. The regional lords who had been waiting to see which way the wind was blowing had subsequently jumped onto my bandwagon and started quelling these uprisings on their own.

On the way back to the royal capital, I visited the Nistonia clan and thanked them for constantly remaining by my side.

"Thanks to the Nistonia clan's efforts in containing the nearby squabbles, the chaos didn't spread any farther. As the kingdom's regent, I offer my deepest gratitude."

It seemed Soltis Nistonia was taken aback by my modesty. For all his ability, he could be such a timid man.

But that timidity had worked out in his favor. It had certainly helped him survive to this point. Half-baked bravado often led one to one's doom.

"No, no, Sir Regent, you are now husband to my daughter Yuca. Fighting for your sake is but my duty. And there were hardly any rebellions of note in this region."

"That is because everyone was well aware that the Nistonia clan was one of my strongest backers. Preventing conflict before it happens is a greater accomplishment than any celebrated general's victories."

"I'm grateful for your words." Soltis let out a sigh. "With the great rebellions quelled, perhaps I'll take the opportunity to pass the reins to my son. If I cling too long to power, I'm sure my son will want to be rid of me."

"Perhaps. But there will be more great conflicts to come, so you might do well to wait a while longer."

Soltis blinked. No doubt from his perspective, this region was now at peace. That wasn't wrong per se.

"We need to bring the West to heel," I said. "The previous king is still attempting to sow discord in the world, and it's our duty to stop him."

There's one last step before I can unite the kingdom.

After my detour at the Nistonia clan, I took the army, which had been joined by the remaining forces, and proudly marched into the royal capital.

It was to show off our quelling of the rebellion to the capital's residents.

According to my rappa spies, the people's reactions were varied.

There were those who believed the regent was the greatest power in the kingdom, while others believed it was terrifying that I was willing to kill my own in-laws. Since they were both stating the truth, there wasn't much I could do about either belief.

Fortunately, I had no relations, blood or otherwise, with those supporting the King of the West. That made the next step somewhat easier.

——So you've finally made it this far.

Oda Nobunaga sighed.

——Akechi Mitsuhide killed me just as all that remained was to advance into the West. You, too, should be careful of that woman Kelara.

No, I'm sure there's nothing to worry about with her.

Although I suppose I may as well go ahead and show her some gratitude.

Since I arrived late in the capital that day, I only sent a messenger to the king, noting that I would pay my respects later, and decided to get some rest.

I summoned Kelara to my room.

"What may I do for you today?"

Kelara primly bowed her head. No matter how far up the ranks she rose, these mannerisms hadn't changed.

"First, I had a question about the old ways for you. Go ahead and take a seat. You don't need to stand while we discuss this."

Kelara quietly moved her chair and took a seat.

"Would a nonroyal be allowed to kill a former king?"

Kelara swiftly raised her head and looked straight into my eyes. "You mean you intend to kill the last king, Paffus VI."

"That's right. As regent, I have a duty to defeat those who resist His Majesty. The ones I've taken down to this point were all of negligible rank, so there was nothing to worry about. But even if Paffus is a threat to His Majesty's reign, a previous king of the realm is a man of the highest birth. Am I, a man born of minor nobility, permitted to kill him?"

"A moment, please."

Kelara began to write out a list of names on a piece of memo paper. I immediately understood that it was a list of kings who had been killed.

"There have been five examples of kings who were slain in battle, two of whom were replaced by a new dynasty, so their own dynasties ended with them. The other three were slain by opponents who had declared themselves kings, so those do not count as examples of kings being slain by their vassals. Further, there have been no examples of kings who had vacated a throne being slain, either."

It was certainly unheard of for a former king to end up a wanderer.

"I see. So would it be possible to kill the former king? If I can't, then I have no choice but to capture him. Then again, if I capture him and bring him to the royal capital, His Majesty is likely to order his execution."

No doubt Hasse would try to eliminate any family members who would be a threat to his reign. I couldn't fathom him letting Paffus live, based on their past conflict. Even the most merciful punishment would probably be exile to some isolated island far from civilization.

"Certainly, it would be questionable if the regent were to muster the forces of his own volition," Kelara explained. "However, the regent is the representative of His Majesty the king. Therefore, it would mean His Majesty is the one who defeats the former king, which I do not believe would be considered problematic."

"I see. So there wouldn't be a problem if His Majesty issued the extermination order."

"Yes. It would be a substantially greater problem to disobey His Majesty's direct orders, and no one would regard it as an act of disloyalty."

I nodded firmly. I felt a small weight lift from my shoulders.

"Good! Then to cement His Majesty's reign, we need to take down these rebels as quickly as possible. The enemy this time is large, but that won't stop me!"

But at this, Kelara's expression clouded a bit.

I didn't miss the change in expression.

"Mm? Was there something odd about what I said?"

"No...it's nothing of significance."

"Don't lie. I can tell you have concerns. Go on, tell me. There's no one else here. I'll even swear to the gods here and now if you wish."

Kelara seemed to be torn, but then opened her mouth as though she'd resigned herself to it.

"Well...Sir Regent, do you really intend to protect the order of the Kingdom of Therwil once you've united the lands...?"

My smile vanished in an instant. It didn't mean I was angry, however. I carefully tried to see where she was going.

"I don't understand what you're asking. Isn't uniting the realms of the kingdom the same as restoring order to the kingdom itself? The rebellions within the kingdom are the anomaly, not the norm."

"Sir Regent, if, as regent, you wipe out the former king and his allies, there will be no force in the kingdom capable of resisting you." Kelara slowly squeezed out the next sentence: "I thought that perhaps, you might be in a position to be handed the kingdom at that point, Sir Regent..."

She averted her gaze. By her standards, she was clearly rattled. She didn't look like her usual calm, steady self.

"So, more succinctly, you want to know if I intend to usurp the crown."

"Y-yes..."

It was quite a question, so Kelara's reply was muted.

"Then let me ask you in turn. Do you think I should become king? Or should I refrain?"

I had no duty to tell her my true intentions. Kelara was still my vassal. She was sworn to obey me.

Kelara's gaze turned farther downward. It was as though she couldn't meet my eyes at all.

——Explain yourself! Why are you playing with fire?

Oda Nobunaga yelled in my head.

——This is far too risky a way to test her! Do you understand you're putting her in a position where she's justified in attacking you here and now?! Why do you needlessly bring up the core of the problem?! If this woman values the past order more than anything else, it's all over!

*   *   *

Oda Nobunaga, it might be true that Akechi Mitsuhide was a conservative reactionary, and Kelara might have some of that in her, but she wouldn't betray someone over this.

That much I was certain of given my own lived experiences.

Surely you don't believe that Akechi Mitsuhide killed you simply out of a love of the old ways, do you? People are much more self-serving than that. They won't act solely on ideals.

——That's true. But that doesn't make this any less dangerous.

I didn't want to keep using Kelara with doubt hanging over her.

After all, Kelara was one of my concubines.

"Well, Kelara? I'm asking you as a vassal. You need only tell me your opinion. I'm sure you have plenty to say."

Sweat beaded on Kelara's brow.

"I believe that…for the sake of a peaceful world…you becoming a king should also be an option…," Kelara finally answered after a long pause.

"You're not lying to me, are you?"

"No, not a word of it…"

Kelara slowly raised her head.

Her eyes were full of determination.

"The Hundred Years' Rebellion has yet to end. In its time, war and starvation have claimed the lives of more people than we could possibly count. So many people have suffered, one must think of them not as individual names, but simply as numbers."

The deep pain of this tragedy showed in Kelara's expression.

"Now, it would be unfair to lay all the responsibility at the dynasty's feet. If the kingdom's regional lords had banded together and protected the monarchy, at the very least there wouldn't have been civil war. Still…the king also has a duty to step away from the throne when he can no longer wield sufficient power to rule… Such was said in the *Royal Peace* over three hundred years ago."

I'd never heard of the work in question, but it must have been well known among intellectuals like Kelara.

"I originally hoped that the current royal family would once again govern these realms. That is, of course, what a servant of the royal family ought to believe."

"But you felt there was a limit to what could be accomplished that way."

Kelara nodded slowly.

"When His Majesty unites the kingdom, no doubt he won't simply leave the regent…you, Lord Alsrod, alone. Your authority has grown to that extent, and has become that inviolable. No matter how you feel, and what you intend, Lord Alsrod, the honeymoon will end…"

Kelara made a point of addressing me by name as a display of determination. My vassals generally called me Sir Regent or "my lord." Pretty much the only one who addressed me by name was Laviala, who had known me since childhood.

"And once you are gone, Lord Alsrod… Whatever your title, when Lord Alsrod the individual is gone, the kingdom's peace will scatter to the winds and return to anarchy…"

"In which case, it would be better that I become king."

It would have been cruel to force Kelara to put the conclusion into words herself, so I finished her sentence for her.

Kelara needed only to nod.

"I'm somewhat different compared to your loyal vassals like Laviala," she said. "If I determined that you, Lord Alsrod, would bring further strife into the world, I might very well turn my arrows against you."

Kelara's voice had the faintest of trembles. Only a determined woman would say those words out loud. Even then, it would be difficult to stay calm while doing so.

I stood up from my chair and slowly circled behind Kelara.

Then I lightly placed my hands on her shoulders.

"I promise to you, I'll make this a wonderful world."

Swearing that oath to her was the most I could do now, and the best thing I could do.

Since I was behind her, obviously I couldn't see Kelara's expression. Still, I felt like I could feel her emotions emanating from her.

A teardrop spilled from Kelara onto the table.

"Yes… Please—don't betray me…"

Kelara quickly wiped at her eyes with her left hand.

"Recently, I've become afraid of myself. In my dreams, I send out troops to slay you, Lord Alsrod, when you're at a cantonment… Those dreams have come up more often of late. There are times I'm so frightened I don't know what to think…"

"That's probably because of your profession—Akechi Mitsuhide."

Kelara's profession was the name of a vassal who'd killed Oda Nobunaga in the past. It wouldn't be strange for that profession to be subconsciously influencing Kelara's thoughts.

"If you fear me to be a threat, I think it may be better to kill me."

Because of her extremely serious personality, Kelara probably meant it.

"A man who can't make use of a skilled general like you isn't worthy of being a regent or a king. No matter how wild a horse you are, I'm confident I can ride you."

"I understand. However, I've said all I ought to say. If you wish to be rid of me, you need only do it…"

"Forget that. I want to bed you."

I honestly voiced my desire.

"Right after a talk like this…?"

"I told you I'd ride you, mm? Besides, pleasure is excellent medicine for lifting a gloom. That's not a joke. I'm serious."

Kelara undraped my arms from her shoulders and, standing, murmured, "Pardon me," before kissing me.

After that, we switched locations and enjoyed our rendezvous. No—in Kelara's case, it was less like enjoyment and more like she sought me out to reassure herself.

Once we were finished with a rather intense session, we lay in bed next to each other.

"At this rate, I worry you'll be assassinated rather easily."

"Oh, not at all. I only do this with those I truly trust. Particularly given that I'm in a position where I might have to worry about assassins more than His Majesty himself."

I grasped Kelara's hand under the covers.

This hand won't ever try to slay me, I thought without the slightest doubt.

After all, we knew each other intimately. Surely we were past the point of pent-up frustrations exploding into a knife in the back. If she had any complaints, she could air them to me.

"I, Kelara Hilara, will serve you, Sir Regent Alsrod, with all that my heart can give."

I knew from gazing at Kelara's face: She did love me. Today's conversation was like the reverse of that coin.

That only endeared Kelara to me.

"Kelara, let's do that again."

"I'm a bit tired..."

"Serve me a bit more."

I once again embraced Kelara's dark-skinned body.

I felt an intense satisfaction from having such a pure-hearted vassal.

And I believed this kingdom wouldn't last in the long term with a man like Hasse—who had so readily offered me a vassal like Kelara—as monarch.

I truly needed to become king—for this kingdom's sake.

With my vassals in tow, I attended an audience with the king.

"I have quelled the rebellions and safely returned to the capital. I fear I may have caused you concern during my absence, but rest assured, none can now threaten this, your royal capital."

"Yes, we had trusted in your victory, Brother."

The vassals surrounding the king glanced between the two of us. While many of the king's vassals were those I had chosen myself, there were, of course, several who were the king's favorites, and not all of them were my allies. Plenty of them didn't enjoy the presence of an upstart.

"You may already know, Your Majesty, but it appears this rebellion was orchestrated by the former king, Paffus VI."

"I see—I suspected as much. That fool… Continuing his pointless resistance…"

The previous king, Paffus VI, was both cousin and mortal enemy to Hasse. Indeed, Paffus VI had taken the title of king from Hasse's father.

From his expression alone, I saw just angry Hasse had become.

"As for how we intend to proceed with our pacification plans, I believe it's about time to exterminate the western lords who shelter the former king," I said. "The major lords of the Great Isle Region in particular regard him as their sovereign. We cannot simply let them maintain that facade."

"At last!"

Hasse let out an elated shout. The unification of the Kingdom of Therwil depended upon that plan.

If the unification came to fruition, Hasse would become, in name, the one who had restored order. If the kingdom's history continued normally, he would be known as the one who had revived the dynasty's fortunes. I understood why he'd dream about that.

Nevertheless, several vassals didn't appear pleased.

It was clear they viewed me as a threat. If I went ahead and finished pacifying the entire kingdom as the commander in chief, that meant my authority would grow further.

They were concerned about what I would do under those circumstances.

Their concerns were justified, but they couldn't very well remove me without any evidence. Moreover, without me, the world would fall further into chaos. There was no telling what would happen if the previous king attacked from the West in my absence.

I might be poison for the dynasty, but the disease known as the previous king couldn't be stopped without that poison. It was a painful situation to be caught in.

"I believe we will begin preparing to finish our task of completing the reunification of the kingdom by defeating the Counts of Talmud and

Samuur, the main supporters and major regional lords of the Great Isle Region. Of course, it will require many soldiers and enormous amounts of supplies. I would like your permission to raise a temporary tax to pay for those matters."

I respectfully bowed my head to Hasse.

The next fight would not only be a long campaign, it would be an excessively large-scale one. It would require meticulous planning. A single large loss in a field battle could very well tip the odds back in the favor of the previous king.

Hasse nodded magnanimously.

"Yes, you bring up good points, our brother. We must leave no stone unturned in preparing for this fight. After all, we are restoring order to a long-fractured kingdom. I myself have a great many ideas."

Hasse was probably just thinking about a victory parade in the royal capital.

Of course, that much would be on any king's mind. There was no point in criticizing him there.

Hasse wasn't a particularly good king. I was aware of that from our many meetings.

Which wasn't to say that he was particularly dim by the standards of the past, either. No doubt he would have been adequate if he had reigned during a peaceful time.

A king isn't a hero. It was enough for a king to stand at the top of a kingdom and check to make sure the politics remained relatively fair. At the very least, I'd never heard any rumors of Hasse enacting bad laws and raising the ire of the citizens around the royal capital. He could at least fill the basic role of king.

If anything, the evil, ruthless monarchs who had left their mark on history had all tried to create new laws and thrown their own kingdoms into confusion. In other words, tyranny and incompetent rule were the result of those with a desire to wield power simply misapplying that power. Supposedly the figurehead king in Oda Nobunaga's time also became oddly motivated, and that was how he ended up in conflict with Oda Nobunaga.

The current problem, however, was that this era of strife needed a great leader.

Which was why, as reward, I would eventually take this kingdom.

"So, Brother, we have a request for you concerning the next stage of the unification campaign. Will you listen?" Hasse asked as he leaned forward in his throne.

"Yes. What do you wish to command of me?"

"We would like to command the army and fight in the campaign."

I almost let my displeasure show on my face, but I managed to keep it hidden. In a word, he was going to get in the way.

"I see. If we can have you encouraging our forces, I would appreciate it beyond measure. No doubt our generals will be motivated by your presence, Your Majesty."

"No, we mean to have you sit out the next campaign and rest, Brother."

At first, I didn't understand what he'd just said.

"We believe that the king should be the one to finish unifying this kingdom. Otherwise, no one will accept our sovereignty. Simply sitting upon this throne here in the capital doesn't make one a king—rather, it is accomplished solely through fighting for the people and gaining their respect, is it not?"

Hasse's words sent a murmur through the room.

Many of the vassals present likely hadn't thought about this.

My personal opinion of Hasse went from "merely average" to "incompetent." He was about to stick his hand where it didn't belong and be bitten for it.

"Your Majesty," I began, "the next campaign shall not be an easy one. It is one we must approach by covering all of the possible outcomes. Please, could you leave the campaign to I, the Regent, who have long been accustomed to battle?"

"We understand what you wish to say. But we have concerns…concerns that can only be addressed by fighting as a king."

Hasse's voice grew quieter. Here was something that was difficult for him to say to me.

"There are those among us who believe that if you, dear brother-in-law, continue to gain laurels, the people will believe you worthy of being king rather than I myself. It goes without saying that you have never betrayed us, of course."

Several people looked down at the ground. They must not have been expecting the king to say those words out loud.

"Even if you have no intention of doing so, Brother, the people will typically support those who win in battle. In which case, if we complete this campaign, then the crown will be secure… That is what we think."

"I see. Very well…"

Looks like this is going to end up being quite the hassle.

It was true that if Hasse could manage to reunify the kingdom, opinions of him would change. That would only apply if he was actually able to accomplish it, of course.

"In any case, there are many preparations to attend to, so let us take our time to plan this out," I said in order to avoid getting into a debate at that moment.

◇

That day, I visited my official wife, Lumie, for the first time in a while.

As I had been on campaign for so long, I hadn't had any opportunities to see her. Besides, since I had just met with Hasse, the king, it would reflect poorly on me if I visited one of my concubines instead.

And I thought I could grumble a bit to Lumie.

"Goodness, my brother is being quite the bother, demanding to make himself the supreme general."

Lumie said it before I could.

Lumie had her pet, a long-haired cat, on her lap, stroking it. It was a gift from some region of the country. When it came to the regent and his wife, just the number of gifts we received was ridiculous.

That said, I wasn't seeking additional wealth, which was why the ones giving the presents also tried novelties like the cat in an attempt to curry favor with us.

At the very least, Lumie was extremely fond of the animal, and she pampered it. Perhaps she was particularly fond of it because she hadn't had a child yet.

"It isn't as though my brother has never fought wars at all. He has taken up a sword or spear when his life was in danger a few times. However, he hasn't survived this long due to his skill and courage. He was just lucky."

"Luck is an important thing to have. After all, the unlucky don't survive very long. Surely there's never been a king, now or in ancient times, that faced no assassination plots."

Fortunately, I didn't have to be the one criticizing Lumie's brother to her face. If anything, I was defending him.

"Yet my brother appears to believe he has some skill and courage of his own. Of course, even he doesn't believe he can defeat you, but I suppose it's true that he's yet to lose in his life."

Lumie drew her pet cat to her chest. The cat didn't squirm and remained calm. It must have fully accepted Lumie as its owner, or perhaps it thought of her as its mother.

Come to think of it, I suppose none of my other consorts had quite the maternal presence of Lumie. Her growing up in a convent meant she had been raised with a great deal of compassion.

If I were to become king, Lumie would become queen consort—that is, the mother of the country.

However, if Lumie didn't bear any children, would Seraphina end up becoming queen consort?

Conflicts have played out multiple times in history among a king's consorts.

For instance, the queen consort killing the king's favored concubine after the king dies, or the reverse, one who had climbed from being a favored concubine to being queen consort destroying the families of the other concubines... There were plenty of these off-putting stories of palace intrigue.

Frankly, that was one thing I wanted to prevent at all costs. Perhaps I was getting ahead of myself, as I was not yet king, but I intended to avoid seeing the people I love felled by tragedy, no matter what it took.

"I understand His Majesty's feelings of wanting to be remembered as the reviver of the dynasty," I said, "but the next campaign will truly be the one that determines who controls the kingdom. It would be a problem if His Majesty, with little experience in war, were to be out on the front lines. At worst, if something were to happen to him..."

I left my words vague, but Lumie couldn't have possibly missed my implication.

If King Hasse were to die, the former king would loudly proclaim that he was now the sole monarch. It could change the perception that he was the legitimate king practically overnight.

"Indeed. While my brother has children, two of them are daughters, and one a son who is still in infancy. Not a reassuring presence to have as next in line for the throne."

"That's right. I would like His Majesty to show a bit more restraint."

True, Hasse's death would make legitimate possession of the crown an extremely tenuous claim.

Even if he existed only because of my support, there were plenty of lords who only recognized Hasse's legitimacy because he was an adult male. If he were to be succeeded by an infant ruler, the situation would change dramatically.

An infant ruler has no power of their own. It's one thing if the king's in-laws are influential, but Hasse's wife was no such thing.

Which was why Hasse exposing himself on the front lines for me and for the kingdom was nothing but risk for no discernible benefit.

"Lumie, there's quite a bit of time to prepare until the next campaign. I'd like to ask you to try to dissuade His Majesty from participating in battle."

Lumie nodded with a smile.

"Yes, I, too, believe that my brother would be happiest were he to stay quietly in the capital. He should not be setting out to war."

It seemed we'd settled that matter for the time being.

The rest of the evening was dedicated to staying with my wife. I placed my hand on Lumie's shoulder.

"Could you shift your affections from the cat to me? It's been so long I've almost forgotten what your skin feels like against mine."

"Mm, but I'm sure you had plenty of fun while you were out on campaign."

Lumie pouted. She must have learned that expression from Laviala or Seraphina.

I wasn't exactly innocent on that score, so even I had trouble responding. For example, there was Talsha, the Margrave of Machaal's younger sister...

"Oh, seems I hit the mark. I'm afraid I must resent you for it," Lumie teased, and then she nodded again. "However, my misfortune was decided the moment I married a man such as yourself. Please, for now, at least, focus your love upon me."

Lumie had really grown into a beautiful wife. Not just her body, but the elegance of her mannerisms. She was truly a matchless woman.

No doubt there were many men who'd dream of bedding a woman like this once in their lifetime.

For me to have Lumie all to myself... Well, being regent has its perks. There was certainly worth in continuing in the job despite all the dangers.

As I lay in bed sleeping, Lumie clung to me.

"Oh, I've just remembered. I have something I needed to tell you, my dear."

"Here? Now?"

What could this be about?

I stroked my fingers through Lumie's hair as I asked. Even in the dark room I could see her milky form well.

"A few days before your return, I paid a visit to the temple of the god of fertility. There, I received a revelation—that I would be blessed with a child today."

I pulled Lumie closer once more.

“If you’re concerned about the fact that you don’t have a child as my official wife, don’t worry. I won’t neglect you over something like that.”

Perhaps Lumie felt some urgency from watching my son with Seraphina grow up.

“I’m not worried. I’m just noting that I will also be bearing you a child.”

Lumie was smiling. True, it didn’t appear as though she was worried at all.

“I received some herbs from the temple as well.”

“Try not to take anything you’re not sure about…”

I was more worried about Lumie than about any potential children.

“It will be all right. No doubt this child will be beautiful, like a jewel,” Lumie said with conviction. “A child descended from you and royalty.”

Those words stuck with me for some reason.

Lumie’s child would be the nephew or niece of King Hasse.

A while later, as I was planning a great mobilization of military forces while dealing with administrative work, Lumie made an announcement to me.

“It appears I really am pregnant. Lately I’ve been experiencing that—what is it called? Morning sickness?”

“Really?! You’re sure you’re not just overthinking things?”

“Dear, this is something I suppose a gentleman may not understand, but there is no mistaking it. Please believe me.”

I embraced Lumie tightly and rejoiced from the bottom of my heart.

At the same time, I thought of a particular scheme.

It was still beset with uncertainty, and it was a dangerous gamble, but it was a scheme nonetheless.

I paid a visit to Yanhaan under the pretext of participating in a tea ceremony. Of course, I still went through the proper motions and treated the ceremony with respect. In fact, I thought my skills had improved quite a bit.

Yanhaan was, in a way, one of my political advisers. But I didn't have her propose multiple policies to me. I simply talked with her and came to a decision based on that conversation. Yanhaan was something of a philosopher, and she helped me examine matters from various angles.

Neither merchants nor generals can avoid leaving something to chance.

No matter how much one plans, the plans can never be perfect. Even an undefeated warrior might die from a stray arrow. A ship full of cargo could sink, and suddenly you're left with enormous debts.

Hence why talking to a dyed-in-the-wool merchant like Yanhaan settled my nerves.

I drank the tea quietly during the ceremony, feeling the liquid enter my throat.

"It's good."

"Why thank you." Yanhaan narrowed her eyes as she smiled. "Are you perhaaaps wondering about what highway to use in waaar? I can't imagine what else you might be thiiiinking of," she said languidly. Given that she brought the question up herself, she probably knew that wasn't what I'd come for.

"Can I consider what we discuss here to be in confidence?"

"Yes, that goes without saying. A merchant's trust is their biggest asset, after all. Further, it's forbidden to leak the contents of a tea ceremony to outsiders."

I let a moment pass in silence.

That silence allowed me to check for any spies by feeling for their movement. The more caution now, the better.

"His Majesty is insisting upon fighting as the supreme commander in our next campaign."

"So I hear. Kings, after all, have been leaders of warriors since ancient times. It's only natural, I think." Yanhaan's eyes widened a bit. "Still, if His Majesty is short on good strategists, then perhaps the regent could do his planning for him. That shouldn't pose any issues. What is most important for the regent at the moment is to avoid losing. Whatever else you are to do, first you must unify the kingdom."

Her statement presupposed that I was planning to usurp the throne.

"As for that, for example, and I do mean as a hypothetical example…," I started, gazing intently into Yanhaan's eyes. "What's our chance of winning if His Majesty dies in battle?"

I could see Yanhaan swallow.

Probably because it was a question that required her to take a moment to think through.

Essentially, I was asking: Could we get rid of the king in this campaign and win it at the same time?

If that plan succeeded, I would be able to effectively take over the Kingdom of Therwil. No matter who was to become king, he would have to be young, and if the man responsible for reunifying the country was still around, then it would naturally work out that way.

"I'm not an expert in matters of war, so I don't know the precise details," Yanhaan replied. "However, it would be far too dangerous. It would be fine if you could win, but if you were to be chased by the former king's forces…"

Perhaps the former king's reign was justified after all—at least, that might be what many people would start thinking. That was simply how risky this bet would be.

If my own allies defected to the previous king, one after another, then I would be done as regent.

"However, if I execute it well, then my authority would become much stronger. No, let me say it plainly. There would be no one above me in this kingdom."

Of course, someone other than I would likely inherit the crown.

Even then, it would be one of the young children of the deceased Hasse. They wouldn't be able to do anything. And their mother's family had no power.

At which point I would have no choice but to rule the entire country. If I departed, the country would fall into utter anarchy. No one would want that. The kingdom would finally have been unified. Those who were tired of war would try to maintain that stability.

And I had one more trump card.

Rather, if I hadn't had that card, I wouldn't even seriously consider this idea.

"Lumie is pregnant—meaning there will be a child descended from both myself and the royal family."

Evidently surprised at my words, Yanhaan glanced down.

"At the very least, things are not yet in place for that child to take the throne...," she said.

"That much I know. But it does mean the possibility of the royal family's bloodline continuing has increased."

Of course, if all of Hasse's children died, then the main royal line would go extinct, and the children of Lumie's husband—that is, the princess's consort's children—might be able to ascend to the throne. But that likely wouldn't happen unless something like a plague conveniently occurred.

Besides, if there was such a plague, there was no guarantee my own children or concubines wouldn't become victims themselves.

"In any case, His Majesty still intends to participate in this campaign as the supreme commander," I added. "If His Majesty were to die in battle, it's necessary to think about how we'll regroup. It's always important to be prepared for every contingency."

"You're right... If you accomplished enough to overwhelm the loss of the king, then perhaps there wouldn't be a problem."

Seemed like Yanhaan had regained some of her calm.

"For example," she continued, "if the previous king were also to die in battle, then there would be no issue concerning the current royal lineage, no?"

I realized that a smile had made its way onto my face.

"Both sides of the dynasty taking each other down, huh?" I said. "In that case, one of Hasse's children will take the throne and the dynasty will continue."

It wasn't a bad proposal. Of course, it would be dangerous.

Besides, this wasn't something I myself could make happen.

If the previous king didn't appear on the front lines, we couldn't kill him in battle.

As for what it would take to lure him out into battle...

The fact that Hasse was out in the front as well.

It's not an impossible plan.

But if I'm not extremely careful, it'll look like I orchestrated it.

I suppose the quickest option is to persuade the king.

◇

"My brother is extremely stubborn..."

Lumie, who appeared to be slowly showing signs of her pregnancy, grumbled to me.

"All he talks about is restoring glory to the royal family... If I tell him it's dangerous, he says he understands... That's not understanding. It's as if he's infatuated with his own self-image..."

"Lumie, if we continue fighting His Majesty on this, he may think we have ulterior motives. I'm starting to have no choice but to bend on this one."

"Huh?"

Evidently she hadn't expected me to say that, and she peered curiously at me.

"I suppose that's true... I'm sure there are those who believe you're aiming for the royal family by becoming supreme commander..."

No one was saying that quite so directly, but some must have been thinking as much. Someone with authority over the military also has the power to rule over the rest of the country.

"Still, he could put himself at risk. I will explain that to him, and make sure that he understands, before he makes his decision. There's never been a regent that's fought through as many battlefields as I have."

"Yes... I certainly hope he'll reconsider..."

If he changed his mind, then I would just do what I needed to do with that.

I formulated my plans, taking every possibility into account.

◇

"Brother, no matter what you say, we intend to participate in this campaign! To restore this kingdom's realms under its rightful, traditional banner, we can't very well sit atop the throne waiting from start to finish. If we don't take a sword in our hand, future generations will mock us as a cowardly king."

After arguments from vassals other than me, it seemed that Hasse had grown even more obstinate.

"We will command the soldiers on the battlefield and obtain a glorious victory! That will put an end to this age of chaos!"

I suppose his obstinance had been unavoidable. There was no bridging the gap between the argument that it was too dangerous for him to participate and Hasse's belief that he understood the risks. It would just be an argument without end.

"I understand the strength of your conviction, Your Majesty."

"We recognize your feelings, but— Mm? You've finally understood?"

"So I would like to form our plans based upon the assumption that Your Majesty will be on the front lines. No doubt you have heard this repeatedly and you're tired of hearing about it, but anything can happen on the battlefield. There are none who know battlefields as well as I, your regent. If you're willing to listen to my explanations and are still willing to do so..."

"I see, I see! Yes, please do explain!"

Hasse was obviously happy with the development.

A murmur rippled through the other courtiers. Evidently, none had thought I would let Hasse go.

"While care on the battlefield is important, so, too, is care of the residence that you leave vacant. Please set out by taking the greatest precautions."

"Indeed! You're completely correct!"

"So, first, please appoint a crown prince before you leave. After all, you have yet to specify who will be your successor," I said softly.

"But my children are all young. Is it not too early to decide?"

"Going out to the battlefield means the possibility of death. If, in the worst possible event, Your Majesty were to die and if there was no decision on who was to take the throne, the kingdom would fall into anarchy… It could very well endanger the lives of your children…"

"You're right… It's as you say, Brother. If our death throws the future of the kingdom into doubt, there could very well be those who start to believe Paffus ought to be king…"

"In order to avoid such worst-case scenarios, if you are to participate in this campaign, I ask that you do so after appointing a crown prince. Once that is done, and there is a system in place for the vassals to support Your Majesty's successor, then the kingdom won't easily succumb to such an upheaval."

Several vassals made noises of agreement.

The proposal itself was perfectly decent, and not one that would benefit me directly. If I could reduce any unnecessary suspicion, that was good enough.

"Very well. Then I'll pick my eldest child, Attmus, to be my successor."

And so little Attmus, who wasn't even three years old, became the crown prince.

The anointing ceremony of the crown prince was conducted solemnly.

Of course, the crown prince himself didn't seem to comprehend what was going on, but that was understandable given that he was just two years old.

The ritual was conducted with a splendor that would have been difficult to imagine given the depleted royal family of recent years. Thanks to my conquests in the various regions, taxes had started flowing back into the national treasury.

For both Hasse the king and for me, to be able to strengthen the state's authority with this wasn't a bad thing. It was crucial to show off that the royal family now had power.

With this, the possibility of Hasse going to the battlefield went up a notch. At the very least, I could minimize the confusion should Hasse die on the battlefield.

That didn't mean it had advanced to becoming a plan to kill Hasse.

That would happen only if things could be executed in the right way. Currently, Hasse and I were still allied. Without a unified kingdom, I couldn't form a new dynasty, after all.

If those around the kingdom regarded me as a usurper, I'd end up with resistance from all conceivable corners. That would make things harder, not easier.

If the king were to die in war, it was true that things would be easier in some respects. Times of war required a powerful leader.

Perhaps I should ask my profession, who had been down this road before.

Oda Nobunaga, how did you end up driving off the king?

——How unusual for you to ask me a question.

That seemed to put Oda Nobunaga in a good mood.

——My country had a peculiar system. The king, I guess you could call him, had always existed, and there was a supreme general, called a shogun, under him. The shoguns created a system in which they served as the effective kings of the country.

I see. So it was a military government. Pretty common, isn't it?

——The Ashikaga shoguns never held much military power of their own, since it was a bit different from a military government, but it was true that the shogun stood at the top of the military hierarchy. They had the highest court rank among the military. Rank was something provided by the king without the actual authority.

*　*　*

Oh, I see. In that case, you would have justification if you were able to outrank the shogun, right? If you could become higher in rank than the shogun, you no longer had reason to be subordinate to him.

——Yes, you're certainly sharp. That is absolutely correct. Hence why I didn't need to worry too much when I was taking power. Eventually, I thought the court would provide me with a higher rank. When I was of higher rank than the shogun, Ashikaga Yoshiaki, I would gain the right to form my own government.

If there's a separate, objective rank, that would definitely make things easier.

If you could become more highly ranked than the man you had served, it wouldn't be a betrayal of any sort.

——Of course, before that could happen, Yoshiaki rebelled against me and got himself into all sorts of unnecessary mischief... He was annoying, but if I killed him, I would suffer a reputational loss for it. That was what I wanted to avoid at all costs. There were those who had killed shoguns in the past, but none of them had advanced much after.

This Oda Nobunaga might seem reckless, but he was actually quite prudent. All the more reason to listen to his anecdotes.

——Listen. Now is the time to be concerned about your reputation above all else. Humans will subconsciously try to avoid helping traitors. There aren't many who will freely participate knowing their side is considered the wrong side. It's easy enough to drag down a ruler. The question is what comes after. That's true of everything, is it not? Breaking a teacup is easy—the cleanup is what's difficult.

I'll be sure to etch those words into my mind. Yes, the next step is one I have to think carefully about before I try it.

So far, I had only been thinking abstractly about taking down the factions that supported the previous king in the Westlands. Now if Hasse gained renown, it would change the dynamic.

——It would be simpler if there were a system like zenjou in this kingdom. Of course, that didn't exist in Japan, either, so I suppose one shouldn't be greedy.

And what sort of system is this "zenjoe"?

——When an emperor—well, a king, that is—realizes he does not have enough karma to rule, he will peacefully transfer the title to one who is more worthy. At least in theory. Most of the time, a military officer would gain too much power and force a transfer. Then, once the transfer was done, the family of the original ruler would be massacred.

Well, of course, if you didn't do that, your opposition could very well haul them out at any point.

——Exactly. Even then, if people knew that such a system existed, they wouldn't feel as much discomfort at the idea of this transfer of power occurring.

I see.

Then what should my next plan be?

Perhaps I would need a better tactic than the campaign against the Westlands. Fortunately, my home base of Maust, having been cleaned of rebels lately, was as peaceful as ever. Perhaps it'd be better to think of a plan in Maust, even.

In the middle of the anointing ceremony, I let my mind wander.

What's the fastest way to become king?

What's the most secure way of becoming king?

It would be pointless if the monarchy ended with me.

If I don't create a system with which my family can pass down sovereignty from generation to generation, I'll end up a mere hero in an age of war. That would make me no different from Ayles Caltis.

If I don't win in the end, I'll simply make countless people around me unhappy.

I saw Lumie, next to me, cast a sad glance toward her brother, Hasse.

Hasse had tears in his eyes as he watched his son become the new crown prince. But he and Lumie were teary-eyed for very different reasons.

"What is it, Lumie?" I asked. "This is a magnificent ceremony. That sort of depressed expression doesn't belong here."

"I know. However…this means my brother can now step onto the battlefield."

In the end, I was unable to grant Lumie's wish.

"As regent, I couldn't continue to turn down His Majesty's will. Forgive me."

"Yes. My brother made his own decision on this matter…but recently I'm increasingly worried…"

Lumie pressed herself close to me and said in a voice only I could hear, "…that you…feel that the royal family should go ahead and die out…"

I didn't react with any particular surprise. After all, that had been on my mind for a while. I was sure that plenty of the king's vassals shared that same fear, and several had probably voiced their concerns to the king himself.

I possessed the greatest military force in this kingdom. That much was an immutable fact. To phrase it differently, if I were to betray the kingdom, it wouldn't survive in its current form.

There's a saying about an old man keeping a pet tiger. The old man is secure so long as the tiger's attention is fixed outward. But if the tiger attacks the old man, he has no chance of surviving.

The problem was that this was the first time Lumie had voiced such concerns.

I loved my wife and wanted to make her happy. There was no lie in that.

But if Lumie, as the king's sister, wished for the royal dynasty to continue, then we would forever be at odds.

I'd always known that. I'd known it from the moment our marriage was decided. At the time, I'd thought I'd simply make use of the girl and felt no guilt over it.

But as time passed, I ended up deeply in love with Lumie, and surely she felt the same about me.

There's no answer in this world that leaves everyone happy.

In any case, I'd grown too powerful for a mere regent. Even if I served the king loyally, he still might regard me as a threat. That's what it means to be the second in command.

Even if I were to live out my natural life span, it was possible my children could be purged instead.

I'd crossed the point of no return a long time ago.

I pulled Lumie closer to me.

With everyone focused on the ceremony and the music, I doubted anyone could hear our conversation.

"Don't say such things. I'm doing what I must as regent. His Majesty is aware of that. The fact that he's never tried to take my authority over the military is proof."

"Yes. You've certainly served my brother loyally. There's not been a trace of doubt in your behavior till now." Lumie's voice quavered. "But...if you believe in your heart of hearts that the royal family should die out... Imagining that fills me with fear... What should I do...?"

"Lumie, it's not good for the baby for you to dwell on your fears. Try to think of happier things."

"I'm sorry..."

With that, Lumie fell silent. I needed to have a serious conversation with her.

Staying in the capital would probably make her all the more uncomfortable. This was a good opportunity for us to return to Maust until Lumie gave birth.

"Lumie, the weather is better in Maust. Why don't we return there for a while? I'll go with you."

"But I'm sure you have your political duties as regent..."

"If I make a mark as regent here, that'll only make you worry further. I'd rather be given some leave and spend time with you."

Lumie pressed her face to my chest and wept.

"I'm so sorry for causing you all this trouble..."

"Don't worry about it. I haven't been able to think about your concerns."

"I know this is a sign of your love for me. I've never doubted that you love me. That—that's why...as a daughter of the royal house, I'm so afraid..."

I wondered what would be the best path to take if I were in Lumie's position.

I couldn't find an easy answer.

That night, I discussed the matter with Seraphina.

"You're such a rogue, my dear husband."

Seraphina chuckled. Part of it was the effect of my profession, but her appearance hadn't changed since she married me. If anything, she might very well be more seductive now.

"It is what it is," she said. "We live in an age of strife. Women end up weeping. I've wept plenty myself."

Right—Seraphina's family had just been extinguished. That was exactly why I was consulting her, but she cheerfully treated it as something that didn't affect her.

"I mean, shedding tears isn't much to have to bear. After all, for men the price isn't their tears, it's their heads."

I was reminded of just how much of a pragmatist Seraphina was.

"That's true, but I'd rather not make my wife cry if I can help it. Lumie's still flesh and blood, and so am I."

"You've fallen too deeply in love with that girl, darling husband. You should have been more blasé and discarded her." Seraphina purposefully phrased it harshly. She often would say things just verging on a taunt. "Of course, I understand why, given how beautiful she's become."

"When you put it that way, I've got nothing I can say back. I shouldn't have spoken to you about this..."

I'd come here hoping for a serious conversation, only to end up being teased. It was a nice distraction, so I wasn't irritated. I'd known Seraphina for a long time.

"You've already decided to return to Maust, right? Then there's nothing for me to say about that. And she'll probably see her family fall at some point. The fact that she said such a thing to you means that while she may seem oblivious, she's starting to notice."

"Yeah, I guess that's about right."

I knew that realistically I needed to come to a clear decision eventually. At the end of the day, telling Lumie of my plans was just a matter of how I felt.

"But returning to Maust now isn't such a bad thing." Seraphina's expression hardened slightly.

"You have something planned?" I asked.

"Let's raise your importance for a bit, shall we? Show the men who think you're after the throne, dear husband. If you can teach them that this kingdom can't do anything without the regent Alsrod around, they'll return to you with hats in hand, begging for you to return."

With that, I understood Seraphina's intent.

"Meaning let the king and his underlings try their western campaign while I'm holed up at Maust."

"Of course, since they won't be able to muster much of an army without you, they'll only be able to do some skirmishes, and I doubt the enemy will muster tens of thousands on their end, either."

The soldiers that Hasse could muster between the royal army and his vassals numbered, at most, around twenty thousand. And that would be the entire force. He couldn't very well leave the capital undefended, and unless there was a particularly dire emergency, the most he could move was probably about half of that.

That being the case, the chances were good that the enemy would only raise a force large enough to match it. The former king's frontline bases were far to the rear, while his main fortifications were across the sea in the Great Isle Region. They wouldn't gamble on an all-out decisive battle.

Seraphina understood that well. I didn't think she was wrong, either.

"Which is why you can watch safely from Maust. I doubt a single loss would lead to an emergency."

"If the royal army suffers a string of defeats at that point, yes, they'll realize my importance, but what if the royal army strings together wins while I'm not there?"

There was no real reason to believe that Hasse would lose the skirmishes just because his army wasn't particularly powerful.

The enemy could just bide its time in multiple small fortifications. It's the tactic to employ when you leave your main body in the rear and wait for the enemy to deplete their resources. In that case, on the surface it would at first look like Hasse was winning battle after battle.

If Hasse were to gain authority and power, it would be a problem for me.

However, Seraphina remained calm.

"That's fine in itself. I mean, it's not as though you'll be losing any soldiers, right? You can wait and conserve your strength."

It seemed that Seraphina was contemplating a rather long-term strategy. Perhaps she was able to take the long view because she didn't participate in battles herself.

"It'll give you time to figure out your long-term plans. They won't consider you a threat, either. Doesn't that seem ideal?"

I see. It's not such a bad thing for me to show I have no intention of usurping the throne at the moment.

"Dearest husband, you've been fighting for so long now. Perhaps a rest would do you some good."

"Thank you. It's made me look forward to returning to Maust."

"Yes. This isn't a retreat, it's an advance."

After chuckling, Seraphina took my hand. "Stay the night. While your official wife is pregnant, I'll stand in for her."

She shot me a seductive, come-hither look.

"Got it. I'll make love to my former official wife tonight."

"Tch, such a mean way to put it."

I pulled Seraphina to me. She was surprisingly light.

We then went to our bed. This time, Seraphina raked her nails against my shoulders. It made me think of a pet cat playfighting.

"There are plenty of examples of men who've been deposed despite wielding more power than the king. What's important is how you proceed from here. Everyone's watching your every move."

"You're right. I need to show that I'm a tiger with no teeth. There's also the constant worry of assassination."

"I don't think there's anyone foolish enough to assassinate you while the outcome in the West is uncertain. But there could be assassins working for the former king as well."

Seraphina pressed her ear to my chest and listened to my heartbeat as I basked in the warmth of her skin.

"What you should do, my dear husband, is prepare to increase the number of your supporters. You made the warrior girl of Seitred, Margrave of Machaal, one of your concubines, yes? She seems quite the handful, though."

"Ah, Talsha. She's a warrior to the core. I don't know if it's part of being a northerner, but she's an aggressive one."

Despite the fact that she was almost a prisoner of war, we got along surprisingly well.

So much so that I'd be fine with leaving a division under her command. That was how much I trusted her.

"Make sure that you draw that sort of faction into your orbit. That way, if in the worst case you can't take the throne, you can at least secure an independent kingdom within the kingdom. If the former king and the current king's factions end up fighting each other, they'd be too depleted to go after a new country anyway."

Seraphina could really chatter on and on about planning.

"Can't you talk about something a little more sensual while we're in bed?" I said with a dry laugh, running my fingers through Seraphina's silken hair.

"I want to be a conqueror's wife. That dream hasn't changed. No—if anything, I'm giddy because it's closer to coming true."

Seraphina squeezed me into a tighter embrace.

I tightened my embrace in return.

But despite all that she'd been speaking about, there was one thing Seraphina hadn't mentioned.

Kaito Shibano

Part of me thought it better not to bring it up at all, but I also felt that would be dishonest. I'd never hidden anything political from Seraphina.

"Once Lumie's child is born, it might be harder to make your son a king."

I had no idea what the political situation would be in a few years. And if even I didn't know, pretty much no one else in the kingdom had the slightest clue. It might not be all that constructive to discuss the future, but…

If I were to usurp the throne, it was likely I would argue that I was a member of the royal family due to my marriage to Hasse's sister.

Lumie's child would definitely be of royal blood, making them a much more persuasive successor to me than my eldest—my son with Seraphina.

"You've hit a nerve there," Seraphina said with a sad smile. But I couldn't be sure she was wholly serious.

"To be perfectly honest, I'd like my son to be king. But I'm not such an optimist that I think that sort of revolution can happen. Maybe it'd be better if I were so self-absorbed I couldn't see the truth."

"I'm sorry. It's probably not something you want to hear, but I wanted to make sure I told you everything."

"It's not a problem. But in exchange, I'm going to keep watching all of your conquests at your side. Closer to you than Lumie or Laviala."

I'd always felt something akin to friendship between Seraphina and me.

And that probably wouldn't ever change.

I requested an audience with Hasse and informed him I wished to return to my home castle of Maust.

Both Hasse and his trusted courtiers were abuzz. A military officer who served as a pillar of the kingdom was asking to leave his position at the capital, and right before the Western Pacification Campaign was about to kick off in earnest.

"Brother. Wh-why...must you return to Maust at this time...? Are you unhappy with something...?"

Hasse couldn't hide his concern. Based on that, it seemed Lumie hadn't said anything to him.

I realized again that Lumie sincerely loved me.

She could very well have told Hasse that I had my own ambitions, or at the very least mentioned that I intended to return to Maust.

That she hadn't done either told me she was acting solely in her capacity as my wife.

Lumie was a virtuous wife too good for an age of strife—no, too good for *me*.

Which was why I wanted to do everything I could to make Lumie happy.

"The reason is simple. My wife is with child. And in terms of climate, the nearby river brings a warm breeze to Maust, making it much more temperate than the capital."

That he would ask why I was leaving showed Hasse's weakness as a king. There were countless reasons I could bring up. In the end, any reason would only serve to reassure him, nothing more.

"Further, the capital is tense as preparations continue for the western campaign. Leaving my wife in such an environment would keep her in a state of agitation detrimental for both mother and child. For now, I'd like to take her back to the peace and quiet of Maust and watch over her until she gives birth."

There wasn't a single lie to those words. Leaving the capital was the right thing to do if I wanted the best for Lumie. The greatest way to keep Lumie from being tortured by her thoughts was to take her to a land as far from the idea of war as possible.

"A-ah, understood... Lumie has never had the strongest constitution, either... We understand your feelings, Brother..."

Hasse couldn't react too strongly given that I'd brought up his sister.

"Yes. My wife's child will be Your Majesty's nephew or niece. I would beg Your Majesty to consider the health of your relatives."

"But we must still decide the timeline of the western campaign. If you're not in the capital..."

"As you have been saying, Your Majesty, you could lead from the front, taking direct control of the preparations. For the sake of restoring the crown's authority, I beg that you take control of the situation."

Everyone here knew that Hasse himself had long wanted to participate in battle.

Which should keep him from rejecting that proposal.

"While I am a loyal servant of Your Majesty, I have spent too much time at war. There are those who doubt my trustworthiness. It is true that military officers have often rebelled since time immemorial... The skepticism is warranted. Which is why I would like to put those doubts to rest by refraining from participating in this campaign."

Several of the courtiers blanched. They were concerned that Hasse might blame them for my decision to withdraw. It seemed they hadn't anticipated that I would willingly refrain from participating, never mind my return to Maust.

"That's...a generic argument... Myself as king first and foremost, none of us believe you would betray us, Brother..."

"Most certainly. However, the position of regent is far too powerful, and as a result, may appear to be tyrannical to others. Fortunately, our bureaucracy is far stronger than it was under the former king. The government will not cease to function because the regent is absent."

I had no intention of yielding on this one. Surely no one would argue that I was rebelling by returning to Maust. If they were to send an army from the capital toward me, the former king's faction would roar with laughter.

In that case, there was even the possibility I'd ally with the former king.

Risking internal division before the western campaign was something even my most hated rival wouldn't try.

"Very well... More than anything, Lumie's health is of the utmost importance. She was raised in a convent, far from conflict; the capital would not be good for her... You have permission to return to Maust."

"My sincerest thanks, Your Majesty."

Based on his reaction, it seemed Hasse had planned from the start to borrow some of my forces to conduct the western campaign. I had no intention of playing along with that.

"It need not be said, but if there is a danger to the crown, please call upon me. I will assist you as needed," I said with a smile as I lowered my head.

Go and see what you can accomplish on your own, Hasse.

This is a fight for you to regain your crown's authority...and failure will mean losing whatever authority you have now.

The more people lose faith in the crown, the more my own value goes up. The more people believe you to be unworthy of being king, the closer the end of the Kingdom of Therwil becomes.

——Hrmph. Just like how Ashikaga Yoshiaki couldn't rebuild the bakufu, this man won't accomplish anything. It's not a peaceful age where mere tradition allows a man who can't fight to rule.

My profession had already foretold Hasse's failure.

Well, if Hasse wins, that'll be fine as well. The previous king's faction, which I'll have to take on eventually, will be that much weaker. It won't all be negatives for me.

Either way, there's plenty for me to do at Maust.

With the defeat of rebels such as Ayles Caltis and Brando Naaham, I had more realms under my direct control. I wanted to turn my attention toward actually governing them. There was also no disadvantage to making friends with the other regional lords in the hinterlands. That sort of diplomacy, which was hard for me to conduct in the capital, would be easy to accomplish in Maust.

I should check with the Margrave of Machaal to see if we could renew our friendship.

I'll do everything I can to increase the cards up my sleeve.

"I will pray for your success as general from my place in Maust. Glory to the Kingdom of Therwil!" I declared, not meaning a word of it.

◇

I decided to move all my vassals to Maust at once.

While the kingdom's bureaucrats technically served the kingdom and couldn't leave the capital, most were practically my vassals, meaning I'd have reports from them even when I was elsewhere.

Speaking of which, a few days before I left the capital, Hasse dismissed several of his courtiers—all those who had warned him that I might betray the crown.

Because I had chosen to return to Maust, the crown saw a substantial decrease in its available forces, and those courtiers had been dismissed for their part in causing that situation.

That meant I had fewer enemies, so things worked in my favor.

With the departure of my forces, the remaining number of military officers was rather thin. Not only was that true in terms of sheer quantity, but given that I was the only one who had been fighting for a long time, most of the best generals were also my vassals.

Since they had all left, what remained in the capital was the royal army. While the crown would probably assemble forces from the neighboring lords when it went to war, there wouldn't be any notable generals among them.

"You know, the air feels cleaner away from the capital," I said offhandedly to Laviala, who was riding next to me.

"It's not that it feels that way, it actually *is* cleaner. Or rather, the capital's air is dusty and awful. Maust isn't that much better than the capital compared to Aweyu Forest, though."

"I see. So there's that big of a difference for elves, hm?"

I might have made the comment to the wrong person.

"How do you think things will play out in the kingdom?" The next question came from Kelara, who was riding on my other side.

"What do you think, Kelara? I'm interested to hear your thoughts."

Kelara bowed briefly before replying.

"It's likely impossible to not conduct a western campaign at all, so they'll probably send out forces. I do not know what the scale of the forces will be… I doubt they would wish to admit defeat, so they will probably try to muster a fair number of troops…"

"Agreed. Which is why the capital will be quiet, at least on the surface, for now. They'll try to carefully determine just how many of the western lords are part of the former king's faction."

Hasse had formally claimed the title of King of Therwil. And his argument was that the rebels had dug in in the West.

But that was the perspective from the capital. The previous king, Paffus VI, maintained his own claim to the throne, and he argued he had merely moved the capital to the west.

I didn't know whether he believed that himself, but unless he continued to make that claim, he couldn't have the lords around him raise armies and urge them to fight Hasse.

Technically, there were two claimants to the throne within the kingdom's territory.

And the western lords had all agreed to support the claims of the previous king. At the very least, they had no intention of falling under my command.

The question was which of the two sides would move first.

Put simply, the previous king's supporters wouldn't attack the capital if they weren't certain of victory. The farther east they went, the farther they would go into Hasse's territory, and the more supplies they'd need.

On the other hand, the farther the army from the capital advanced into the West, the easier it would be for the western lords to make use of the terrain to defeat the advancing army.

The enemy's plan was likely to force Hasse's army to extend its supply lines too far, cut it off from retreat, then destroy it in a surprise attack.

If Hasse's army were to be destroyed in that fashion, then there would be more lords following the previous king, changing the balance of power.

"The former king doesn't have the nerve to bet everything on a single throw. At the very least, they had been assuming I would be the one commanding the army, so their plans must have changed. They'll likely stare at one another for a while in a stalemate."

"Then I hope we can get what we need done during that time!" Laviala said brightly. "Let's make sure we take firm control of the lands we haven't been able to directly govern until now! If we do, then we have nothing to fear from either the current or the former king!"

"Of course, I intend to do whatever I can. That's why we're returning to Maust. Well, that's not the only reason… I'd like Lumie to relax and get some rest."

Lumie was in a well-sprung carriage along with her attendants.

No doubt she was still conflicted about heading to Maust. I was about the only one who could help ease those feelings for her.

When we arrived in Maust, I would need to have a talk with Lumie.

I didn't want to keep her in the dark.

Of course, if she then decides that she wants a divorce and declares me a traitor, what will I—?

"Lord Alsrod, depending on the outcome, I'll take care of the unpleasant work," Laviala said with a serious expression. "We haven't gotten to this point by doing everything aboveboard. There haven't been many women who've stood in your way, Lord Alsrod, but—"

"Laviala, you need not say more." I stopped Laviala with a firm expression.

"My apologies… I was out of line…"

"No, I understand what you're saying. After all, a conqueror has probably killed the most people in their country."

At the very least, I'd have to take measures if Lumie were to show resistance.

But it'd be difficult to convince Lumie that I had no intention of usurping the throne. She couldn't ignore that threat any longer.

"It's a husband's job to deal with a wife. Otherwise, such a useless husband deserves to be divorced."

No doubt this sort of thing had happened countless times over the last hundred years. Lots of men and women had experienced such conflicts. I would overcome this, too.

"Sir Regent, please don't weigh achieving unification and your love life upon the same scale." Even Kelara made sure to drive home the point. "It's because we're in a world where truth and lies intermix that it's best to be honest at times like this."

Once I entered Maust Castle, the regional lords immediately sent envoys offering their felicitations.

They were all quick to congratulate me on my official wife's pregnancy.

I felt like word had gotten around rather swiftly, but every regional lord was desperate to survive. Each of them probably had at least one agent in the capital, and of course they would celebrate the good news for the kingdom's largest power.

Lumie hosted these envoys with a smile. I told her to rest, as it was a needless strain on her body, but she insisted, "It is a wife's job to meet with envoys."

She wouldn't budge from her stance. I felt this sort of stubbornness was where she was similar to Seraphina.

All my consorts, even if they were different in personality, were very strong-willed. Could it just be that I drew that sort of woman to me naturally?

I'd returned to my residential castle on the river, but that didn't mean I was without work to do. If anything, there was more because I'd returned for the first time in a long while.

I had put Fleur in charge of the personnel decisions involving girls at the castle, such as the maids, and the various nunneries scattered about the domain. Fleur was perhaps more of an aide than a concubine. She calmly went about her work. She was extremely skilled with administrative tasks, but rarely showed any sign that they were any burden for her.

"Sir Regent, I believe the time is right to begin building your formal wife's household agency here within Maust Castle."

While we were sipping tea during one of our rare breaks, Fleur brought up the subject.

People like the formal wife or heir of a king or great lord had the right to form small governing organizations with themselves at the top. This was because they had to manage their individual landholdings or the churches where they held authority.

As the younger sister of the king, Lumie held territories in her own right. But until now, while she had gotten help from bureaucrats or my subordinates, she had generally managed her holdings on her own.

However, as her pregnancy progressed, that was going to get more difficult. Before it did, she should create her own household agency and have them conduct her official business.

"True. But I intend to speak directly to my wife first about the matter."

I hadn't had time to be alone with Lumie since I'd returned to Maust Castle.

While it was true that I had a backlog of work to do, we were probably both using that as an excuse to put off meeting with one another.

Then again, I couldn't afford to be at odds with Lumie while things were in disarray.

"Your wife appears to be struggling from being too pure-hearted."

"That makes it sound like your heart's corrupted, Fleur."

"At the very least, I felt relief that my clan would continue when I became your concubine. My first thought went to my clan."

Fleur laughed self-deprecatingly.

"Whatever your motivations, Fleur, you've been loyal to me, and I'm extremely fond of you. I can still remember when we held hands on our first night together."

I also hadn't forgotten just how happily Fleur had smiled that night. I had a pretty good memory. Apparently Oda Nobunaga rarely forgot anything he heard, either. Although that was coming from the man himself, so I didn't know how just how true it was.

"Discussing such matters during the day is a bit naughty, isn't it?"

Fleur giggled, holding her hand over her mouth.

Our relationship was close enough that we could exchange these sorts of remarks.

I hoped to eventually have a relationship like this with Lumie as well, but Fleur and she were in far different positions: the daughter of a clan facing annihilation versus the younger sister of a king, no matter how weak. It wasn't right to expect the same thing from both of them.

"I'd like to talk with Lumie tonight. As her due date approaches, no doubt she'll be more tired."

"Yes, that sounds like a good idea."

Fleur nodded with a businesslike expression.

◇

That night, I dressed formally and visited Lumie.

I was more visiting the king's sister than I was entering my wife's room. And since I was in formal attire, I had my sword equipped as well.

"Dear, you seem awfully intimidating today."

Lumie welcomed me in with a sad smile.

Her attendants had also been dismissed, so it was just the two of us in her room.

"Lumie, I have something very important to tell you tonight. I want you to listen to me carefully."

"I understand. Please begin."

We sat facing one another with a table between us.

"My wish is to turn this kingdom into a truly peaceful place. Not a peace that will last a few years, but one that will last centuries."

"A laudable goal."

Lumie had the air of a royal. I felt it was something that came from the blood of those who had long ruled this kingdom. She seemed far more stately than the current king.

"In order to achieve that, I want your child to ascend to the throne," I said as I gazed deeply into my wife's eyes.

Her own gaze never wavered.

"Does that mean you intend to start a new dynasty?" she asked.

"There's no one in the Kingdom of Therwil with more power than me. I will stand at the top of this kingdom and begin a new dynasty. It's what's best for the sake of peace. But for that, Lumie, I need your help."

"No matter how I parse it, this sounds like sedition."

"If I unify this kingdom, it won't be sedition."

We continued to stare straight at one another.

It almost felt like a contest; the first one to break eye contact would lose.

"In that case, no doubt my brother's fate will not be a pleasant one."

"I want to fight for my wife's happiness. My brother-in-law's happiness takes less precedence."

"Th-then, what if..."

It was at this point that Lumie glanced away.

Her eyes filled with tears.

"What if I said I was going to report all of this to my brother? In that case...you will have no choice but to kill me... It would make your words about wanting to do everything for the sake of your wife...a lie..."

"That's a meaningless question."

"Why is that...?"

"Because my wife loves her husband more than her brother. I'm certain of that."

I stood up and embraced Lumie from behind.

"My wife wishes for my happiness. Which is why our interests are entwined. Isn't that so?"

Lumie buried her face in my chest and sobbed for a long time.

"If I had hated you, perhaps history would have changed..."

"Bear me royalty, Lumie." I quietly whispered my wish into my wife's ear.

The conversation I had that night with Lumie cleared the air between us.

Of course, that didn't mean it had resolved all of Lumie's concerns. Each time something happened, she would struggle with it. But still, Lumie had chosen her path.

She had sworn to accompany me.

Eventually, I was summoned to a room where Seraphina, Laviala, and Fleur were waiting for me together.

"Lord Alsrod, I heard from Lumie about what happened, but this time you were far too reckless. Just what were you planning to do if Lumie didn't listen to you?!"

Based on Seraphina's expression, she felt similarly. Probably because I had basically charged headlong into this.

"I wouldn't have done anything. Though in that case, perhaps I would have had to explain myself to the king. Though I may have put Lumie under house arrest, but if I did that, the information would get to him, and the result would be the same. In which case, maybe it'd have been better to just send her back to the capital."

"O reckless husband, did you seriously not consider what you'd do if things went sour?"

Seraphina looked exasperated.

On the other hand, Fleur remained silent, a cool expression on her features. It seemed she had known what I would do.

"No, rather the opposite. It's because I was so honest to the point of recklessness that Lumie decided to commit herself to me."

If I don't love this man, he might very well destroy himself—I won the moment that thought went through Lumie's mind.

Laviala laughed dryly and said, "That's cheating." She appeared to understand.

"Honestly…how is it you're so confident of being that loved despite the fact you have so many concubines…?"

Seraphina let out a theatrical sigh as she rubbed her forehead. Apparently she had come to terms with my actions as well.

"Of course, Sir Regent, if you were suspected of sedition, I'd imagine you would have at least joined with the former king and attacked the capital with him," Fleur offered in my defense. "In that case, the capital would have easily fallen. It would complicate matters afterward, but I'm sure you could have at least taken down the former king."

Yes, she more or less had it right.

It had looked like I'd left everything in Lumie's hands, but in reality, I'd had plenty of paths to victory when I'd returned to Maust Castle.

Even if Lumie had called me a traitor, I would have simply defected to the former king's side, continued the war, and ruthlessly driven out Hasse.

Of course, it would have been a departure from my original plan. It wouldn't have been ideal.

But it wasn't the worst possible case, either. It was a path that had enough value to pursue.

And more than anything, in the end, I was able to value Lumie's wishes.

All I had to do now was work my damnedest to make Lumie happy like I did with my other consorts.

"Thinking about it, Lord Alsrod has also developed a habit of being reckless on the battlefield," Laviala noted. "It makes sense when I think about that as applying outside of the battlefield."

"Thank you for understanding, Laviala. I'd expect nothing less of my milk sister."

"It's not a compliment. I'm still exasperated."

But it was true—I did tend to pick the slightly riskier path over the one that was too conservative.

"For my part, I'd thought it might be kind of interesting if she'd step away from being your official wife, but I guess it didn't work out that way," Seraphina teased. No doubt she was being at least partly serious.

"I'd like my consorts to get along..."

"I know. But if you spend too much time loving me or the other concubines, Her Highness the official wife might change her mind, so you should be careful, O husband of mine."

I'd left myself wide open for Seraphina to say whatever she wanted to.

"I mean, last night, after you visited me, you went to Laviala's place, then finally stopped by Fleur, I'm told. I've heard heroes have strong libidos, but aren't you overindulging a bit?"

Laviala and Fleur blushed at Seraphina's remark. This wasn't a subject to bring up in front of others.

"You went to Fleur's place after you visited me… L-Lord Alsrod, y-you're a little too virile…"

"I just was in the mood… There are times when I feel that way after I get something off my chest… Besides, I feel more at home in my own castle than at the capital…"

As I wondered if it had to do with my profession, Oda Nobunaga shot back with *"Don't drag me into this."*

◇

The next day, I called Kelara to my room and had a detailed discussion on the governance of my direct realms.

I was now able to muster the largest force I had ever been able to mobilize. I even needed to create a new division to place some of them in.

I discussed with Kelara who would be suitable to lead that division. As something between a bureaucrat and a general, she made for an ideal adviser.

"I believe it would be best to employ this individual who had a long history of service with the Caltis clan. We have no idea how much they'd be willing to fight if we assigned them someone who had no connection to the clan."

"You're right. No doubt these men still have a lingering attachment to the Caltis clan era anyway. This is a good place to treat a surviving retainer of that clan well."

"So I believe we're done for the moment."

Kelara seemed to think that she was done working, but I wasn't finished yet.

"Um, Kelara, sorry, but I'd also like to ask you to serve me with your body…"

Kelara glanced down and answered, "As you wish…"

I was certain I'd settle down eventually…it was just that my mind and body were still worked up after my escape from the capital.

* * *

Once we were finished, Kelara said in her usual overly formal speech, "Sir Regent, there was also the matter of the Northern Problem."

"Yes, we need to discuss that. I had planned to do that at another time, but—I suppose this is as good as any."

I discussed the Northern Problem with Kelara.

"—That about sums it up. Kelara, what do you think?"

"Oh, yes..." Kelara glanced away, as though blushing. "Ah...it's impressive how quickly you can switch from matters of the bedroom to matters of strategy..."

Having her actually point that out made me faintly self-conscious.

"Oh, come on... You were the one who brought up this subject after our matter in the bedroom. You were the one who switched tracks first. Don't pin this on me."

"No...I had planned to come to this subject after the discussion of your territories. It was then that you brought up wanting my body..."

Kelara's face was bright red. It felt like Kelara had become more womanly, or rather she had just developed a wider range of emotions.

Perhaps she was just that in love with me. That was something that felt pretty good to me as a man.

"All right. You win. So let's return to the subject at hand," I said with a laugh. "So, do you have any concerns after hearing about this plan? I want your honest opinion."

When making large moves, it is enough to ask a small number of trusted advisers for their input.

Those who are uninteresting fear making the move itself and can't come to decent decisions.

Further, those without a fixed view tend to get pushed to side with the majority.

"I don't think it's a bad plan. So long as the other side isn't excessively stubborn."

Kelara had regained the expression of a senior adviser. Indeed, Kelara was the one who could switch gears quickly.

"Yes. It's all a matter that involves an opposing party. But it would be best to secure our control over the North during this opportunity. It would greatly expand our options."

No matter what Hasse accomplished in his western campaign, if I controlled the North, I could make my own country. My position as regent of the Kingdom of Therwil itself would no longer be of any use.

"Thanks. The rest of this I'll settle by talking with Talsha directly. I've gotten your approval, so it's time to bring in the one who'll actually be involved."

But hearing the name Talsha made Kelara furrow her brow ever so slightly.

"Are you perhaps planning more intimacy…?"

"No! I'm plenty satisfied with that right now… Still, I don't really know how Talsha herself feels…"

I brought Talsha's disposition to mind.

Driven and energetic in everything she did, she was a woman who was pretty much the embodiment of everything people from the capital imagined when they thought of a Northlander.

But there was one thing that made her different from the Northlanders imagined by those in the capital. Northlanders aren't barbarians. If anything, they value honor far more than the capital's residents.

Of course, considering how often the authority in the capital changed hands, living according to an honor code and standing by one's honor could very well get one and one's entire house killed, so perhaps in the end it's a matter of geographic differences. If there's no one to pass on tales of your honorable death, it's simply a pointless death.

The moment Talsha entered my room, she immediately closed in on me.

"I need to calm my emotions before we can discuss politics… Alsrod, please…"

This woman was oddly passionate. She was the personification of her clan's heritage.

"All right. I need you to actually listen to me. Do what you need to settle down."

Talsha and I spent a long time making love.

Of course, if I could get Talsha with child, it would push my strategic goals along nicely, but that would be asking a bit too much of a woman who wasn't a concubine.

"Now then, what is it you wished to discuss?" Talsha asked me in bed, her face so close that our noses were practically touching.

"Talsha, I informed your brother Seitred, the Margrave of Machaal, to abdicate his title in favor of you. Or rather, it was to notify him that he'd abdicated his title to you." I shook my head slightly. "As a matter of personnel within the Kingdom of Therwil, you've already been named the Margrave of Machaal. Talsha Machaal, you're now the Margrave of Machaal."

"Well, that's rather sudden notice, but good news is always welcome, no matter where one hears it."

Talsha laughed with an expression that was worthy of a great hero. It was certainly not an attitude a noble woman from the capital would show. This woman was a born warrior.

"But, as I said before, I can't believe that my brother will so easily turn over his title to me. My brother is a brute, but he believes he's used his strength to protect our lands. And there is a part of him that thinks less of me because I'm a woman."

"I know. Which is why you need to take it from him by force. I'll lend you the troops that I promised you in the past. No—I'll accompany you." I grinned and pulled Talsha to my chest. "Now that I've returned to Maust, I have time I can take for my own ends. I can at least give you aid. That'll make driving out your brother easy, won't it?"

"I see. You'll go that far for my sake." Talsha also smiled and embraced me. "I will become the strongest, no, the greatest ruler among the Margraves of Machaal! I will swear that to you here! My brother's lands are too small to contain me!"

"That's right. I need you to expand much farther out."

Talsha had a profession called Takeda Shingen.

It's not a profession for one absorbed in defending their current lands.

"Go with the intention of ruling the entirety of the North. Then, if you think you can trust me, lend me your troops. We're going to unify the kingdom together. If you think I won't manage it, then turn your spear upon me."

"I have no desire to fight you. Worry not."

Talsha chuckled against my chest.

It was the softest sound I'd heard her make all day.

"I have fallen in love with you. It would be strange to fight to the death with the man I love. Alsrod, even if you are left as the last surviving warrior, I will be your ally!"

"If there's misfortune for me, it'll be that I won't see you for some time once you become the Margrave of Machaal."

It's hard to be separated from a woman who loves me this much.

"Which is why we're going to make love while we still can," Talsha said. She kissed me passionately.

At the very least, in bed, I lost to Talsha.

◇

I immediately had those in my domain ready troops for an invasion of the North.

The objective of our campaign would be to send in Talsha as the new Margrave of Machaal.

Many were at a loss because of the sudden decision, but I had them prepare without complaint.

We had a good chance of winning even without a large army. After all, the new Margrave of Machaal was no figurehead, but a hero who exceeded her predecessor.

On paper, we were sending soldiers to the North to place the North firmly under the kingdom's control while Hasse was planning his western expedition.

There was nothing strange about this. We had already started the conquest of the North, and it had only been temporarily suspended because of the rebellions. Which was why this wasn't a military adventure done at the whim of the regent.

Of course, there was still the chance that the campaign would be canceled.

That would happen if Talsha's brother, Seitred, agreed to abdicate in favor of his sister.

If that happened, all Talsha had to do was ride confidently into her new castle.

In the end, Seitred didn't reply to me before the deadline. He intended to fight me. Oda Nobunaga said he'd known this would be how it ended.

——Shingen's father was also quite the brute. He unified Kai, then tried to expand into Shinano, but that was when he was driven out by Shingen. Shingen couldn't have executed such a plan on his own, so he had already obtained a great deal of support.

I figured as much. A coup d'état could only be maintained with a fair number of allies.

A coup d'état executed without a military advantage would be immediately suppressed. At the very least, one needed forces equal to the old regime's, and even then, it was still risky. Humans tended to be conservative and opposed to change.

——I've only heard what the situation in the world is, but this Seitred sounds like a similar man. He's good in war, but sloppy in matters of politics. It's likely he's not particularly esteemed by his vassals. If there's an outside invader, they will close ranks with him to resist, but—

If it's a proper member of the Machaal line, they'll probably side against him.

——Don't preempt me. But yes, that's right. Just in case, send letters in Talsha's name criticizing Seitred's poor governing to the various lords of the North and to Seitred's vassals. It would be a small price to pay if it reduces the number of enemies.

Thanks. That's a good idea. The less fighting the better, as far as I'm concerned.

A long, protracted war would bring unneeded scrutiny from the capital, and it would deplete my own forces. If that ended up ruining my ability to participate in the western expedition, it would be defeating the purpose.

I first moved Talsha up to a fort farther north.

The northern lords naturally gathered at that fort. Many of them admired Talsha's talent. There were evidently even lords who were moved by the fact that she had finally risen up to claim her rightful title.

Eventually, there were those who left Seitred's side to join her.

As those numbers slowly grew, I took my own force of seven thousand to join Talsha as reinforcements.

The total forces reached a bit over twenty thousand.

"They gathered so quickly here that it was almost too easy. It's almost as if I'm the margrave." The moment I saw her, Talsha said something odd.

"No, you already are the Margrave of Machaal. The enemy you're going to fight are rebels who are resisting you."

Talsha realized her mistake and broke out in laughter.

"Ah, of course. Then it means I can't afford to lose, can I? It would be a problem if I lost my first battle as margrave."

Talsha finally set off to attack her brother, who refused to hand over the margravate.

It wasn't that there were no enemies trying to stop her along the way, but she made short work of them, crushing them with hardly any losses to her own forces.

I watched her command from the rear, laughing at what I saw.

If my forces were like a sharp blade that sliced its way into the enemy, Talsha's forces fought like a giant hammer that pulverized the enemy.

She was extremely adept at commanding them, and all her generals were eager to put everything they had on the line for her. She had a natural charisma.

With a whip crafted from a horse's tail in hand, Talsha smartly took command. She made a perfect general.

This must have been the power of the profession Takeda Shingen. There was nothing particularly unique about them, but her tactics were extremely well executed. She knew just when to attack to do the most damage.

By the time she entered the margrave's territory, scores of the Machaal clan's most trusted vassals had flocked to her side.

"Ultimately, we serve the Machaal clan itself. Given that there has been a formal order appointing a new Margrave of Machaal, we will obey it," said a grizzled man acting as their representative.

"Yes. I will become the greatest of the Machaal margraves. I look forward to working with you. I have no intention of exercising dictatorial power like my brother. If you have complaints, feel free to air them to me."

Talsha welcomed them with a gentle smile.

At that point, the gap between her and Seitred had become decisive.

The only ones on Seitred's side were those who had quarrels with families who had gone to Talsha's side. Meaning they were hesitant to participate, and there were few who believed that Seitred had any chance of winning.

The vassals were concerned first with protecting their own clan over their lord. If there was little chance of winning, they'd make excuses such as illness and be stingy with their troops.

Talsha brought down the fortresses one after another, and was steadily cornering Seitred's faction.

It seemed his loss to me was still dogging him. The northern lords no longer viewed Seitred as their leader.

Five days after our arriving in the margravate, after we had joined with the clan's most important vassals, Seitred surrendered and formally handed over his title and lands to his sister. Because he had disobeyed a royal command, Seitred was to be imprisoned in one of the domain's temples.

The fate of a man deemed unworthy of being a lord was a sad one.

But he was perhaps fortunate that his opponent had been his own kin.

Kaito Shibano

◇

Talsha entered the capital of the margravate, Wulhere Castle, and rewarded her generals.

It was then that she finally appeared in attire suited to the position of margrave.

"This dragging cape is somewhat bothersome… Perhaps I'll grow used to it in time."

Everyone sucked in a breath.

There was an ideal ruler standing there, combining elegance, beauty, and courage.

I, too, was moved by the sight.

"Sir Regent, I was able to secure my title because of your help. I don't know how to thank you."

Talsha bowed her head to me.

She'd been calling me by my name all this time, but it seemed she was capable of addressing me by my title after all.

"The kingdom swears to support you," I told her. "I look forward to your contribution in bringing peace to the Northlands."

"I hear and I obey. Please tell His Majesty that he may leave for his western expedition secure in the knowledge that we will hold the North."

It was a formal exchange for show, but Talsha and I enjoyed doing it. There was something entertaining about playing the roles.

"So, Lady Margrave, whom do you intend to bring in as your groom?" I asked half-jokingly.

"Having only recently taken this position, I have yet to consider such matters. However, if I could wish for one thing"—Talsha looked me in the eye and smiled—"whether a son or a daughter, I hope to have a child that's strong like you, Sir Regent."

The vassals, who were likely not aware of our relationship, laughed in response.

Given that this was Talsha, she was probably serious.

"No doubt you are tired, Sir Regent. Please rest well."

* * *

It took a while for Talsha to let me go that night.

"I didn't even get to fight a proper battle. To have this many boring battles in a row, there's nothing to douse the flames within me..."

Talsha had shown up in the room for visiting dignitaries that I was staying in.

I felt like it might not be a good idea to advertise the fact that we were doing this the day she took residence in this castle, but Talsha paid that no mind. She was pressed tightly against me.

In that sense, Talsha was loyal to her principles and to her desires. You could say her lifestyle was easy to grasp.

Our time together was rather intense, and it was less making love than desperate mating.

"I mean, I know your personality, but surely you can do something about this? It's not like I can always be by your side...," I said while swallowing a yawn. *Please let me sleep. I'm tired from all the travel...*

"Then we could have a duel with blades if you'd prefer. That would settle my spirit as well. But that runs the risk of killing you."

She was assuming she'd win. This female lord was a piece of work.

"For my part, it would completely wreck my plans if you died the day you became margrave. So there's no way I can accept that sort of challenge."

"Right? So this is the only other option."

She wouldn't listen to my complaints, so I simply replied with a sigh.

At the very least, I was able to leave the North in the hands of someone I trusted. That was a massive gain for my side.

"Besides...if I can, I'd rather have my heir be a child from you," Talsha said slowly, as though squeezing out the words.

It seemed she had reservations about saying that out loud. She was shy about the oddest things.

"Margrave isn't a position that can be filled by the virtuous. Even the slightest weakness can put my title or my life at risk...which is why the only one who could probably carry on the line would be a child with your blood. That's why...that's why..."

Oh, right, I remember talking to Oda Nobunaga about Takeda Shingen's children.

Oda Nobunaga had defeated Takeda Shingen's son and ended that clan. Further, Takeda Shingen's son had been trying to find a way to become in-laws with Oda Nobunaga's children.

In other words, perhaps Talsha desired me at a subconscious level.

Of course, there was no clear answer. But the fact was that I loved Talsha—that was all that mattered to me.

"All right. Then make sure you bear my child."

I exchanged embraces with Talsha yet again. I'd lost count.

"But don't you dare die in childbirth. I don't want to make any women I've associated with unhappy."

I doubted the protections of Seraphina's profession of Saint would reach Talsha this far away. The number of women who died in childbirth wasn't low. No matter how strong she might be on the battlefield, it was still a possibility.

"I'll live. If I die, not only will your plan be derailed, but the history of my bloodline will end as well. No one else in my clan is capable of taking the reins."

Talsha now bore the entire fate of the Machaal clan upon her shoulders.

That would be an enormous burden on anyone, no matter how strong. In a sense, it was harder and harsher than being king in a stable era.

While I was approaching the endgame of my plans, Talsha was still only starting out.

After being given the helm on the high seas, Talsha had decided to bet everything on me.

The only thing I felt at her choosing me was joy. Nothing else came to me at that moment.

"Talsha, I swear that I'll make you happy. I'll make sure that the bloodline of our children will continue for hundreds of years. Just wait a while longer."

"Of course. Alsrod, claim the throne. You're the most suited to finishing off this moribund dynasty."

After discussing our commitment in bed as comrades, we roared together in laughter.

"First, I'll make the lords around here bend the knee to me. There will not be a single northern lord who will turn their blade against you. Don't worry about watching your back."

"Thanks. Actually, now that I think about it, you just want to fight more, no?"

Talsha laughed. It seemed I'd hit the mark.

◇

As she'd promised, Talsha—now the Margrave of Machaal—renewed her push to get the local lords to swear fealty to her.

Her rapid gains were quickly conveyed to me over in Maust.

Uncomfortable with the stuffy atmosphere of the governing office, I was in Fleur's room, reading a letter that reported she'd managed to force a lord I'd never heard of from the middle of nowhere to offer up a hostage.

"Seems the margrave is making remarkable progress. It would appear she's working with hardly any rest."

Fleur smiled gently. The reason I was in Fleur's room was that Fleur had political instincts far sharper than your average strategist's.

"Of course, it's right after she's taken over. It's a period when she has to demonstrate her ability to those around her."

"Exactly. It would be a problem to have others underestimate her. Still, I doubt there's anyone in the kingdom's North who's not heard of Talsha's reputation as a warrior."

"Even if we refer to the North, the conquest of Misroux Prefecture hasn't progressed much prior to this, so she probably intends to fully draw it into her area of influence. It seems she'll complete the conquest of the two northern prefectures before long."

The vast region in the North of the Kingdom of Therwil was split between Machaal Prefecture in the East and Misroux Prefecture in the West. Both prefectures were geographically much larger than those near the capital, because they had once belonged to other peoples and had been slow to come under the kingdom's political control. They also had relatively low populations due to the mountainous terrain.

Originally, the Margravate of Machaal had been based out of the most populous city in Machaal Prefecture (and the one closest to the royal capital), Wulhere. The margrave's residence had to date remained in Wulhere Castle. That had meant the margraves hadn't exercised sufficient control over the northern reaches of the prefecture.

The margrave had only started to extend his influence into the northern regions of Machaal Prefecture and the neighboring Misroux Prefecture during Talsha's brother Seitred's reign.

Seitred had probably rebelled against me because he had confidence as the leader of the northern lords.

However, in the process of expanding his sphere of influence, Seitred had gone to some rather large extremes. Of course, that wasn't something limited to Seitred, but trying to force authority structures where they hadn't existed before was bound to create friction and resentment.

His hopes were dashed, however, when Talsha, who had gained a reputation as a warrior, then came crashing into the North and declared herself Margrave of Machaal. Many of the lords abandoned Seitred, who had lost to me.

"She really doesn't need to be in this much of a hurry, though," I said. "Hasse hasn't even gone on his western expedition yet."

While the king, Hasse himself, was eager to go, there hadn't been any notable progress on that front. The fact that I had taken my forces and withdrawn was still having an impact on his preparations.

"Even if His Majesty serves as the supreme commander, there will be several generals required to serve as his subordinate commanders," said Fleur. "There aren't any people with that sort of skill around the capital. They all seem to be finding one excuse or another to decline the appointment."

"Well, that sounds about right for the king's retinue. According to Yanhaan's reports, Hasse's becoming quite impatient with the fact that his Western Pacification Campaign plans aren't coming to fruition. He's evidently been yelling at his less enthusiastic retainers."

Information about the capital was being supplied primarily by Yanhaan. Since she was technically a bureaucrat serving the crown, she hadn't left the royal capital. Of course, that was simply an excuse; there were bureaucrats who had accompanied me to Maust. In Yanhaan's case, she was also a merchant, which was the real reason she couldn't leave the capital.

"Still," Fleur continued, "it's taking much longer than it should. It seems that those around His Majesty are doing whatever they can to avoid war."

Indeed, Fleur was every bit as sharp as I'd thought.

"They probably do want to avoid it. In an extreme sense, the king's retinue doesn't care about reunifying the kingdom. Many of them have never really even left the capital itself. They're more like rats that have made their nest in the capital than anything attached to the king himself."

A former vagrant like Hasse didn't have his own bureaucrats or vassals. Once he entered the capital, he had taken on those who had been oppressed by the former king—those who had served during Hasse's father's reign.

Those people were concerned only that the monarchy should not revert to the lineage of the previous king. If anything, they'd be in deep trouble if there were multiple wars and the royal lineage was overturned. If the former king returned, they'd all be out of work.

"Ah. So all they care about is holding power, and they don't desire anything further," said Fleur.

"Most people are reactionary. If anything, I think I'm the exception. I mean, if I had been given the title of viscount to start with, I might have only been concerned with protecting that."

The age for that sort of peace-at-all-costs parasite was rapidly coming to an end, but they seemed determined to cling to it at all costs. They were less incompetent and more simply incapable of living any other way.

"Which is why the retinue wanted to push you away from His Majesty. To them, a revolution would be the worst possible thing to happen."

"Yes. I'm probably a bigger threat than even the former king in their eyes."

Even if Paffus returned to the throne, they could still possibly switch sides, whereas if I created a new kingdom, there'd be no telling what would happen there.

"Fleur, can I rest my head on your lap? I'm a bit tired."

"Yes, of course, Sir Regent."

I dozed on Fleur's lap. It really was peaceful in Maust at that moment. If the capital was also this peaceful, I was sure there were those who'd prefer that it stay that way.

"But there will be conflict. Beyond their reach, I imagine," Fleur said as though peering into the future. "If there's two factions bordering each other, there will eventually be a military confrontation. If a lord swearing fealty to His Majesty loses, he won't be able to simply abandon him."

I quietly gazed up at Fleur's eyes.

Yes, Fleur knew the travails of minor lords better than anyone, as the daughter of a minor lord.

"If possible, I'd rather they'd wait another four months or so. Surely they can last that long."

◇

Talsha's victory reports continued thereafter, and she was close to securing the two northern prefectures.

She was planning not a loose alliance, but a political structure with herself as the top power in the two northern prefectures. She had basically succeeded.

It was the right call. The days of small lords surviving on their own were coming to an end.

I had been aware of that, just as the now defeated Ayles Caltis and Brando Naaham had been. That was why we all tried to expand the reach of our own power.

Ambiguous alliances can betray you unexpectedly, as had happened to me. For safety's sake, it was best to simply expand your own strength.

Among those victory reports, there was one notice that stood out.

"Hmm, so she's expecting…"

Apparently Talsha was pregnant. The letter said the child was mine.

Seraphina teasingly asked if I "intended to bury the kingdom in my children." With her sharp nose for gossip, Seraphina had heard the information and immediately come to my office.

"That's going too far. At least let me defend myself."

"Very well. What sort of excuse are you going to come up with?"

Had Seraphina recovered from the loss of her family? Or was this exchange one of her minor acts of revenge?

"There were plenty of kings with even worse libidos and more children than I since time immemorial. At the very least, I don't have children with city girls whose names I don't even remember."

"That doesn't prove that you don't have a womanizing streak, dearest husband. It only proves that there were those with a bigger womanizing streak."

Seraphina was the only one at Maust Castle who teased me this way.

How do I put it? It felt like in front of Seraphina, I could break out of the heavy shell called the regency.

"Yes, I like women. But what man doesn't? Aside from the most eccentrically pious priests and the like, that is."

"Oh, so now you're not even trying to justify it. Still, I'm sure that Talsha girl is relieved to have an heir…… No, I suppose one's uneasy until a child is born, so I guess I can't be sure about that."

Honestly, I couldn't give an opinion on that front, not being a woman, but I was sure there was still some anxiety. All I could do was pray that she gave birth someplace clean and that both mother and child would be healthy.

"The letter said that she'll be appointing the next margrave in case the worst comes to pass. Given that the father is in Maust, she'll be choosing a relative who's friendly to me."

If a ruler dies, the spouse will often serve as the acting head of the family. Their authority holds even if they're a groom or bride not related by blood to the ruler.

But Talsha wasn't married, which complicated matters.

If the vassals would accept me as the Margrave of Machaal, it would remove the contradiction on paper. However, that would be difficult from the perspective of the vassals.

I was a man who hadn't even married into the family and had merely impregnated their lord. As far as that went, I was sure Talsha had spoken with her vassals, but it was still a special case. At the very least, it would be safer to choose the next margrave from among her relatives.

"I thought she'd be pretty brutish in that regard, but it seems she's quite cautious. I'm impressed," Seraphina commented.

"Talsha's a woman with the character to be a great lord. That's for certain. Which is why she decided it would be most effective to claim that the child is mine."

"Oh? You sound as though you're convinced it's not your child," Seraphina said with a hint of displeasure.

"Well, the truth is that she needs an heir, and in her position she can have a lover, no? Besides, they can't prove it, so she may as well insist it's my child..."

"You know, O gallant husband, you are a politician and a military man, but you don't understand a thing about women."

Seraphina let out an exaggerated sigh. This was how she acted when she was really exasperated with me.

"That woman truly loves you, my dear. Of course, thinking about the dynastic politics, taking a lover makes sense, but I doubt she'd do such a thing. It's your child, dearest husband."

"You're awfully confident..."

"I know—I'm speaking as someone in love with that same man," Seraphina said rather proudly. When she put it like that, there was no way I could argue. "The more a person's been self-reliant all their lives, the more they'll fall for someone who defeats them. There aren't that many people who'd draw their interest, are there? That interest is romantic love."

"For romance, she sure demanded my body rather quickly."

At first, I'd thought Talsha was possessed by a wild animal or something.

"It means she's just that passionate. Regardless, I suppose I'll pray that your child grows up healthy up in the North."

Like one of her profession of Saint ought to, Seraphina softly closed her eyes, clasped her hands together, and offered a prayer.

While she laced her words with sass, Seraphina was actually an extremely good-hearted woman.

Profession and personality are, to some extent, related. If she weren't capable of wishing for another person's happiness, Seraphina would have never been given the profession of Saint.

"Seraphina, I get the sense that I'll be causing you more headaches from here on, but I'm counting on you."

"You need not ask me. I'll keep supporting you, O dearest husband of mine. You won't be rid of me so easily. I plan to support you for decades yet. The period before you become king is really just a rounding error."

I may be a womanizer, but I'm blessed in the types of women I attract.

"Seraphina, I love you."

"I'm sure you've told all your other consorts the same thing, but it's still nice to hear. If you didn't love me despite everything, I'm sure you'd end up punished by the heavens or something."

Seraphina beamed.

The North had settled down before anything happened in the West.

Now it was time to continue the preparations I could make here in Maust.

I immediately sent out a messenger to congratulate Talsha on her pregnancy. The letter I gave the messenger noted that I regretted not being able to be by her side as her husband. Those were my honest feelings on the matter.

But I wasn't so idle that I could leave Maust unattended for a long time.

I was having a census done of the territories under my rule. There were many lands where I didn't have a good sense of how many soldiers I could muster. I could leave it to the individual lords to declare their numbers to me, and none would purposefully report more people than they actually had, so there was a need to have a precise count.

"It's perfect, since it looks like you're just dealing with internal governance on the surface," Laviala said as she helped with my work.

"Yeah, I'd much rather have the capital think I'm focused on running my territories. Besides, I came to Maust to allay their suspicions, so it'd be a problem if they didn't think that."

"Of course, that's just on the surface."

Laviala grinned with amusement. It didn't feel like the sort of atmosphere where we were actually talking politics, it was more relaxed.

"This will make your armies much stronger, Lord Alsrod. Yes, it'll make it the kingdom's most powerful and largest army! An army that'll eliminate any foe when Lord Alsrod tells it to fight!"

"I really hope that's the case."

Compared to the optimistic Laviala, I couldn't help but feel I was being cautious, even for me.

There'd been plenty of people caught off guard despite being the most powerful person around. There could always be some pitfall or shortage that I hadn't accounted for.

After all, Oda Nobunaga died a step before he could finish unifying his country.

——Don't bring me into this. Damned rascal.

My profession complained to me.

——But it's true that I died when I had only a little left to accomplish. Truly, a revolt was unfair. No one can truly eliminate the risk of rebellion or assassination. Damn! And damn again! If I had another opportunity, I could have worked in a way to avoid having Mitsuhide come after me!

Well, I can't do anything about that. You could always be reborn into a new life, but you can't redo your old one.

——-Yes, I suppose that's one way of thinking about it.

Seemed Oda Nobunaga had come to a certain realization.

——One can't relive one's old life. That is a truth. But to put it differently, I've used the memories of that life and live on within you. I may not have a beating heart or arms and legs at my disposal, but I remain as a consciousness.

Right. To the point where I feel you're a little loud sometimes. Though on the whole, I appreciate what you've done.

——In other words, perhaps I'm borrowing your body to retry unifying the world. That must be why I appeared in this world as a profession, no? Yes, that must be it. I did have at least that much regret when I died.

* * *

It was a theory that we couldn't prove unless God came out directly and told us, but I understood what he was trying to say.

That would explain why Oda Nobunaga existed as my profession.

Considering the share of nobles among the population, even though Oda Nobunaga had become a profession with his consciousness intact, the probability that he would become the profession of someone with effectively no status, like a farmer or city-dwelling peasant, had been much, much higher. And it would have been far more difficult to create a kingdom starting as a farmer than starting as a regional lord.

——If that's the case, it would explain why the dwarven girl who is this world's Mitsuhide hasn't betrayed you. No doubt Mitsuhide regretted killing me. After all, his entire clan was wiped out as a result. I wouldn't be surprised if he wished he hadn't rebelled and had quietly continued to serve me.

Which would mean that when he emerged as a profession, he would appear in a position where he could be a loyal retainer.

I see. Kelara serves me so faithfully perhaps because she has guilt and regrets over betraying my profession in a previous life. It's a pretty attractive theory.

——Yes. That proves it. The reason the Shingen woman challenged you was that Shingen had always wanted to fight me, and it would make sense that she gave in after witnessing your strength. Shingen had believed he was the strongest, but believed I was the next strongest after him. The moment he learned he couldn't win, he must have chosen to serve you. Yes, that makes sense.

Oda Nobunaga seemed quite pleased.

I couldn't really say since I didn't know anything about the original people, but…

It was true that people from a specific era, from a specific world, were being reborn in a cluster in this age.

In carrying out the census, I had an opportunity to check the past census records for confirmation. There were regions that also recorded professions. Swordsman, Wizard, Farmer, Rancher—all common jobs.

There had never been any mysterious professions that appeared to be names of people. Even among the nobility, for whom there were more surviving records than for the peasantry, there hadn't been any examples of such odd profession names in the past.

Which seemed to mean there was a high probability this was something unique to this era.

"—lsrod, Lord Alsrod."

Laviala was calling for me.

"Oh, sorry. I was thinking about something."

"Lord Alsrod, at times you seem to be staring off into the distance. No, that's not the right way of phrasing it. It's as though you're so focused that you can't hear the outside world."

I hadn't told even Laviala that I could talk with my profession. I had yet to meet anyone who had experienced the same thing, so no doubt it'd be hard for her to believe.

"It appears that Yanhaan has arrived," Laviala announced. "She is likely here with information about the capital."

That reminded me—Yanhaan had a profession called Sen no Rikyuu.

——Rikyuu was a rather interesting man. He seemed to be enlightened, yet scheming at the same time. The world was all the more interesting with someone like him in it.

I wondered briefly if collecting people like that around him was why Nobunaga had things like rebellions happen to him, but that would just be arguing from hindsight.

"All right. I'll arrange to see her immediately."

I had already built a tea room in Maust Castle.

Yanhaan, whom I hadn't seen in a while, was dressed in loosely fitting clothes that befitted a merchant.

"It has been a while, Sir Regent."

Yanhaan bowed with a calm, mature smile.

"How is the capital? No, I suppose it's uncouth to start with that sort of talk. First, there's something I want to show you. Come with me."

I took her to a ceremonial tea room small enough to look almost like a miniature.

The entrance was so low that one needed to kneel to enter.

Inside was a table, designed so that a host and a guest could face each other.

"I had this built in order to spread the art of the tea ceremony. I'd like to hear your opinion."

"It's quite looovely." Yanhaan immediately knelt and entered the tea room. "I see, I see… The inside is well-built, too. If I had to critique it, it's perhaps a liiiittle too ostentatious. Simpler materials would work better."

"It was because the workers feared making it too rough. No doubt they feared being punished by me. I told them ahead of time not to make it too fancy."

"Still, it'll do for a tea ceremony. Shall we have a cup? I have brought the needed tools."

That had already been my intention. That was practically why I'd built this room.

Yanhaan quietly began preparations for tea. A dignified air dominated the small space.

The bitter green tea wasn't bad even when consumed outside the capital.

"The tea's flavor feels different. Have you changed something?"

"Each serving of tea is a special moment in time. No doubt each occasion provides a different flavor."

When she was conducting a tea ceremony, the mercantile cynicism in Yanhaan seemed to melt away. Instead, I felt as though I were sitting with a nun.

The fact that she could so easily change the atmosphere around her was, no doubt, partly due to her own abilities, but likely also due to the small space we occupied. Entering this room let me reset my emotions.

"How does it taste?"

Yanhaan's face was serene, like that of a mother in a painting.

"It's bitter. But not an unpleasant bitterness. It has a reassuring flavor."

"I'm glad to hear that."

Yanhaan smiled faintly, as though she were a carving.

The room was briefly veiled in silence.

It wasn't an uncomfortable silence.

Rather, it felt like it was scrubbing my soul clean.

"Now, may I speak about the situation in the capital?" Yanhaan asked.

"Please do—and in detail."

We finally touched on the main subject. Of course, the proper main subject within a tea room ought to be the tea ceremony itself.

"The plans for the western campaign have finally been settled. The Supreme Commander will, in fact, be His Majesty. As for his subordinate commanders, three were chosen from the dukes and marquises who are his relatives."

Yanhaan continued to present additional information. It was an unnervingly precise description of the military situation.

The fact that this amount of information had reached Yanhaan's ears was proof that Hasse was bad at maintaining the secrecy of critical information. I wonder what he intended to do if information on the actual strategic plans leaked to the enemy.

"I knew that the lords didn't want to participate, so I guess it means in the end he's sorted it out among those of royal blood. And if he fails, he can push the responsibility onto the subordinate generals."

"Yes, it seems he convinced the lords to chip in their forces by making it clear that even in the event of failure, the responsibility will remain within the royal family."

Members of the royal family couldn't keep turning down entreaties from the king, and in a sense they were tied to the king's fate, so they would be motivated to fight the former king.

"Better than having to rely on war-weary nobles, I think. But only better, not ideal."

"Then is it best to consider this war an unwinnable one?" Yanhaan asked.

"It's possible that the enemy is even less competent than Hasse's forces, but the commanders of the royal army are essentially amateurs. If they lose the initial engagement, I doubt their drive to fight survives it."

If the royal army could win the first battle, they might have a chance—the enemy probably understood that as well. And at least that wasn't out of reach for them.

"They'll strike the elite troops from the front and break the royal army's momentum from the start, and, if possible, take out a general or two. If they can do that, then most of the lords who've been dragged into participating will probably give up."

"For whatever it's worth, the royal army has somehow mustered twenty-two thousand, while the enemy is an alliance centered around the Viscount of Kark of Orba Prefecture. His Majesty would have roughly twice the number."

While Ferth Morrissey, the Viscount of Kark, didn't have much in the way of territory, he was at least a head above the other lords of his region in terms of skill. Which must have been why he was chosen to lead the collection of forces assembled by supporters of the former king.

I smirked.

"Watch him lose with over twice the numbers. Hasse's army will collapse overnight."

So it was about time to consider the path the army would take.

"Once the royal army loses and begins its return, I need only wait here in Maust. But if Hasse dies, then I need to immediately advance upon the capital."

"I see that you wish to see His Majesty die in battle."

"I didn't say that. I do worry about the former king's faction gaining too much power. I don't know which would be preferable. But—I'm just going to consider all of the possibilities when I act."

I also got confirmation from Yanhaan of when the expedition would depart.

There was still time. The expedition would begin a little bit after Lumie was due to give birth.

"It seems we are about to see some large-scale fighting." Yanhaan gazed intently into my eyes. "Three years from now, you will either be on a throne or in a tomb."

"I pray I'll be on the throne. But just praying won't be enough."

While we were still in the tea room, I hadn't noticed that my hands had gotten a bit clammy.

It seemed I was a bit excitable.

Your Majesty, I'll be fighting off in the distance in a way, so please go and fight the enemy to your heart's content. If you don't, the enemy will come looking for you instead.

Remember, don't put those you can't trust in front of you. Do remember the very basics of tactics.

◇

Walking the gardens of the castle, I ran into Altia and her two daughters as they were planting flowers.

"Listen up. You'll have to water them every day. If you do, you'll get pretty flowers."

Once Altia said that, the older daughter nodded and replied, "I promise."

"Flowers, mm? I hope you'll get large blooms."

The two daughters quickly ducked behind Altia upon seeing my face. It seemed they were still afraid of me. But I supposed it was better than their hating me as their father's killer. Although I might find it easier if they hated me for it.

Given that I'd killed countless people, I was sure there were plenty who hated me whom I didn't know about, but that had never really been something I'd thought about. Which was probably why I had been able to keep fighting until now. The ones who felt guilt each time they killed people probably had their spirits broken before long.

Altia, meanwhile, seemed to have moved on to some extent.

She smiled at me like she used to.

"Brother, aren't you supposed to be working? You sure you should be wandering around?"

"I've already given the necessary instructions. Now I just need to watch how the situation progresses. Also, there's another thing I need to look after."

Altia's eyes narrowed as she smiled.

"Lumie's birth, right?"

"Yes. The first birth is particularly scary."

"Yeah, I'm pretty sure I know what Lumie's feeling better than you do, Brother. It's as difficult as going to war."

That probably was not an exaggeration. Indeed, there were old books that described birth in the same way.

"If only I could shoulder some of her pain—but there's no magic of that kind. At most, there are medicines and magic that reduce the pain."

"The physical pain is bearable. It's something you can justify as part of the process."

Altia seemed to glance off into the distance.

"I'm sure Lumie will also be struggling with the fate of her family as she's fighting. That's got to be much harder."

There was a weight to those words when Altia said them. While there was a difference between birth family and family by marriage, Altia had experienced what it means to lose one's family.

"But that much is a given. That's how women fight."

Altia gently smiled and placed a single flower on my tunic.

"You just need to keep fighting to end war. There will be people like me who will end up crying, but nothing will happen if you stop each time that happens."

"I don't actually expect you to forgive me."

I'd had my reasons. But that wasn't enough to make her forgive me for killing her husband.

"Forgiveness, resentment...those things are minor things when it comes to you, Brother. Which is why you don't have to think about it," Altia insisted. "It's not something a king should worry about."

Altia had grown a lot stronger when I wasn't looking.

I wondered what had done it. Was it because she was the mother of two children? Regardless, there was no sign of the frail girl she used to

© Kaito Shibano

be. She was dignified enough that one could believe she was a lord in her own right.

"Take the throne, Brother. What I'm most worried about now is that you might worry about the small things and end up missing the great goal. If there are those who stand in your way, you need only kill them. There's no other way."

It was essentially a command.

"If you end up not becoming king, then that's when I'll resent you. Because I'll end up feeling that if you couldn't take the crown, you should have let my husband kill you."

Ah, so now I was carrying the lives of the dead upon my shoulders.

So if I failed to achieve my objective, it would make their lives meaningless.

"All right. I swear I'll become king, but I need you to wait just a little longer. I don't think it'll take much time."

Altia beamed.

It seemed my answer wasn't too bad.

"Oh, and another thing," added Altia. "Brother, you're constantly underestimating the strength of women. It's probably because you judge everything in terms of warfare. But you don't need to be overly protective."

Now she had the expression of a sister warning her brother.

"Think about it. Seraphina, Fleur—they're all very strong. They've all got nerves of steel. They all love you."

When she put it that way, I could merely nod intently.

"True," I replied. "None of them have lived a quiet life."

The only people left around me, men and women, were strong ones. Conquest wasn't achieved alone. At the very end, I'd have to trust my consorts and my vassals.

If I couldn't trust them, I would lose my footing.

"Altia, I'm proud that you're my sister."

"Yes, because I'm the sister of a king."

"Can I hug you?"

"Go ahead, Brother."

I slowly took a step forward and pulled Altia into a hug.

Her body was as slender and fragile as it had always been. But then, I guessed her strength came from her spirit.

"You're always so warm, Brother. But maybe a little too strong."

"Just bear it for now. That's an order from a future king."

Altia softly chuckled to herself. I found myself laughing as well.

Altia's two daughters, who had been cowering from me, started to lightly pat at my legs. Maybe they trusted me a little now.

I hope you two grow up strong. Like your mother.

By the time you're old enough to marry, I'll make sure the age is one in which you won't lose your husbands to war. That I swear I'll accomplish.

After I left Altia, Oda Nobunaga spoke to me.

——She's very similar to my younger sister. She's tough—much stronger than your average warrior.

That's not surprising in a conqueror's sister.

——Yes. You must become king. And make your sister's daughters happy.

I found myself in agreement with Oda Nobunaga quite often that day.

◇

As Hasse was about to set off with his army from the capital, Lumie's water broke.

I took Altia and Laviala with me and offered a prayer at the temple in the Maust castle town.

The priests in front of me lit a fire and were fervently offering rites for a safe birth.

Because they were repeating the same sorts of phrases again and again, I gradually fell into an almost drunken, trancelike state.

I crossed my arms across my chest and stared at the priests.

On either side of me, Altia and Laviala watched in similar poses.

While these were rites for a safe birth, I kept thinking about Lumie's safety. In an extreme case, I would be fine with a stillbirth so long as Lumie was all right.

I was torn between whether I wanted a boy or a girl. And it felt like thinking about such political considerations was less worthy than worrying about Lumie's health.

The voices from the chant that spanned about an hour faded away, and the priest in charge noted, "We are finished." He was referring to the rite that we were participating in. The chants themselves would continue until Lumie gave birth. But if we participated until the end, my concubines and I would be exhausted.

"All right. We'll rest a bit in a different room before we leave. No, perhaps I should stay until she finishes giving birth. I don't want to pace around the castle."

"Lord Alsrod, let's get going either way. It's hot in here with the fires..."

With Laviala's comment, we quickly left the room.

——You're an oddly pious man.

Oda Nobunaga, on the other hand, didn't strike me as much of a believer.

I don't actually believe in a god. It's just that the only thing I can do right now is offer my prayers. It's not as though someone else can have the child in Lumie's stead.

——That's true. If you believe that luck has a divine element to it, then I suppose I thought of gods quite a bit myself.

Right? None of us would struggle if things would just go according to plan.

Of course, I didn't know what my plan was in this particular case.

I had told Lumie to bear me royalty. But I hadn't told her to bear me a son. While the plan would change depending on whether the baby was a boy or a girl, I hadn't thought about that part.

——Well, at times like this you can be forgiven for just worrying about your wife's safety. I may have called myself the Demon King, but in the end, I was only human. If I had been a god, I would not have died from a mere rebellion, after all.

You know, you seem to have mellowed out quite a bit of late. It might just be my imagination.

——That is probably because your position is closer to where I was in my own life. I can give you advice if it's about taking down a lord or two. But from here on out, all that's left is for you to decide on your own. So I will leave it in your hands. Let me dream with you.

I couldn't help but smile. Oda Nobunaga was less a profession and more an old friend, a steady comrade in arms.

"You seem cheerful, Brother. Like God told you all will be well," Altia noted as we walked down the hallway.

"Well, I doubt us moping around would make anything better. If anything, I'm preparing myself so I can greet my wife with a smile."

"True. Yes, the birth will probably go fine."

I hoped Altia's words would end up becoming true.

"Yes. After all, no one who's given birth to one of Lord Alsrod's children has died in childbirth. We can keep extending that record," Laviala teased.

Having her say that in front of my sister was a little embarrassing.

"Our daughter's starting to act just like you, Laviala. Her ears are even pointed like an elf's, too."

I called our daughter Little Laviala. I'd named her after her mother in the hope that she'd be as energetic and healthy as her namesake.

"Actually, I think she would have been an active little girl no matter which parent she ended up resembling. In that sense, there's no real difference who she takes after," said Laviala.

"Well, I never expected her to grow up to be well-mannered, so that's fine."

"You know, when you put it that bluntly, it bothers me a little bit..."

Altia chuckled as she listened to our exchange.

Once we got to the other room, we passed the time with small talk. We chatted about all sorts of nonsense, as though we were kids again.

When I was a child, I didn't even think about inheriting the title of viscount. I just lived as though I were one of my brother's vassals.

As the son of a regional lord, I knew that I'd be dragged into complicated situations and conflicts when I grew up, but I tried not to think about it that much.

Altia had a fragile constitution and couldn't go play around in the woods, so Laviala and I would go to Altia's room and bring her things like fruits from the trees and tell stories about the forest. They were normal days, but that was nice in its own way.

It had been quite a while since those days.

We all had children of our own, and Laviala and I had a daughter together. If our past selves could hear what would happen to us, would they believe us? No, I doubt it.

After two or so hours of small talk, the maid in charge of receiving guests announced the arrival of a messenger.

Given the messenger's expression of joy, I knew they brought good tidings.

"I bring news, Sir Regent! Your wife has given birth to a healthy child!"

"I see. Thank you for informing me." I tried to sound distinguished, but I couldn't hold back a smile. "So is it a boy or a girl?"

"A princess, Sir Regent."

"Ah, so a girl."

I needed to put aside the question of royal succession for the moment.

"I hate to ask this of you, but return to the castle and tell her, 'Thank you.' I won't go myself until mother and child are settled."

After the messenger left, I sat in a chair and let out a big sigh.

"It sort of feels like I've just fought three straight battles."

"You were merely that worried, despite it looking like you were enjoying our chat," Laviala pointed out.

"Of course. I was like this when you were having our daughter, too."

◇

Because she had been raised as a princess and wasn't as physically strong as someone like Laviala, Lumie spent a bit of time in bed after delivering her baby. Still, her body was healthy, and I was told that she'd eventually make a full recovery.

When I first visited Lumie after she gave birth, her complexion didn't look too bad.

"I gave it my all."

"Yes, I know that well. You did amazingly. We have a daughter who bears the blood of kings."

"But don't you believe things may have been better if it had been a boy?" Lumie said with a faintly teasing tone.

"Truthfully, I hadn't actually thought about that at all. The only thing I wanted was for you and the baby to be safe. I have witnesses. You can ask Laviala and Altia if you'd like."

"I understand. You may do your share of scheming, but at heart you're a good man. I have no reason to doubt your words."

I felt like Lumie's face was now that of a mother.

Women's faces change when they give birth.

"She may be a girl, but she comes from royalty. There's no problem at all."

Either way, my policies were going to be pretty flexible and would change depending on how Hasse intended to act.

"I have also been informed of the situation in the capital. I believe the expedition is about to set off."

"Right. The enemy is led by the Viscount of Kark, a lord of Olba Prefecture who stands at the entrance to the former king's sphere of influence. Paffus's forces have gathered there and number about ten thousand. Well, it's basically just an early skirmish."

Because of the distance involved, the core of the enemy faction—the Counts of Talmud and Samuur—hadn't committed much in the way of troops. They'd decided to wait until Hasse sent forces deep into their territory.

The prefectures of Talmud and Samuur that these two giants in the former king's faction occupied were in the Great Isle Region, across the Sanado Channel. Once forces were landed there, they had no choice but to fight on enemy terrain. It would greatly increase the risks to Hasse's western campaign forces.

"I know you might be worried about His Majesty, your brother, but for now, focus on your own recovery. The ones accompanying him in the expedition know they need to protect him at all costs. I doubt he'll get so much as a scratch."

"Yes. Thank you."

I did my best to avoid lying to my wife.

Surely the western campaign's army wasn't so incompetent that they'd let the king die in battle. It may be an odd thing to say, but for most of those participating in the campaign, so long as the king didn't die, a loss wouldn't really have much of an effect. It wasn't as though the former king's forces could immediately make a move toward the royal capital.

"We also have to decide on a name for our daughter," said Lumie.

I'd already chosen one.

"I think Lumie will do," I replied.

"The same name as me?"

Lumie looked nonplussed. Based on her expression, the idea must have never crossed her mind.

"She's a daughter of royalty. She should bear a name from the royal family. But I can't very well just pick a name myself without permission—that would be out of line. In which case, what's the only name left that I can use without anyone complaining?"

Lumie smiled in amusement.

"You're right. No one would complain if I gave my daughter my own name."

"Right? Also, I have a confession to make: I'm not very good at names… Personally, I'd like to name any daughters after their mothers…"

I'd named Laviala's daughter after her. Little Laviala seemed to like her name. She was not at an age yet where she'd offer flattery, so I thought I could trust that.

"Also, I know some people who put the least amount of effort possible into naming their children, so I felt it best to avoid emulating that."

Lumie seemed completely confused by that comment. Not surprising, considering she didn't know what I was talking about.

——Was that comment directed at me?

Oda Nobunaga sounded irate.

Yeah, that's right. You named your daughter Dog or something like that, didn't you? Perhaps it had some sort of magical meaning, but why would you name your daughter Dog?

——In my country, people were rarely referred to by their given names, so it didn't particularly matter what you called someone. Also, I gave my boys odd names, but only during childhood. I gave them proper ones when they became adults.

Sure, naming conventions might be quite different between your world and mine, but still, naming your daughter Dog? That's too much.

——Well, yes, I suppose.

I knew it—the problem was his taste in names. No, actually…it was that he'd chosen that name knowing full well how odd it was.

Anyway, I don't have the nerve to call my own daughter Dog. After all, her mother is the king's sister; naming her something like that would look like a clear sign I was planning to rebel.

——I suppose that's true. I think Lumie is a good choice.

Since my profession agreed, surely no one could complain.

◇

After I named Lumie's daughter, messengers on horseback began regularly visiting Maust Castle.

The reason was simple. The war was about to start.

However, the really important information was being relayed by the rappas. Their intel was also more reliable.

That night, Yadoriggy appeared in my room. If Yadoriggy herself was here, there must be some movement on the battlefield.

"There's no one else here. You can speak freely. If anything, go into detail."

The kneeling Yadoriggy curtly answered with an "As you wish."

Yadoriggy's appearance hadn't changed since the day I first met her. She'd looked like a young werewolf woman all this time. I didn't know her actual age.

"The royal army and the Viscount of Kark's forces have collided. The former has roughly twice the numbers."

"Sounds about right. The enemy has a bit more than ten thousand, while the royal army was a bit over twenty thousand."

"Yes. As for conditions on the battlefield, the enemy's defenses are tough, and the royal army has not been able to break through. They are currently attacking several forts, but they do not appear to have many generals with siege experience."

That sounded more or less accurate. Numbers alone were enough for a battle on open ground, but not when it came to taking down forts. The discretion of the individual generals was essential under those circumstances.

And Hasse's army wouldn't have any decent generals, given that he had chosen all his seconds from the royal family.

Further, Hasse had been wandering the land on his own prior to his kingship, so he didn't have any trusted vassals. While he could gather up an army for the sake of making a show of force, it would just be too difficult for him to actually carry out an attack on an enemy.

At this rate, there was an extremely good chance that Hasse would end up losing. There was no point in gathering twice as many people as your enemy if your own numbers didn't have a clue how to fight.

"Then what does Hasse plan to do? Does he plan to push forward anyway? Or does it look like he'll quickly give up and run?"

This was the important question.

The damage was going to change dramatically depending on when he chose to retreat. While horse messengers were enough to tell me about general changes on the battlefield, when it came to the king's own thoughts, I needed the power of the rappas.

In his position, I would retreat immediately. Of course, one needed to be careful not to get attacked while retreating, but at the moment the situation was at a stalemate due to low-quality troops. In that case, if the royal army forced an attack, it would just pile up casualties. It would be fine if it had decent generals, but there was nothing to do when that asset simply didn't exist.

"It appears almost certain that they'll force an attack," Yadoriggy replied. "The king surely wishes to avoid his first expedition ending in failure."

"In which case, it won't just be a loss, it'll be a rout."

I grinned.

If he was going to throw away his own authority, it was good news for me.

Further, if he were to ask me for help, that would automatically raise my standing.

My dream of unifying the kingdom was falling right into my lap.

"Of course, it's unclear if the king will immediately ask for reinforcements from you, Sir Regent. That would essentially be admitting his own lack of competence, so he will probably try to find a solution that doesn't involve you."

Yadoriggy hadn't blinked yet. She was probably making sure there weren't any intruders nearby.

"He won't immediately call on me, mm? That's fine—just fine."

Go ahead and keep digging your grave.

Then, once you've run out of options, come and beg me for help.

By that point, I'd be facing a rather motivated army from the former king's faction. That would be an interesting challenge.

"Yadoriggy, from now on, focus your efforts not on the royal army's movements, but on the former king's faction. I'd like to know what the enemy is up to when I face them."

"As you wish."

With that, Yadoriggy left my room through the window.

I could see a single wolf running through the yard.

Returning to Maust had been a gamble of sorts. If Hasse had won too many laurels while I was here, my dreams of unification would have slid a bit further away.

But it seemed I'd won the bet.

I needed only to continue to amass greater power and jump in at the best moment to bail the king out of his predicament.

◇

I immediately began drilling my newly added soldiers in full combat training.

It took time to learn how to wield a Tri-Jarg spear. But once they got the hang of it, the rest was very easy. Specifically, it made the war easier.

Any weapon that keeps the enemy from closing in is plenty powerful.

No one wanted to feel death's approach, save for myself, who would rejoice in that feeling. Most famous warriors were a bit different from the average person in that regard.

I'd also started production of an even longer-ranged weapon: the guns I was having Ortonba the dwarf produce.

I shot a wooden target with my personal gun.

After a sharp, earsplitting roar—

—the target had been pierced with a hole about the size of a thumb.

This firearm felt more accurate than before. But in the end, use made master. While it cost quite a bit in ammunition, accuracy went up immensely once the wielder had gotten enough practice.

Next to me stood the gun's creator, Ortonba.

"Sir Regent, that is a prototype of an improved model. How did it feel?"

"I don't know where precisely the improvements are, but it performs well."

"It's lighter than the old models. Further, I've added a rain cover so that it can fire in wet weather."

Ortonba continued with a long description of the new weapon. He took immense delight in talking about his inventions. He was a stereotypical engineer in that regard.

"All right, then, Ortonba. I need you to ready about three thousand of these guns. Can you do it?"

"Three thousand...?"

Ortonba's expression froze for a moment. I understood I was asking for a lot.

"You can include the old models in that count as well for a total of three thousand guns. With that many, I should be able to win a decisive victory against the former king's forces."

After a brief pause, Ortonba pounded at his thick chest.

"Very well! I'll make sure they're ready by then! This'll be an opportunity to shine that may never come again!"

"Well put. Good, that means all the preparations are finished."

First, I would take all the lands leading up to the domains of Talmud and Samuur—that is, the lands between where I was and the Great Isle Region.

After that, it might be a long campaign. The enemy would face us with a certain degree of commitment and defenses. If necessary, I'd step in myself and take down the enemy directly.

If I could then wipe out the former king's faction, that would remove every last foe who could resist me.

Then, all that would be left would be to take the king's position.

There would be plenty of options, from making him abdicate to going with brute force.

"Ideally, His Majesty can hold out for another month or so."

"I see," replied Ortonba. "You need about that much time to prepare to be able to bring all of your forces to bear." He didn't seem to have read between the lines.

"That's one way to look at it," I told him.

If Hasse were to retreat after dragging the fighting out for a week, his standing would plummet. No doubt the soldiers returning to the capital would look dirty and disheveled.

He would then not be able to declare he'd lead the army, and he'd come to me for help.

All right, then, Hasse, make me a hero. I'll tear the enemies that trouble you in half as though they're made of paper.

I waited for Hasse to give up and come asking for my help, but this was harder than I thought.

Evidently my personality wasn't suited for sitting on my hands and waiting.

But there was a problem I had to resolve before making my next move.

It was, in a word, a domestic problem—something I had to solve on my own.

That day, I visited my concubine Yuca's room.

"Oh…Sir Regent…I apologize for the mess…"

How do I phrase it? Yuca wasn't used to her room—or rather she wasn't used to life at Maust Castle in general.

Despite her being the daughter of the Nistonia clan—whose lord was now a count—there was still something rustic about her. No doubt that was something she had been born with. There was a world of difference between her and Seraphina, another lord's daughter.

Still, it might also be because she hadn't been my concubine for long. Ours was a far too obvious political marriage, and I hadn't visited Yuca much. Our marriage so far had overlapped with a period of heavy military movement.

Even today, despite being the mistress of this room, she was in the corner, trying to make herself look small.

"Yuca, you aren't a servant. You're allowed to relax a bit more. Is my face that scary? I don't think I look like an orc or ogre."

"No, that's not..."

For some reason, watching this girl's frightened behavior tickled at my sadism, making me want to tease her. I tried my hardest to keep a lid on that desire.

"Or are you afraid of being at the side of someone who has killed so many people?"

"N-no, not at all... That's not it at all... I'm just in awe... I still can't believe that I could be one of your consorts, even if I'm the least important one..."

Yuca simply didn't have any confidence in herself. To an excessive degree.

Of course, I didn't necessarily blame her. History was being rewritten at breakneck speed. It wasn't surprising that there'd be people with no idea what they needed to do in that environment to survive. If they chose the wrong path, it could spell the end for themselves and their entire families. It must be much more stressful than being a lord in a stable era.

The vast majority of people were either pretending not to be frightened or too dense to be frightened.

Still, having one of my concubines be like this was a problem for me. After all, there would still be uncertain days awaiting Yuca. I wasn't going to primly stay in my place as regent. While I wouldn't be declaring my own kingdom overnight, at the very least I'd be out on the battlefield.

All the more reason to settle this quickly.

Of course, there was the political matter with the Nistonia clan, but my relationship with her as my concubine was more important.

I slowly approached Yuca, who stood up and edged away toward the wall, which made it look like I was chasing her.

"Why are you running away, Yuca...?"

"Um...I'm sorry..."

I ended up pushing her up against the wall.

"Eep!"

This just makes me look like a villain...

"Yuca, I apologize for frightening you, but surely running away when your husband approaches is a bit much...?"

"My apologies... I still am not used to dealing with men... No, that's not all of it... I also feel rather intimidated by your other consorts..."

Yuca was so earnest that she ended up voicing everything that was troubling her.

Even after she had officially become my concubine, she had shut herself into her room.

At first, some of the other consorts had tried to invite her out. Seraphina had been among them, but according to her, "Yuca was harder to budge than I expected. She's a challenge." Evidently the women had given up, and at some point they'd stopped inviting her out. I supposed Seraphina and Yuca had polar opposite personalities.

To make matters worse, our marriage had occurred right before I departed for my northern conquest campaign, which meant that I hadn't been near Yuca much since our engagement.

Because of that, Yuca had found herself isolated in the salons of my consorts and my retainers. No, that's not the right way to phrase it. Yuca herself had wanted to be alone. She hadn't gone outside much when she was still with the Nistonia clan, either.

"Intimidated... I see. Well, I'm here to try to solve that," I said as I gazed into Yuca's eyes. I slowly moved my face closer as well.

"Solve it...?"

"Yuca, it's just you and I right now, so let me be blunt. I want to make love with you, Yuca."

Yuca shuddered.

Yuca and I were married, but we had never consummated the relationship.

This wasn't a rare occurrence. Most political marriages are for the sake of the clans involved. In the worst examples, I've heard of lords who imprisoned their consort in a tower the day after they got married.

But that doesn't make it right.

If I didn't consummate the relationship at all with Yuca, it would mean I'd simply used her for political expediency.

"To make my excuses, I was extremely busy. But you yourself were very shy, and there was part of you that was afraid of me. Which is why I kept putting it off, telling myself that in that case I shouldn't push you too far."

"No, it's not your fault, Sir Regent... I'm not as beautiful as your other consorts, which is why I felt it was natural that you wouldn't visit me. And I had found that to be reassuring."

I'd figured that would be the case.

Compared to an extrovert like Seraphina, there was something unadorned about the introverted Yuca.

It wasn't true that she wasn't as beautiful. She just had a different type of beauty.

"If you'll allow me..." I gently took Yuca's hand between both of mine. "I'd like to make love to you tonight. As my consort."

No doubt she had no experience at all. Yuca's troubled eyes stared back at me.

"If it frightens you, I won't push the issue. There's no point in making you suffer. But I think if we simply let time pass, then you'll only grow more frightened. Because I'll probably be off at war again."

I slowly waited for Yuca's answer.

I hadn't been able to do much waiting up to this point. My personality was better suited to taking the offensive, just like during war, which was why I hadn't been able to settle this issue with Yuca.

Now I'd wait—until Yuca communicated her feelings with her own words.

If it ended up that she was afraid of me, then there was nothing to be done. I could only back down.

Yuca took a while to speak.

While our eyes met, Yuca's gaze started to waver.

I wondered if my approach was too extreme... I supposed treating her like I did Seraphina or Laviala would end up confusing her.

I really felt that Yuca, her status aside, was a thoroughly normal girl. There had been quite a few girls like her when I had been ruler of a country village. As I became a lord, I stopped seeing such girls.

"If you're afraid, we can just take a walk through the garden while

holding hands. If even that's too much…then I'm fine with just having tea together. Let's do something that'll make you happy."

I did feel like I was trying awfully hard.

It was as though I were attempting to woo a girl I'd fallen in love with.

No… This was me being actually in love with the girl named Yuca.

Until now, I had been a lord. While I could love someone, I had never tried to romance someone. It had been practically guaranteed that a desired partner would look my way, so I'd had no reason to try to get someone to look at me.

I was trying hard to get this girl Yuca to look at me. This was something I'd never done before.

No doubt men of the cities and villages had to put this sort of effort into wooing the women they fell in love with. Then they'd have to gain their trust, or end up being dumped… I guessed they went through the motions over and over.

——Ba-ha-ha-ha-ha-ha-ha! What are you doing, the man who would be king? You're nearly thirty years old! Why are you spending so much time wooing such a simple girl?! It's as though you're a child of fourteen or fifteen!

Even my profession was laughing at me. I supposed desperately wooing a girl was hardly the sort of thing a man aspiring to be king should be doing.

I just wanted to make my consorts happy.

And I had made this girl my concubine in name, but had neglected her.

I just wanted to make amends for that.

——There was nothing wrong with your plan. To make the Nistonia clan commit troops, your plan was to head to Siala Prefecture while you had that chance. It wasn't a mistake. If you showed your face, Soltis Nistonia would ally with you. Siala was also close to the capital. He would serve as an excellent watchdog.

Oda Nobunaga began to go into a detailed analysis in my head.

——But then you started thinking about the girl you made your concubine, who was a daughter of the Nistonia clan. And then, before you realize it, your head is full of this woman. Of course, there's nothing better than to be able to report to her father that you have an amiable relationship. But you're the regent, he doesn't expect that much from you.

Look, like I keep telling you, I just want to make my wife happy.

I didn't want to make any more tragic women like my sister Altia. But to claim that and not be able to look after my own concubines made my oath seem hollow.

Yuca then looked up at my face.

"Heh-heh! Sir Regent, this is so funny!" she said, and she broke out into laughter. But there were tears in her eyes.

"I'm merely the boring daughter of an average lord. I'm nowhere near as beautiful as Lady Seraphina, Lady Lumie, Lady Laviala, or Lady Fleur. But still—in spite of that…you're so earnestly looking at me…"

Yuca pressed her weight against my chest.

"I apologize for my inexperience, but I ask that you love me tonight… I don't know anything, but I'd like to do whatever I can…"

"Thank you, Yuca."

I squeezed Yuca's body. She felt so light in my arms.

After that, I had my first night with Yuca. It had taken far too long.

Yuca looked like she was struggling, but in the end she held my hand under the sheets.

"This might sound presumptuous, but I think I found the secret of your strength."

"The secret?" I said with a smile.

"There wouldn't be any other gentlemen who would be so intensely earnest in their pursuit of someone like me. We're already beyond mere gains and losses. To go beyond gains and losses and want to accomplish something in spite of that isn't something that most people can do."

"Oh, I see what you mean."

There had perhaps never been a regent who put this much effort into loving a single woman.

But one thing about her statement bothered me.

"Yuca, don't use the expression 'someone like me' from here on out. That's an order as regent," I said, hardening my voice just a touch. "You're plenty beautiful. Don't put yourself down like that. You're one of the regent's concubines."

"...Yes, I'd like to try not to do that from now on." In bed, Yuca once again buried her face against my chest. "I'm so truly happy to be loved by you. Truly, truly happy..."

It had taken time, but I thought we were able to love one another properly in the end.

If possible, I wanted to maintain this relationship from now on.

Tomorrow, I was planning to head to the Nistonia clan, but I was sure I could stand to lose a little sleep.

That night, I sought out Yuca for a second time.

I arrived at the Nistonia clan's capital of Port Nistonia in Siala Prefecture with Yuca at my side.

It wasn't a particularly long journey if taken by ship from Maust and then along the coast. We were able to take advantage of the tides and arrive at Port Nistonia by that evening.

"Welcome, Sir Regent. It must have been a long trip."

The count, Soltis Nistonia, came to welcome me. It was late at night, but I suppose he couldn't exactly ignore the regent's arrival. I must have caused him some trouble.

"You can simply call me your son-in-law."

At my joke, Soltis Nistonia waved his hands and insisted, "No, no, that would be presumptuous..."

"I'd heard that the western conquests are not going very well. I thought you would know more," I said to him.

That was the excuse, but Soltis wasn't a fool. No doubt he'd guessed my real reason for being here.

"It's late tonight, so perhaps it would be best for you to get some rest. One does not think well when fatigued, after all."

"I'll take advantage of your offer. Thank you. Also, Lord Soltis...," I added with a smile. "Your daughter and I are quite intimate. Yuca is one of my dear consorts. I will guarantee that I will make her happy."

With that, I put my hand on Yuca's shoulder.

Soltis looked momentarily taken aback, but then replied, "Thank you, Sir Regent. My daughter is a lucky woman to be loved by you."

I could see from his expression that he was relieved.

Even if she was a political chip, there was no such thing as a parent who didn't care about the happiness of their child.

◇

The next day, I had Soltis clear the room, and we discussed the subject at hand.

Soltis had been my ally since before I became regent. He had always been loyal to my cause. Given that I had been betrayed by my father-in-law and brother-in-law, it wasn't an exaggeration to say he was my most trusted in-law.

"About the western conquest—does it seem like it won't happen without my participation?"

"Yes, that would appear to be the case. It was certainly beyond the limits of His Majesty's capabilities. Of course, it wasn't just His Majesty's responsibility. The soldiers were weak and the generals all lacked in experience... The whole situation made winning an upward climb..."

Soltis described an understanding that was identical to my view of the situation. That was just how good my intelligence sources were.

"The Viscount of Kark isn't some specialist in defensive siege warfare," I said. "There aren't any particularly skilled generals in Orba Prefecture. Yet, if they're struggling to win in the attack, then the problem is with the western expedition's forces. While I returned to my castle of residence to lift the suspicions directed my way, I fully intend to march to help His Majesty the moment he asks for my help."

Soltis nodded slowly.

"Once you make your move, Sir Regent, this enemy won't stand the faintest chance. At the very least, you'll be able to easily conquer the two prefectures of Orba and Bilgund. I doubt you have any intention of struggling in any of the territories before the channel."

"No. And I would like you to participate in this campaign as well, Lord Soltis."

Soltis's face tensed. Still, it didn't seem to be out of displeasure. He had probably been expecting me to ask this much of him.

"Of course, I will help… However, the battlefield will be inland this time, in Orba Prefecture, so there won't be much role for the navy. I don't know how useful my forces will be for you."

"I'm not asking that you commit to the very front lines. But if you will participate with a large force, I'm sure the other lords will also commit troops to the cause."

Soltis's expression changed. It seemed he understood my intent.

If the lords who hadn't moved when Hasse went on his expedition were to suddenly act when I, the regent, arrived on the front, just what sort of impression would that make on the others?

It would drive home the point that I was, in fact, the leader of this kingdom.

However, there was no point in testing each lord's loyalty individually. Most lords were cautious. They had no choice, given that one misstep would doom them.

Put another way, if a great lord would step up and lead the effort, the others could participate with confidence.

"I see. So you need me to serve as an example to pull in those who are conflicted about committing troops."

"For the ruffians who didn't commit troops to His Majesty's expedition, I imagine they will become more cooperative if you take the lead in providing military forces for my reinforcements. I will use my own elite units to actually handle the task of taking down the enemy. The western expedition's duration has meant we've obtained information about the enemy. We should be able to defeat them."

I'd already obtained information about the enemy's inner workings from Yadoriggy. It seemed they didn't have much in the way of supplies, and if we sowed confusion among their rear echelon, I was sure they'd end up making an opening. After all, they had a rather large army for a protracted defensive.

While the Viscount of Kark and his forces probably had high morale from defeating the western expedition's forces, that morale was bound to collapse when they faced the reality of starvation.

"I will also advise His Majesty to ask for your help, Sir Regent. I believe His Majesty is seeking an opportunity to pull back as it is."

I couldn't help but smile.

That would be appreciated. At the very least, it would make it much easier for Hasse to nod the affirmative than if I offered my troops to him directly.

"Thank you, I'm looking forward to your efforts. Let's do our best to secure the kingdom's future."

"Indeed. For that we must have your help, Sir Regent."

Soltis and I stood up from our chairs and exchanged a firm handshake.

Then I added in a calm aside, "Please, Lord Soltis, don't betray me like Ayles Caltis or Brando Naaham."

I could immediately tell that Soltis's face paled. I had thought I was smiling, but perhaps that smile was even more unnerving than anything else.

"I will swear upon this, but I have yet to cut loose anyone who has served me loyally to this point. I will always reward loyalty to my cause. I will make sure the Nistonia clan progresses further. So please, do take care to choose the right path."

"Yes… That won't ever happen… Besides, who am I supposed to side with if not with you, Sir Regent…?"

"True, I'm afraid I was worried about nothing."

That should have culled any hostility.

Just serve me loyally. That would be to your family's benefit. Don't make a stupid decision like the ones who ended up destroyed.

"I look forward to continuing our cooperation," I said with a serene smile.

The Nistonia clan would most definitely continue to serve me loyally.

◇

After confirming the next step with the Nistonia clan, I immediately boarded the ship to return to Maust Castle.

It was a ship journey, and Yuca was by my side. We both sat in bed. If the ship were to move erratically, just lying down on the bed would relieve the seasickness.

While she hadn't traveled much by ship when she was younger, for some reason she wasn't really affected by seasickness. Perhaps it came from the blood of the lords of a port city.

"Um...is the reason you love me so much for the sake of this alliance?"

Her voice was faint and she didn't meet my eyes, but there was an implied criticism to her question.

"I would be lying if I said it had nothing to do with it. Yuca, you're not some peasant girl, after all, but a count's daughter," I said while wrapping my arm around Yuca's shoulder. "But I think you know my feelings. Yes, I know I have several consorts, but that doesn't mean I don't love you, Yuca."

"Yes...I understand that..." Yuca leaned against me. "I appreciate the fact that you gave me a chance to meet with my father. After all, if we're unlucky, we might never have seen each other again."

"Is that what you were thinking, Yuca?"

It was rare for her to speak in such drastic terms.

"No, that was what my father told me when we were talking alone. That there will be battles that were far larger than before, and there was too much that he couldn't read or account for."

Evidently Soltis had completely steeled himself for what was to come.

Of course, I intended to win. I'd been preparing to make sure I would. But that didn't mean the enemy would come unprepared, and it was possible for the unexpected to flip the results in an instant.

There were plenty of examples in the history books of a smaller force miraculously defeating a larger one.

We didn't know what would happen next. It was possible that my allies could be killed in the process. There had been one among Oda Nobunaga's brothers who was killed by the enemy while on campaign. Many among his vassals also died. There was no such thing as a unification campaign without losses.

The most I could do was keep those losses to a minimum.

——Oh, what's this? You're being rather sentimental and pessimistic today.

Oda Nobunaga, in matters like this, a little bit of pessimism isn't such a bad thing. Great commanders shouldn't just rely on things working out for the best, should they?

——Fair enough. In the end, you won't know until you actually take action. The path of a conqueror is a lonely one. You've started to become used to that loneliness. It's proof that you've grown. Unification will soon be in your grasp.

I'll take that as a compliment.

Oda Nobunaga, I'll unify the world in the way that you failed to achieve.

I don't know where you are, but just watch me.

Two weeks after I returned to Maust Castle, the king's messenger finally arrived with an update.

"I bear news, Sir Regent. The Western Conquest Army under His Majesty's command was attacked by Ferth Morrissey, the Viscount of Kark, and is already on the verge of being forced to retreat… If neglected, the traitors will gain momentum. Would it be possible to have you take over the campaign in the current army's stead…?"

The messenger explained the situation, appearing on the verge of tears.

I didn't know whether it was an act or the army was actually in that dire a situation.

"Am I correct in assuming that His Majesty and his forces will retreat, while I am to continue the fight with only the forces I bring to the campaign?"

"Y-yes… We don't have much left in the way of supplies… So we must ask that you secure your own lines of supply…"

Hasse was shouldering the costs of delaying his cry for help to the very last minute.

In exchange for bailing him out, I was going to go ahead and do what I pleased with this campaign.

"Understood. I will accept the assigned task. However"—I placed an extra note of emphasis on *however* and continued in a sterner voice—"this is a matter of the utmost urgency. I, Alsrod Nayvil, the regent, will lead the forces directly as commander. I will not have time to receive His Majesty's blessing. Do I make myself clear?"

The messenger hesitated.

No doubt he hadn't been handed the authority to give this level of autonomy to me.

That said, he was in a position where he couldn't afford for me to refuse to commit my forces over quibbling about the level of command autonomy. If that were to happen, the messenger might as well not bother going back, as he would be finished.

"Yes. Because of the dire situation, I believe it is unavoidable… You remain the only one in this kingdom capable of mustering and commanding a large army."

"Very well. I will begin gathering my forces immediately. Rest easy. It won't take long."

I had already prepared the supplies. I had also, of course, begun to mobilize my forces.

I supposed I'd start by taking down Ferth Morrissey, the Viscount of Kark.

◇

I sent the advance force under the command of Little Kivik three days later.

Behind him followed my main force and the armies of the other lords.

After the death of Altia's husband, Brando Naaham, Olbia Prefecture had fallen fully under my command, so we would be taking the Olbia Prefecture's main highway.

Because the prefecture had been divided into multiple small fiefdoms, highway construction had been slow, but in preparation for this campaign I had put emphasis on having it upgraded to serve as a proper road.

By the time I arrived and deployed my forces where I planned to fight the Viscount of Kark, Hasse had already retreated, and all that remained of his army was led by a single member of the royal family, left to serve as his representative. He held the title of marquis, but he was a marquis in name only, with no substance beyond his title.

"I'm sincerely grateful for your help… The enemy has switched from a policy of strict defense to sporadic attacks, and has been chipping away at our forces. The attacks have sapped the morale of the Western Conquest Army, and as we faced the possibility of a complete rout, our council of war concluded that we had no choice but to ask for your reinforcements, Sir Regent."

With his low-slumped shoulders, a mere glance showed that this man wasn't used to the battlefield.

No doubt he was struggling to deal with the unenviable role foisted onto him.

"It's my sworn duty to fight for His Majesty. Rest assured, I will crush the traitor's army."

The Western Conquest Army had fled with remarkable haste back to the capital.

Since it was just my forces left, I was going to fight as I pleased.

I immediately gathered my subordinates and conducted a war council.

"So how do we take down the enemy forts? I know I phrased that as a question, but I've already decided on the tactic to use. I'll leave it to you to find the right answer."

Kelara quietly raised her hand.

"First, we wait. Then, when the enemy attacks, we'll counterattack and quickly dispatch them. Assuming there are no problems, we should then continue on and attack the enemy castles."

"Explain your reasoning."

"The fact that the enemy has started conducting sally attacks rather than remaining behind their walls is evidence that their supplies are running low. It appears they wish to drive back the besieging forces as quickly as possible. If their soldiers are poorly fed, then we should have no problem defeating them if we handle their attacks properly."

"Good. That's correct."

Indeed, Kelara was good at this. She was the second-best gift that

King Hasse had ever sent me. The best gift being my wife Lumie, of course. I can't imagine ever having a reason to switch those rankings.

The Viscount of Kark, a member of the former king's retinue, had recently switched from a purely defensive strategy to one of making sallies to attack the Western Conquest Army's forces. This was in spite of the fact that he had been doing well simply focusing on defense.

Which suggested there was a reason he had been forced to switch tactics.

It wasn't as though the Western Conquest Army had suddenly grown larger with an influx of reinforcements, so the cause had to be on the defending side.

Clearly the reason was that their supply situation was worsening.

My rappas had reported that when the sallying troops attacked, they had done things such as stealing supplies and attacking the Western Conquest Army's supply wagons. Of course, attacking the enemy's supplies was effective even if the attackers weren't suffering from hunger, but given that I had also received reports that the traitor army looked quite gaunt, my hypothesis was probably correct.

"His Majesty missed an opportunity. If he had buckled down and refused to budge, the enemy may have called for quarter. However, because his forces were so ill trained, the enemy's attacks had the intended effect. Once that happened, the demoralized soldiers would simply start cowering before the enemy. They lost their ability to maintain the siege."

That was why I had been called in.

"We should be grateful that they weakened the enemy for us. At this point, we could win by just forcing them to commit to defense. We also don't run any risk of being attacked from behind, so we don't have any supply concerns for the moment, either."

Laviala understood that this would be an easy fight, and was therefore quite unruffled by the entire situation.

"Yes, we could win by just forcing them to stay behind their walls. But that won't leave a great impression. If we're going to do this, I would rather take down the castle by force. For that, I'd rather have the enemy out here when we fight them, but that's all up to the enemy. The most we can do is pray they're in a fighting mood."

"We should deploy our supply wagons to lure them out."

That was Kelara's advice. I immediately approved of her proposal.

◇

Three days later, Ferth Morrissey, the Viscount of Kark, sallied from the main enemy castle with a large body of men.

I could tell from how the enemy soldiers were moving that they weren't well nourished. Their movements were far from sharp.

"On the whole, they seem to be lightly equipped."

With her keen eyesight, Laviala could evidently see the state of the enemy troops from quite a distance.

"Part of it must be that they plan a quick assault and retreat, but it also probably means they simply can't bear the weight of heavy armor. The reason they're all infantry is probably that they've already eaten all their horses."

"Well then, shall we get started? Archers ready!"

At Laviala's order, the archers turned to aim their bows toward the supply wagons.

The enemy then began to file into that space.

The archers loosed several barrages of arrows. Enemy soldiers fell one by one as the arrows found their marks.

Their attack had always been a move driven by desperation. So long as we reinforced our defenses, they wouldn't present a serious problem. The reason the Western Conquest Army lost was that they'd turned their backs on the enemy out of fear. One can't defeat even a weakened enemy when turning one's back to them.

This was less a battle and more just a methodical butchering of the enemy. The archers scythed down the approaching enemy ranks.

Eventually the enemy charge lost its momentum. They became even easier targets. It would probably have been more efficient to employ guns against them, but they weren't an enemy worth using firearms against.

"Seems they're quite weak. They may as well be zombies at this point," Laviala said to me as she herself shot down enemy soldiers. Laviala, with the profession of Archer, could hardly miss such targets with her bow. She didn't have to aim precisely; the enemy was a disorganized rabble. There were no generals to speak of.

"I suppose it's more merciful to kill them than to leave them as living zombies. All right, time for us to switch to attacking. Personal guard companies, are your three companies ready?"

Orcus of the Red Bears, Leon of the White Eagles, and Dorbeau of the Black Dogs were all ready to attack.

As they answered with a loud cheer, I barked out the order, "Attack!"

The enemy forces, thinned by the arrow fire, began getting swallowed up by our forces. Once we'd broken up their charge with our archers, the enemy was left with a pathetic rabble of malnourished troops.

The massacre started in earnest. We practically wiped out the entire army that had sallied out of the castle.

But our attack didn't end there. No, this was just the beginning.

A part of the enemy force fled into the enemy's main castle.

With them were operatives from Dorbeau's Black Dogs company.

Their specialty was opening holes into forts and castles. They'd thought of every means at their disposal for that purpose.

We began our assault upon the enemy castle.

In the midst of our attack, flames flared up from within the castle and the castle gates opened.

It seemed the Black Dogs had done their job. Dorbeau had used this method to force open walled cities and plunder their riches. That experience carried over into castles on the battlefield.

All that was left was to send my army into the castle.

Thanks to my profession's special ability Conqueror's Guidance, the trust and concentration of my troops had doubled, while their attacking and defending abilities had been increased by 30 percent. This strengthened army charged into the now-open castle.

Do your worst.

I needed to show off my strength not only to the former king's supporters, but also to those who had fled back to the capital.

The battle ended quickly.

Not long after, I received a report that Ferth Morrissey, the Viscount of Kark, had been captured alive.

"All right. First torture him and find out everything he knows."

We didn't have any detailed information about the former king's faction's plans. It'd be fastest to hear it from the lips of a frontline commander.

"As you wish. We'll force him to divulge his secrets with the rappas' traditional techniques."

"I'm counting on you. I'll go and bring down the other forts. Of course, that probably won't take long."

With the fall of the main castle, there was a steady stream of surrendering soldiers and deserters from the other forts. We finished our pacification work in about a day.

It was a simple battle.

Of course, I'd had no intention of having any problems this early.

This opened the way to advance farther west. I was going to advance the western conquests.

I planned to wipe out the entirety of the former king's faction.

◇

According to the information that Ferth Morrissey, the Viscount of Kark, provided under torture, the plan had been to thoroughly corner Hasse's Western Conquest Army.

The former king's faction had believed it could achieve that with about half of the Western Conquest Army's troop total.

That calculation sounded about right. It's said that the ideal is to have three times the number of the defending forces when laying siege to a castle. The Western Conquest Army only had about double the forces of the defending army, and the defenders had been winning the sporadic skirmishes that occurred around the forts.

However, if there had been a problem with that plan, it was that the Western Conquest Army had been more stubborn than they expected. The Western Conquest Army had taken much longer than the faction had anticipated to retreat.

There were many reasons for this slow retreat, such as Hasse's desire to save face and the fact that Hasse simply wasn't a good-enough general to know when to retreat, but the result was that the defenders were faced with a problem. Their supplies had nearly run out.

Which was why the former king's faction's army under Ferth Morrissey had switched to attack. This had succeeded admirably, and Hasse had chosen to retreat. Had it ended there, the campaign would have been a great victory for Ferth Morrissey.

But that was when I'd arrived with a new army of my own.

I listened as Yadoriggy gave me her report in the village mayor's house that was serving as my headquarters in our cantonment.

The village appeared to have been ransacked when Hasse's Western Conquest Army had retreated, and it was sparsely populated. Though I didn't put it in writing, I informed the locals that I would catch and execute those who had ransacked the city. Hopefully, that would defuse some of the resentment of the victims of the pillaging.

"I see. It was worth it to learn that the enemy's main force won't be facing us for a while."

"Yes. It does appear that they plan to fight the decisive battle in the Great Isle Region," Yadoriggy replied softly.

The enemy's plan was to place their main headquarters far to the rear and force our army to bleed as we pushed through an endless string of small fortifications. Given that each region had its own lords, while we could take them one by one, that would take a great deal of time.

If it appeared that they could take down the Western Conquest Army at some point along that route, the enemy would do so; otherwise, they would force the Western Conquest Army to stretch its supply routes and take it down the moment it crossed the Sanado Channel. It was basically the strategy that we had been expecting them to employ.

The rest of the information included specifics on the names of the enemy lords and the sizes of their holdings as far as Morrissey knew. Given that he had simply been in charge of the first line of defense, he didn't have a particularly detailed grasp of that information.

"And how is the Viscount of Kark now?"

"He bit off his tongue in the middle of the interrogation and died."

"I can't believe you'd make a mistake like that. If I had to guess, you finished interrogating him, then gave him an opening to kill himself. Perhaps with a touch of encouragement?"

"To be truthful, yes," Yadoriggy answered matter-of-factly, without so much as twitching her lip in a smile.

"Understood. The plan doesn't change for the time being. We're going to continue our advance, reducing enemy fortresses and placing our own garrisons in them. If possible, I'd like to advance as far as the channel, but if not, I'd at least like to conquer these two prefectures."

There'd be no point to advancing and conquering territory if the enemy simply recaptured it once we retreated. Which was why we'd need to place garrisons with appropriate commanders and reinforce the defenses of each conquered territory.

"I believe there won't be much in the way of opposition for a while," said Yadoriggy. "There aren't any lords with large holdings until the channel, which is likely why the former king went to seek shelter from the Counts of Talmud and Samuur."

"True. Well, it'll be easy work until the channel, but it won't hurt to earn some extra points with the king. Also, how is our secondary force doing?"

I hadn't mentioned the secondary force to Hasse. I do, after all, have sole command discretion for this campaign.

"The armies of Soltis Nistonia and several other nobles are advancing with a total of about six thousand soldiers toward the West," explained Yadoriggy. "There aren't any forces that would present a threat to them, so I believe they should be making good progress."

I nodded coolly. "Then there's nothing that worries me. You're dismissed."

Yadoriggy bowed before leaving the room.

I had assigned Soltis Nistonia to advance westward from Ayles Caltis's old territory of Brantaar Prefecture. His orders were to attack enemy lords belonging to the former king's faction.

The goal was to quickly secure and expand the territory under the kingdom's control. No, not the kingdom's—under *my* control.

I would, for the time being, have complete discretion to govern the territories acquired as part of this military campaign. Because Hasse's mortal enemy, the former king, was holed up beyond these territories, Hasse would have no choice but to accept the arrangement. It was a time of war. I didn't have the time to scrape and bow for permission from the king for every last thing.

Then I planned to turn these lands into my own private property. I would treat them like my own feudal holdings.

If possible, I intended to keep them even after disposing of the former king.

If I maintained control of the conquered lands, then the majority of the lands in the kingdom would be under my rule. That would make it possible to push for the king's abdication and to choose Hasse's son to marry Lumie's daughter.

This campaign wasn't just a battle against the former king and his supporters. It was also the campaign to get me the crown.

——The expression you're wearing now suits you. Never change.

With you as my constant companion, Oda Nobunaga, I don't feel particularly alone even when there's no one else around.

——A conqueror's path is a lonely one. Nonetheless, a conqueror must have the ability to enjoy that loneliness. Remember, you are the only one in the world who gets to witness the scene unfolding before you.

That's what I intend to do, of course.

I would become the king. Hasse would be the last king of Therwil.

Whether I changed the kingdom's name would depend upon the circumstances, but at the very least, historians would treat the next king as the start of a new dynasty.

In the midst of all this, I wrote a letter to Hasse myself.

It stated that I had defeated the traitorous army and liberated the lands from its rule. Furthermore, the traitors to the north were on their way to defeat and I would liberate all the territory from here to the channel. I imagined Hasse would think that declaration was merely for show.

But I fully intended to fulfill that promise.

◇

My offensive continued after I defeated the Viscount of Kark.

Because Paffus's forces had gathered around the Viscount of Kark to conduct their defensive war, I met no resistance for a while after.

I was engaging in less of a war and more of a campaign of issuing writs of ownership to the conquered cities and villages. As for the lords who had surrendered because they were unable to put up any resistance, I forced each to hand over a hostage, then incorporated them into my army.

These lands weren't merely areas I was going to pass through, but areas that were to be added to my own territorial claims. I treated them with the appropriate amount of care.

Even when I looked at a map, there weren't any lords worth noting. None of them were above the title of count; the vast majority were viscounts who might or might not control an entire county. Even the few counts in the region had a large number of independent-minded lords in their territories and weren't able to wield much influence.

Of those lords, I made certain to thoroughly crush any who resisted to make them an example to the others.

Fortunately, my forces had been built up over years of hard fighting to be able to shatter the opposition as a warning. My generals, such as Noen Rowd, Little Kivik, and Meissel Wouge, had all grown into excellent commanders. Petty lords who had never seen fighting outside of local skirmishes were hardly a threat.

During the middle of the campaign, I began sending troops along the coastline to the south. There were quite a few prosperous port cities along the coast. I conquered these cities and folded them into my domain.

"Lord Alsrod, things are going far too well. It really is rather dull, isn't it?" Laviala commented one day in a noble's manor, where we were staying.

From the window I could see out to sea, where there were a large number of ships with their sails set. While those in charge of the former king's faction could launch attacks along the coast using ships of their own, so far we hadn't seen any signs pointing to that sort of activity.

"Oh, come now. Had we struggled this early, I'd be stressed over our prospects for the long term."

Our offensive had been proceeding smoothly. At this rate, I would be able to add Bilgund Prefecture, slightly to the east of Yargurtz Prefecture, to my domain. Yargurtz Prefecture bordered the channel on one side and Bilgund Prefecture on the other.

"You know, these seas are awfully calm in this region. The waves are quieter. It's almost like a lake."

It must have been an unfamiliar sight for Laviala. Which meant it was true for me as well.

"This area has a lot of islands. Those islands form a sort of gulf and act as a protective barrier that keeps away all the larger waves. Which is why so many merchant ships come here. I've heard there are even ships from other continents."

"Wow… That's a world I thought I'd never see and still have trouble believing that I'm living in. I always thought I'd spend most of my life in Nayvil County and pretty much never step foot outside of there."

"Yeah, that really was the case just two or three generations ago."

Hearing Laviala put it into words was a shock. It really drove home just how far we'd come.

Rural lords would spend their entire lives ambling around their little territories. That had been the norm until very recently. The exceptions were few. Noble lords whose estates were near the capital might go visit the capital to pay tribute to the king and things of that sort.

For quite a while, there were no lords with the power to send their army this far afield. As for the Nayvil clan acquiring land that bordered the sea? I doubt any of my ancestors ever gave that possibility a second's thought.

"Eventually this entire kingdom is going to be ours. I'll probably end up having to assign lords to govern various sections of the country, but at least in name, as king, it'll all be mine."

"Having traveled the world with you, I'm fully aware of just how amazing your ambitions are, Lord Alsrod." Laviala heaved a theatrical sigh. "Look at me, the concubine of such a ridiculous personage. I'm an elf, gazing at the sea. An elf, breathing in the salt air. I'm probably the first one in my family to have seen the ocean."

"Are you planning to change your family name to reflect that you visited here? Maybe name yourself after something near this city?"

"Never. I'll continue to proudly bear the name Aweyu that shows we're a family of Aweyu Forest."

Laviala puffed out her cheeks like a pouty child.

"It took a while to plan out our campaign, but once it started moving, it didn't take long," I noted.

The effort to sweep aside the former king's faction was going extremely well. The final question would be how to fight the enemy on their own home terrain.

"We were really fortunate the king's so inept at war. If he had advanced all the way to the Sanado Channel, you would have lost the opportunity to make these territorial gains, Lord Alsrod."

"Quite a few lords submitted out of fear when they heard I was advancing on them. If it had been Hasse, I'm sure it would have been much harder for them."

Killing Hasse would be a certain ticket to advancement for a member of the former king's faction. That, and the fact that the Western Conquest Army had struggled to raise its morale and was tired from its long march, would have made the enemy far more competitive.

Besides, the core of my regular army wasn't a levy raised primarily from peasants. As a professional army, it had a morale that was much harder to break. There were still a fair number of peasant conscripts, but they were primarily employed in roles where they didn't have to fight directly, such as in support roles behind the lines.

Assimilating the new prefectures on the way to the Sanado Channel would greatly expand my sphere of influence.

Further, if I could finish off the former king's faction on my own, there wouldn't be a single faction with enough power to resist me in the kingdom.

The dream of unification was so close I could smell it.

The excitement made my palms clammy with sweat. I felt like my kingdom was starting to take shape.

No, I needed to stay calm. It was clear to everyone that I was expanding my influence. If I was too obvious about my plans, there was always the concern the capital might do something unnecessary. I needed to continue to act as the Kingdom of Therwil's regent.

"Anyway, it's long past time that my guest arrived. Guess I may as well take advantage of the lull and relax. I'm sure no one would blame me for taking a day to enjoy the sights of a port city."

"Guest? Just who's coming by?"

Laviala apparently hadn't grasped the situation yet.

"My father-in-law. The one who wouldn't ever betray me."

The next day a messenger came bearing word that my guest had arrived.

"Lord Soltis, the Count of Siala, is here to see you."

"Yes, I'm aware."

The rappas had been keeping me apprised of Soltis Nistonia's movements. There was no way he would betray me at this point, so they were only keeping track of his location.

I had prepared a room in the temple for us to meet in. Given that I was also going to thank him for his work, I brought some alcohol as well.

Soltis Nistonia appeared a bit worn from his long campaign, but because of his victories, his features were full of life.

"Count of Siala, I was amazed by your campaign. You swept through the enemy as though there were no one impeding you. It was a treat to read your reports."

"It was simply the fact that the former king's faction had been deployed expecting only to fight your forces, Sir Regent. They seemed completely unprepared for the possibility that I would attack from the north. I have your superior planning to thank, Sir Regent."

I poured wine into Soltis Nistonia's glass.

"While I did come up with the plan, you were the one who actually defeated the enemy, my dear count. You have more than earned the right to be proud of your conquests. History, no doubt, will regard it as one of the finest military accomplishments in your clan's distinguished history."

"Perhaps, although whether it will be treated as an actual accomplishment depends on how things progress from here."

Soltis thinned his lips as his expression tensed.

Of course, I hadn't called Soltis here simply to praise him for his victories.

"For the time being, things are progressing as well as we could hope for. I'll be placing the newly acquired territory under my direct control for now. Tax collection and the like will be conducted by my own people."

"Meaning that you will be incorporating the new territories into your domain, yes?"

I shook my head theatrically. "No, I'll merely be a temporary caretaker. After all, we're in the midst of a war to secure our country's authority. It'd be far too dangerous to leave lands that could be attacked at any moment by the former king's faction in the hands of lords with no strength."

"Agreed. Your policy is perfectly justified," Soltis said for form's sake, lying even as he grasped my intent. "Once you and your supporters control the prefectures up to the Sanado Channel, that will place much of the kingdom other than the Great Isle Region within your sphere of influence. You will, without a doubt, control enough territory to make it impossible for other lords to stand against you. And in the North, the Margrave of Machaal is continuing her advance."

"Yes. I intend to make the lords east of the capital fully submit as well."

Once I acquired the entirety of this kingdom's military forces, the rest would fall into place.

"Still," began Soltis, "you have to wonder what His Majesty truly thinks of your extraordinary accomplishments." I could understand why Soltis's feelings seemed mixed. "To put it bluntly, he certainly can't be pleased."

I readily agreed with Soltis's assessment. "The regent has defeated an opponent that the king himself couldn't, and he refuses to let go of the territories he's liberated from the enemy's faction. Although the current king wants the former king and his faction defeated, the regent poses a problem of its own—a thorn in his side, if you will. I think it inevitable that the king would feel that way."

"At which point, what will His Majesty do...? I hesitate to even bring up the possibility...but he could very well think of turning upon you, Sir Regent..."

"A distinct and likely possibility. It's only human not to be able to let certain things go." I made a grand gesture of draining my glass of wine. "But we'll cross that bridge when we get to it. Should His Majesty seek to take me out, I'll be compelled to resist him."

I wouldn't show any fear, nor would I show any anger. I'd simply act as a regent ought to. Be it an ally or a father-in-law, I wouldn't give anyone unnecessary information. Spreading that sort of intel was of no help whatsoever.

"Indeed. However loyal a vassal, it would be far too much to ask a vassal to hand over his head without something akin to a guarantee of his clan's survival after his death."

Soltis was also carefully choosing his words. This was a man who'd protected his clan's domains by correctly deciding whom to ally with.

Even if he was now approaching a position close to that of one of my vassals, he wouldn't make any reckless suggestions like recommending that I turn against Hasse.

"My dear count, there's no point to continuing such conjectures. Our task for now is to rid the lands before the channel of the former king's faction in His Majesty's name. I have already had my bureaucrats draw up plans for a temporary tax collection regime."

"Understood, Sir Regent. All there is for me to do is to follow your plans and work for your sake."

Soltis declared his intention to cooperate with me. With that, the day's work was done.

"Thank you. I look forward to your cooperation." I held out my hand for a handshake. Soltis immediately took it. "However, while I know this may sound repetitive—remember that you're working not for my sake, but for His Majesty's."

I would still fulfill my oaths. On the surface, I intended to remain a fully loyal vassal.

If I ended up fighting Hasse, it would be preferable that I be blameless.

The one who would decide whether that was the case would likely be Hasse, not I. That was why there was an element to this I couldn't fully anticipate. If I was to build my own kingdom, then my enemy wasn't just the former king's faction, it was everyone who would stand in my way.

Soltis let out a rather resigned sigh.

"Sir Regent, you are indeed an honorable man. It speaks to why you've been able to climb to where you are at such a young age. I'm glad my daughter is married to you."

"I'm also blessed to have acquired such a good consort. I hope that our happiness lasts a long time."

"If a man of your character had appeared earlier, no doubt this age of chaos would have ended far earlier."

"No, not at all," murmured Oda Nobunaga. I agreed with the sentiment.

"It was because the kingdom was in chaos that I was able to make a name for myself," I replied. "Had it been an age of peace, I would have merely been a lord's younger brother."

◇

I had already asked Kelara and Yanhaan to come up with a number of proposals for governing the conquered territories, anticipating a wide range of local circumstances.

Afterward, I chose to place Kelara in charge of governing the local administration. While I retained the ultimate authority, there were limits to how much I could manage on the civilian side on my own. Not to mention that my deployment was technically meant only to drive the enemy out of these territories, so behaving as the territorial lord would be problematic.

Therefore, I summoned Kelara to maintain the facade.

"—Which is why I will be leaving the administration of the conquered lands in your hands. Don't hesitate to ask for my advice if anything goes wrong. Although I doubt that'll be a problem for you."

We had decided that the coastal prefecture would be governed under Soltis's name, as he had been the one to conquer it from inland. That would make it appear that we were doing it because we had no choice. Of course, Soltis and I were connected behind the scenes.

Kelara primly bowed her head and knelt.

"I humbly accept your order, Sir Regent. If I have any reservation, it is the fact that it is enemy land, so I can't quite anticipate where there will be rebellions."

It was true that we couldn't be fully certain that there weren't enemy generals mixed in among the peasants and city folk. There were practically limitless places for them to hide.

"You have full authority to deal with revolts as you feel is necessary. The enemy are traitors rebelling against the crown. Punish them as you see fit."

"I will do as instructed, Sir Regent."

There was no longer any doubt in Kelara's gaze about the fact that I planned to build a new kingdom. She had truly become one of my loyal vassals.

——To think that you would bring Akechi Mitsuhide to heel... Well done.

Oda Nobunaga sounded simultaneously exasperated and impressed.

——Of course, this is a clear lesson to be learned from my previous life. Had I known Mitsuhide would betray me, I would have treated him differently. Certainly, in retrospect, it was a fatal mistake, but all the daimyo had acted with similar levels of carelessness. Dammit! To imagine there will be those who will try to pin all the responsibility on me is irritating!

Don't get so worked up. You took a country that was mired in chaos to the brink of unification. There's no mistaking that you're a conqueror. A conqueror shouldn't be bothered by what gnats in the future say about him.

——You have a point, but...in the end, the ones who rate historical figures are the ones living in the particular age when that judgment is made. Being treated like a fool for a single mistake is extremely unpleasant. There's a saying about failing to finish a great work, and to fail in that moment is indeed a painful thing to deal with.

I understand. That's something I'll be careful about.

"Kelara, while you're dealing with the occupied territory, I'll capture Nargust Prefecture—another prefecture a step before the channel. For that, I intend to place my base of operations on the eastern part of Nargust Prefecture, toward the capital."

I placed my hand atop the map, then pointed to an inland city named Yagmoory.

"It seems a bit too far east to fight the former king's faction, and a bit too far from the sea—but that's because you wish to keep an eye on the capital, yes?"

Kelara already understood my intentions.

"Correct. On the off chance that I'm attacked from the capital, it needs to be a place where I can hold out if need be. And this location would let the Nistonia clan and Talsha the margrave send me supplies through northern trade routes. Particularly given the prefecture to the north is controlled by the Nistonia clan."

I had already made preparations for independence.

The southern seas risked attacks not only from the former king's faction, but from warships from the capital. Which was why I'd decided to place my central command farther inland.

Not only would it serve for an offensive against Paffus's faction, but it would also allow me to take an appropriate response if Hasse were to grow fearful and turn against me.

"Certainly, there are now no factions with more power than yours. That His Majesty would regard you as his greatest threat is…not beyond the realm of possibility."

I nodded slowly. As things stood, if I were to eliminate the former king's faction and then occupy its territory by force, it would leave the majority of the kingdom in my hands.

Even if the factions to the east of the capital had yet to directly fall under my influence, that would be sufficient military force to corner the capital.

Which was why Hasse hadn't tried to encourage me to cross the channel and take the offensive against Paffus.

The most recent missives from him were primarily full of half-hearted efforts to show appreciation for my work, such as by telling me to take care of my health.

They also indicated that he wanted to send governors for the conquered territory from the capital.

I'd turned down those recommendations by stating that the situation in the conquered territory was still fluid.

That wasn't a complete fabrication. If a governor with administrative experience but no military experience was assigned to the territory, no doubt they would struggle to contain any revolts. I wouldn't be able to trust the territory to them.

But the biggest issue was that such an outsider would just get in the way of my efforts to bring about effective control of those areas.

The conquered lands would eventually be fully under my control. I was going to maintain ownership of them until Hasse accepted that outcome.

"I assigned Little Kivik and Meissel Wouge to advance into Nargust Prefecture from two directions. But I also told them to take their sweet time doing so."

There weren't any lords in Nargust Prefecture who could resist my army divisions. Besides, those ruling the Great Isle Region probably wouldn't try to defend Nargust Prefecture. It simply wasn't worth the effort.

"It's a prefecture we can conquer quite quickly, but, well, we're going to take things slow. I'm sure we can be forgiven for having one war where the goal isn't to actually defeat the enemy."

"It's almost as though you're finding the time to move your center of power to Yagmoory."

Kelara wasn't the sort to joke, so no doubt she was at least somewhat serious about this statement.

"That's reading too much into it. I don't intend to do that. Maust Castle is my beloved castle. I wouldn't move to a place like Yagmoory where I have no connections, even if Hasse ordered me to do it."

I immediately denied it.

But then I looked off a bit into the distance.

"There might be times in the future when I won't be able to leave Yagmoory."

"There are examples where a lord was defending a castle he was ordered to defend by his liege lord, only to have that liege lord lose while he was busy defending it and end up being named the master of that castle by the new liege lord."

If they had come from anyone other than Kelara, I would have thought the words sarcasm, but Kelara didn't have any intention of mocking me.

"All right, Kelara, I'm putting my trust in your governing abilities. I'm going to go provide Little Kivik with some motivation. The plan can't continue if he doesn't go at least as far as Yagmoory."

It was at that moment that Kelara made a statement approaching a joke.

"Isn't this about the time during a deployment when you're starting to miss a woman's touch?"

"Yes. I think it's about time I indulged myself."

I made love with Kelara before she departed.

I felt that we'd come a long way toward understanding one another.

Little Kivik's army slowly and steadily brought down the enemy lords one by one. It didn't take them much time to force the Yagmoory clan, who owned Yagmoory Castle, to surrender.

The enemy in Nargust Prefecture didn't have particularly high morale. They'd already seen a large number of their peers crushed underfoot and had no confidence that they could suddenly start winning.

And, perhaps because it intended to conserve its strength, it didn't appear the former king's faction had any intention of sending serious reinforcements. It wouldn't be odd for the lords of Nargust to believe they'd been abandoned, given that it was, in fact, the case.

The former king, Paffus VI, had already given up maintaining a hold on the continent and had switched to a policy of strengthening his control of the Great Isle Region across the channel. He intended to treat the Great Isle Region as a kingdom in itself and maintain a government in exile.

That in itself wasn't a bad choice. If he could push back the royal armies of Hasse several times, it was possible that everyone would increasingly consider the Great Isle Region an independent kingdom of its own. Indeed, there had been a time when the Great Isle Region was a separate kingdom.

The two great powers of the Great Isle Region—the Counts of

Talmud and Samuur—were already obsessed with protecting their own lands, and Paffus VI was in no position to ignore their wishes.

Of course, the priorities of the former king's faction were of no concern to me.

I took a look around Yagmoory Castle, guided by Little Kivik. Given that it was a small castle, the tour didn't take much time.

"Since the enemy surrendered quickly, things such as the cordon are still intact. It's hardly what you could call polished, so I doubt it's been changed much over the generations."

Little Kivik wasn't quite a fire-breather like his old man, Kivik the Elder. But that didn't mean he was lacking in ability, and he fulfilled his duty well.

The second generation tends to be a bit better behaved. Perhaps because they've watched the reckless behavior of their parents, they grow up to be more cautious.

"This certainly takes me back. Nayvil Castle was at most about this size, too. The ramparts were low and the cordon wasn't designed for fighting a sizable army."

"I have no intention of insulting your ancestral castle, Sir Regent…"

"I know. But it's true that this castle and my ancestral castle are hardly impressive. This castle won't do as it currently sits. For one, it won't fit nearly a large-enough garrison when defending."

——It would at least be entertaining if we could make this castle like Azuchi Castle.

Azuchi Castle was Oda Nobunaga's home castle.

I'd heard him brag about it on more than one occasion. Because it was evidently extremely different in appearance from this world's castles, I couldn't really get a clear image of it in my head, but I could well imagine it had been quite an ostentatious castle, given Oda Nobunaga's tastes.

——Azuchi Castle was a lavish and beautiful structure. No doubt it was the greatest castle in Japan in that era. It's such a pity that it

burned down. If only it had survived in that form, it would have better informed later generations of my greatness. Ah, such a shame, such a shame.

I hate to tell you this, but I have no intention of building a castle just to impress people. What we're building is a military fortification for use in war.

——I know. Even if you knew every last detail about Azuchi Castle, there's no need to build that now. More than anything, there simply isn't enough time.

There are, largely speaking, two types of castles.

Of course, there's no such thing as a castle with no military purpose. However, castles for great lords or kings also function as capitals. They are built not only for war, but also for governing.

Maust Castle and the royal palace were such structures. I guess I can describe them as the sort of castle that peasants think of when they imagine a princess attending a ball.

No matter how unassuming or austere the lord, that's not a castle he can afford to stint on. Symbols of authority are meaningless if they don't stand out. If one attends a ball wearing ragged clothing, that just makes one a disrespectful eccentric.

Then there are castles like the one I was about to build. Their only purpose is to fulfill their military role. So long as it didn't let the enemy in and was built to bleed an attacking army, it didn't matter how ugly the castle itself was. As a conqueror, Oda Nobunaga was well aware of that fact.

——Still, this is an opportunity to build a good castle. Even if Azuchi Castle isn't an option, why not make one like Kitanosho Castle in Echizen?

Kitanosho Castle? In addition to the unfamiliar location name, the notice of a new ability rang through my head.

Special ability Conqueror's Claim acquired.
Allows the use of Oda Nobunaga's knowledge and tastes when building a castle.

Oh, this might prove rather useful.

A list of strange castle names appeared in my head. When I tried choosing one from the list, the basic information about the castle came up.

There weren't many castles constructed of stone. Most were made of earth, with various holes and blocked paths built in to prevent intruders.

I selected Kitanosho Castle from the list.

Although I'd never seen it myself, the castle's design began flowing into my brain.

Things clicked into place. It made use of a large river as a moat on its western side. In that way, it was similar in concept to Fort Nagraad. That made it harder for attackers to approach, so it would be useful regardless of the world it was built in.

But what was most noticeable about the castle was the extremely tall building that towered like a fortress. It wasn't as tall as a tower, but the stone base spread out across quite an area, and it would simply overwhelm an opponent who stared up at it unless they had a particularly large force at their disposal.

Not bad. I think I'll go ahead and build this Kitanosho Castle.

——Of course. This will be a linchpin that will help you hold the northern area. The enemy will quickly be stopped in their tracks. Only those with a particularly large army would be able to take it down.

All right, I'm going to use Oda Nobunaga's knowledge to make the greatest of military facilities.

I turned to Little Kivik.

"Prepare as many engineer units as possible. I also want to begin collecting stone."

"So this will be a stone castle, sir? Then I shall summon the masons."

"That's not technically what it'll be, but masons will be useful to have."

The first thing we did was dig a moat.

Yagmoory Castle had been built near a river, but that river wasn't very deep or wide, so we shifted the location of the new castle farther downstream and decided to deepen the river itself. We added inflow from another nearby river next to the castle.

Still, this was something anyone could come up with. It didn't need Oda Nobunaga's knowledge.

Once the river was expanded, we had boulders brought over by ship. We began piling them up to form a stone wall.

At first Laviala insisted that this plan was impossible.

"Lord Alsrod, even if you can gather enough stone, we don't have enough masons. No matter what we try, it takes time to carve boulders into square blocks..."

"Laviala, there's no need to make flat blocks out of the boulders. This is enough to make a solid wall."

"Huh? What do you mean?"

"I should probably explain this to the masons rather than you, Laviala, but..."

Oda Nobunaga's knowledge included information on stone walls.

The stone walls were extremely odd looking. They were piles of uncarved stone and boulders. They looked like they could collapse at any moment, but the small stones wedged themselves between the boulders and served a role similar to mortar.

That was enough to build up a wall of about three jargs in height. There was a secret to how the rocks needed to be piled up, but Oda Nobunaga had supplied that knowledge to me.

Which meant that Oda Nobunaga was interested even to the detail of the best way to pile up stone. If that weren't the case, he would've left all that in the hands of the masons.

——When I invaded Omi, I saw many impressive stone walls. When I conquered Kannonji Castle of the Rokkaku, I was moved by the elegance of their stonework. Omi also had Mount Hiei's Ano-shu Guild; their approach toward stonemasonry was more advanced than others'.

Oda Nobunaga was fond of explaining. He had a practically child-like curiosity about everything. And he liked showing the fruits of that curiosity to people. The problem for me was that I was the only one he could unveil that knowledge to.

——And so I came upon an idea. If the stones could be piled high, as high as possible, it would make it possible to make far tougher castles than using earthen ramparts. Ramparts made of soil would eventually erode over the years and end up shorter, or the edges would start rounding off. But one could construct a much larger base with stone. You could have countless sharp-cornered corridors within the castle's interior. One could create a castle that was next to impossible to invade—a castle made to massacre the enemy.

I'm definitely going to adopt your ideas. Thinking about it, of course enemy soldiers would lose heart if they saw a castle hardened with stone.

I explained the concepts behind the stonework to Laviala using the terms Oda Nobunaga used. Laviala was still skeptical, but seemed to grasp that I was right when she saw the stone structures that had been started.

The masons were the same way. As the smaller stones settled between the boulders and large stones like little wedges, they held the boulders and large stones in place. It greatly reduced the amount of time spent on cutting and polishing stone.

"The stone really doesn't move… And if a wall this tall ran all around… it'd be impossible to attack the center of the castle." Laviala gazed up the wall as she patted the stone. "And if you placed archers and arquebusiers on top of it, they could fire down without mercy on any attackers."

"Yes, I knew you'd notice that, Laviala. That's exactly right. Shoot through as many enemy heads as you want from here."

This castle was like a labyrinth designed to slaughter the enemy. No doubt I would be able to sleep soundly inside.

"And if the castle still is at risk of being conquered, we can lower a ship onto the river next to it and use it for escape. This will definitely become the center from which we launch our future expeditions."

"It's really well designed. But perhaps the most surprising thing is… that it's only been a month since we started construction…"

True, the pace of the castle construction itself was quite fast. This was a privilege afforded to me because of the sheer number of people I could command.

"We're still in wartime, after all. The plan is to have it finished in about three months. It'll be a castle that'll never fall in my lifetime."

With no real interruption from the enemy, the new Yagmoory Castle was completed in three months.

When the castle was completed, I hosted a small party in celebration with the generals who were there.

Leon of the White Eagles told me that word of the castle was spreading. It was being talked about as the castle where walls of stone loomed over its surroundings. My personal guard companies were always by my side.

"I've done all that I needed to do. From here on out, I'll manage the conquered territories from Yagmoory Castle."

"No doubt that will become a reality soon. However, if there is a concern…"

"Hey now, don't go jinxing things. Leon, you're far too nervous about everything," Orcus of the Red Bears teased.

"Can you think of any man who could conquer this castle? There's no concerns. We'll finish taking out the former king's faction soon. Or are you afraid of getting in a boat to cross the channel?"

"I have no such fears! I don't doubt we'll defeat the former king's faction, either. But if his base is this well fortified, there will be those who believe that the regent is the greatest threat."

Leon was being somewhat tactful, but it was clear what he was hinting at.

"That's why I say you're paranoid, Leon. Even if the king were to be afraid of the regent and attack, the regent would just switch to supporting the former king. The king doesn't have the luxury of making an enemy of the regent."

I tried to avoid getting involved in the argument between my two personal guard captains, but I did feel that I needed to prepare for the unexpected.

If he did end up coming after me, it might be sooner than I expected. No doubt he'd think it would be too late once my rule was established. I was sure there would be those that whispered those things into his ear.

It could very well be that the next challenge would be the trial I faced to become king.

◇

Two weeks after the completion of Yagmoory Castle, a wolf quietly appeared in my room.

"Ah, Yadoriggy. You can speak in human form."

Unusually for her, Yadoriggy was visibly tense. I understood immediately that she brought important news.

"We've discovered that His Majesty the king and the former king have been exchanging letters."

"Oh? It'd be nice if the former king would hand over the Great Isle Region like that. Then the unification would essentially be complete."

"The primary subject of their secret missives involves how to dispose of the hawk that's grown too large."

I sucked in a breath.

So he'd finally made a move.

But to think that the greatest enemy would end up being me...

"A hawk, mm? That's a lovely animal to be compared to."

Had he called me an overly fattened pig, I might have been a bit insulted.

"So have they decided how to dispose of the hawk?"

Yadoriggy had returned to her usual level expression. "No," she replied. "Once they've disposed of the hawk, His Majesty and the former king would be completely at odds in terms of their interests. It appears they're struggling to hash out the details there."

I was struck with an urge to burst out laughing, but I somehow managed to contain it.

"To waste time on a future that hasn't even happened at this juncture…," I scoffed. "Royals are certainly far more leisurely and careless than us mere mortals."

And that leisurely attitude will be your undoing as a royal family.

"However, under the current conditions, I believe they will settle on the king ceding the prefectures close to the channel to the former king," Yadoriggy explained. "Or perhaps the former king will cede the continent to King Hasse in exchange for recognizing the Great Isle Region as a separate country. One of the two."

Yadoriggy still continued. Because she had so much information to convey, it almost appeared she'd suddenly become a talkative woman.

"As the former king and the lords of the Great Isle Region are keenly feeling the danger approaching, I believe they will be willing to compromise to avoid that danger."

"I see. Do you happen to know the ones who encouraged His Majesty to take this action?"

Yadoriggy brought up several names from among the king's courtiers.

They were all men whose only value was as members of a retinue. After all, the actual political administration of the capital was done by people in my camp. The age of courtiers stealing the fruits of the capital had ended.

"From their point of view, I'm sure I'm quite the thorn in their side. But even if their motivation is wrong, they've managed to give him the right advice. As advisers to a king, they've actually done a decent job."

If they had continued to trust me and told Hasse to just sit back, they would have been irredeemably stupid.

"His Majesty tried to ignore them at first. It seemed he didn't want to consider that possibility. However..."

"He saw my policy of governing the conquered territories and felt a prickle of fear."

A general doing as he wished on the front lines was an ancient tradition.

It's not as though I were a particularly villainous example. Maintaining authority in times of war is necessary if one is to be able to fight the enemy. There is no time to go and obtain permission from the king back in the capital. It is a necessary evil.

Of course, the nature of the discussion had changed once the area under my effective rule was greater than half the total area of the kingdom.

When it was a virtual certainty that Talsha, the Margrave of Machaal, and Soltis Nistonia, who had exterminated the former king's faction, were on my side, the amount of influence Hasse, the current king, actually wielded was extremely small.

He must have thought that if the former king's faction were to be eliminated and the Great Isle Region were also to fall under my direct control, he would be next on the chopping block.

"I see. But a hawk can freely soar through the skies. Once it's left your grasp, it's far too late to go after it. There's no such thing as a hawk that would willingly return to its cage."

"What will you do about your children and consorts at Maust Castle?"

At that question, my expression froze.

I hadn't realized I'd been thinking only about myself. Yes, it was true that Yagmoory wouldn't fall easily. It was too far from the capital and too well defended.

But with so many troops deployed away from it, Maust Castle's defenses were more fragile.

I fell silent for a moment.

"Should this pincer attack come to fruition, the former king's faction will cross the channel and strike. Which means if I leave here, the former king's faction will rapidly take land…" I strung the words together as though trying to convince myself. "Even if I were to return to Maust, I can't go and kill Hasse while I'm being attacked on two fronts. If I did, there would be uprisings by those who consider me a traitor. But if I only imprison Hasse, I would have to deal with a newly resurgent force under Paffus's sway and be at a disadvantage…"

The best path for me to become king was practically decided for me.

"I should cross over to the Great Isle Region before returning to Maust Castle."

I didn't want to think about what would happen to Maust Castle during that time.

Considering common practices on the battlefield, they probably wouldn't kill any women. However, I was concerned about how they would treat the consorts of a traitor if they were to declare me one.

"I'll send a letter to my consorts telling them that Maust Castle might be attacked, and that if necessary, they have my permission to surrender."

"As you command."

"However—I'll also tell them to hold out for a bit. Fleur and Seraphina are there. I'm sure they could hold out against a weak enemy's assault."

My last words were less serious.

While that was close to a wish, it was also my sincere opinion.

Honestly, I think either of them might actually be pleased to be able to wield power as temporary lord of the manor.

"I'll advance the plans for crossing to the Great Isle Region. Send word to Soltis as well. There might be revolts in the lands under Kelara's control, so a blitzkrieg advance to take out the former king's faction would be the most effective tactic."

If I were to fall into a defensive stance, that would create new openings for them to exploit.

This was a time when I couldn't afford to ease up on my attacks.

"Understood. Godspeed, Sir Regent."

"Yadoriggy, a rappa like you doesn't need to pray. Just keep a clear eye on reality for me."

◇

While Yagmoory Castle was already complete, it seemed I wouldn't be able to take the time to enjoy it.

I had felt I would eventually end up fighting Hasse, but I hadn't expected him to ally himself with Paffus. I had bet on him not being the sort who would be willing to go to whatever lengths necessary to secure his ends.

It was impossible to know what a desperate person would do. It seemed I had driven Hasse into a more desperate state than I had thought. Or had he ended up resenting me for so easily accomplishing the western conquests that he had failed to accomplish? No, it was a meaningless thing to think about.

The reply from Maust Castle came immediately. Each of my consorts wrote her own reply. The basic contents of each reply were the same, telling me not to worry about them.

However, Seraphina's was a little different.

I won't let them take this castle. As the daughter of an infamous villain, I'll go and conquer the capital myself.

"That's my Seraphina!"

I burst out laughing when I read that.

Fight as much as you want. No matter how wild your life has been, it's not an opportunity that'll come by often.

◇

I sent a formal envoy to the capital.

The envoy wasn't there to wish Hasse well, but to ask a question.

Essentially, that question was, *Was there any truth to the rumors that he was going to ally with Paffus VI and attack the Regent Alsrod?*

Immediately going on the offensive wasn't a good idea. That would make me the villain. The more justification I could claim, the better. It was something my profession would nag me about.

"Do not defy the will of heaven"—that's how Oda Nobunaga expressed it.

In this case, the will of heaven was something like a supreme god. Although the concept of a supreme god had supposedly been rather vague in Oda Nobunaga's world, it had become necessary, which was how the will of heaven came to be.

——The will of heaven can certainly be interpreted as a supreme god, and there were many who viewed it as such, but that is a meaningless interpretation. It's a scam.

Oda Nobunaga interrupted my thoughts again. Perhaps being a profession leaves one with too much free time. No doubt he would have been a lot more entertained if there were a listener there to serve as an audience for his boasts.

——The will of heaven isn't actually anything divine—nothing of the sort. It's public opinion—that is, the opinion of the masses. It isn't divine, but rather as temporal as temporal can be.

I understand. That said, there's something ironic about someone who aspires to be a king not just walking the path of the conqueror but also having to worry about public opinion.

——That's hardly worth complaining about. No one thinks to follow those spurned by public opinion. I tried to keep that in mind with my actions, but I ultimately stumbled at the end. As I grew closer to the ultimate prize, I missed the forest for the trees.

* * *

Even I knew what Oda Nobunaga was lecturing me about.

This was the endgame for me.

That was why I sent a messenger to the capital to question Hasse. It was an unpleasant assignment for the messenger, who could, in the worst case, end up dead.

Of course, if Hasse killed the messenger, the will of heaven would smile upon me.

Or rather, I should probably say that the will of heaven would abandon Hasse.

◇

It was now the messenger's earliest return date.

No matter the response, I was still tense. Perhaps for that reason I was thirsty, so I drank several cups of tea in my temporary quarters at Yagmoory Castle.

I didn't think he'd indict me as a rebel and declare war upon me, but I still couldn't get a good read on what Hasse was planning to do.

It was then that Laviala practically burst into the room.

"Pardon me, Lord Alsrod."

"You should be saying that *before* you enter the room, not after. So what is it?"

"Let's take the opportunity to bring the various consorts from Maust Castle here! We still have enough time to do it!"

So it was a reasonable plan to move my consorts to safety before the capital faction could toss me aside. It was actually a perfectly normal thing to propose.

Though, based on her mood, she was probably having trouble staying put and had burst into my room to suggest it. To Laviala, the other consorts were both colleagues and family. I understood why she'd be concerned.

But I couldn't just accept that proposal.

"Laviala, if I brought my consorts here to Yagmoory right now, it would be used as unimpeachable proof that I was planning a rebellion."

People offered as hostages are, of course, killed the moment their master betrays an alliance. Which is why from time immemorial, generals planning to revolt have been trying to secure the safety of such hostages. While Lumie and Seraphina weren't hostages but sitting in my residence at Maust, that wouldn't change the fact that I'd be moving them somewhere safer. It would be the most obvious evidence in the world.

"I know that, but I'm still making this proposal. At this rate, everyone would—"

I placed my index finger against Laviala's lips.

It was my way of telling her to be quiet, and a gesture I made not to a vassal but to my concubine. I immediately took my finger off her lips.

"If my consorts leave Maust, they could very well be attacked on the way," I told her.

Laviala's eyes widened in realization.

"Compared to being attacked outside the walls, being in Maust Castle is safer. Of course, I wouldn't exactly call it safe."

"You're right… If the king's already planning to attack you, Lord Alsrod, he's probably already got Maust Castle under surveillance…"

"Now's the time to wait," I replied with a nod. "It's the most unpleasant time of this whole affair. Being out on the battlefield is easier to understand and come to grips with."

I retrieved a teacup for Laviala myself.

"Oh! I'll do that!"

"Don't worry about it. I'm just pouring tea for my concubine. You need to have a cup to calm down. Better to have tea in the morning than wine, I think."

Laviala also sipped from her hot tea and let out a slow breath. Warm drinks calm the spirit. Yanhaan had taught me that. Tea was originally a drink developed as a medicine, after all.

"I'm sorry for losing my cool earlier. I've just been so afraid while we wait on the messenger's reply..."

"I know. But I'll do all that I can. Just as I'll do all I can to create my own kingdom."

The next moment, there was a panicked knock on my door. It was one of my squires. I could tell from the sound.

"Yes, come in."

The squire immediately rushed into the room. Perhaps the messenger had returned.

But the squire's report was an unexpected one.

"My lord, I'm here to report you have a guest. Your official wife, Lady Lumie, has arrived!"

"Wha—?! Lumie?"

"She wishes to immediately speak with you! May I show her in?"

I just managed to say, "Please do."

Lumie's expression was pained as we came face-to-face for the first time in a while.

And the moment she saw me, tears flowed from her eyes as she leaped into my arms.

"My dearest, please listen to me! Please listen!"

"What is it, Lumie? I'll listen to whatever you have to say. Tell me."

I'd never seen Lumie this wound up. She was in far less control of her emotions than Laviala.

"I...I heard from the messenger that my brother might attack you. The other consorts also heard the same story."

"Yes. The outrageous rumor came from one of my spies."

I had already told those at Maust Castle to prepare for the worst-case scenario. Seraphina and Fleur were more than ready to fight. They were far more trustworthy than your average general.

Lumie should have also heard the same explanation.

"Which is why I...went to the capital and went alone to speak directly with my brother, the king. I demanded to know whether the rumors were true."

"Huh?"

I was caught completely off guard by Lumie's statement.

Lumie's expression was one of mixed regret and anger. The anger was directed at her brother in the capital.

"Lumie, it hasn't been that long since you gave birth. Have you been all right?"

"This was far too important to worry about that. At the very least, I haven't felt ill up until now."

Indeed, I couldn't imagine anyone this lively being sick. Lumie's complexion was extremely healthy at the moment.

"I spoke directly with His Majesty, tête-à-tête. No—I wasn't speaking to His Majesty, but rather to my older brother. My brother agreed to speak to me."

I imagined the look on Hasse's face at being cornered by his sister.

No doubt he hadn't been expecting his sister to come visit him.

"And my brother said to me that soon there would be no one who could stop you in the kingdom. At which point, even if the former king was slain, the Kingdom of Therwil might come to an end. And that he was considering taking steps to prevent that from happening."

That was essentially an admission that he was going to attack me. And there was a person who had heard it directly from the king's lips. There was no greater evidence than this.

"The information hasn't been made public yet. There hasn't been a royal decree declaring you a traitor. If such an order were to circulate now, you might very well defect to the former king's side, after all. However—I realized that there was no good future for us if you continued serving my brother."

"Lumie, how did you get here? Even if you heard him tell you that... Didn't he try to capture you...?"

Given that she wasn't a spy, Lumie probably couldn't ride a fast horse. Having been told that information, even if she wasn't imprisoned, she would have at least been placed under house arrest...

"I told my brother that I would go to my husband's side—and that if he was going to kill me, he was welcome to send his minions after me, for I would accept my fate and kill myself. That as my child was being cared for by a wet nurse at Maust Castle, I had nothing to fear from him," Lumie said with a burning strength to her gaze.

No doubt she'd told Hasse her feelings with a similar expression on her face.

"And that's why you were able to come to Yagmoory Castle without anyone pursuing you?" Laviala, who was still in the room, asked with a shocked expression.

"Yes, that's right. No doubt my brother hesitated to kill me," Lumie said. I could tell by the look on her face that she felt that was the only natural outcome.

I couldn't help but burst out laughing.

"Lumie, you're a woman worthy of being my formal wife. I'm blessed to be married to a heroine like you. No, I suppose it's that fate chose a woman worthy of the role."

My wife had directly questioned the king and gotten an answer from him about whether he planned to attack me. What I had to do was now decided.

Still, I could only marvel at how unfit Hasse was to be king. To tell Lumie the truth and then to let her slip out of his grasp. At that point, he should have stopped her whatever the cost.

Which was why, after looking at Lumie's expression of pure defiance, I could only sympathize with Hasse.

If he'd tried to place her under house arrest, Lumie would have chosen death without hesitation. In that case, it would be hard to muster the desire to arrest her. Even I couldn't choose an option that would ruthlessly kill Altia.

Of course, he could have gotten away with it if he hadn't told her anything in the first place, but Hasse must have been overwhelmed by his sister's insistence.

The Therwil royal family was finished. Their kings were simply far too incompetent. In all honestly, Lumie was far more suited to rule.

Wait.

A certain idea suddenly came to mind.

"Thank you, Lumie. I'm committed now. I can now go and do what I must do without hesitation."

I embraced Lumie once again.

"You must be exhausted from the long trip. Rest easy for now. By my estimation, this is the toughest castle in the kingdom. Even while I'm gone, not a single enemy will slip in."

"Yes. I'm also extremely glad I was able to be of use to you."

Lumie looked deeply relieved. It was as though, with her task completed, the tension had drained from her.

"Compared to your other consorts, I have been unable to do much for you, so I hope I was of some help this time."

"Yes. It's a feat that'll be next to impossible to match. But there's one more big thing I need you to do."

"What would that be? Please do tell me whatever it is that needs to be done."

Even at times like this, Lumie sometimes showed a little bit of lingering childishness in her expression. But that was what made me love her all the more.

"It's something only you can do, Lumie."

Lumie was at first shocked to hear my proposal, but—

"I will do it. It would be an extreme honor for me as well."

—by the time I finished explaining, she was more motivated than I was.

Soon after, a messenger from the capital arrived with a notice for me.

The contents were mild and attempted to avoid confrontation: Hasse claimed he wouldn't possibly suspect his regent of disloyalty, that he expected me to continue to give my all in the effort against the former king.

In other words: Officially, he wanted to hide the plan to hit me from two fronts.

It was, of course, too late. There was no doubt that Hasse hadn't expected Lumie would show up, but given that he was still waffling at this late hour, he simply couldn't remain on the throne any longer.

I immediately gathered my vassals and held a council of war.

There was a single action item.

"We're going to cross over to the Great Isle Region and advance into the Count of Talmud's domain. We're going to eliminate the former king. It's taken longer than any of us would have liked, but we're now ready to take that step."

The generals, motivated by my declaration, let out a series of celebratory shouts.

In particular, the captain of the Red Bears, Orcus Bright, was like a child who'd been given a new toy, exclaiming, "We finally get to go crush that riffraff in the Great Isle Region!" The personal guard would be without work if there weren't a war, which was probably why he was so elated.

I supposed Hasse would have problems justifying sending an army after me if I wasn't mobilizing my troops against him.

But he could do as he pleased. While he was off sitting on his thumbs, I was going to go crush the previous king and his underlings.

"While I'm gone, there might be those who try to attack Yagmoory Castle. I'm going to have Kelara return from the conquered territories to defend it."

I understood why Oda Nobunaga appeared reluctant. Kelara was the woman with Akechi Mitsuhide as her profession. No doubt to Oda Nobunaga, it'd seem like suicide to leave this castle to a woman like that and cross the channel.

"Furthermore, I'll also have my wife Lumie defend this castle."

My men seemed to take that as a joke. Orcus actually burst out laughing. He was so hysterical that Leon of the White Eagles had to chastise him.

"I actually think it's a hell of an idea."

There was no way that Kelara would betray Lumie. She was perfect for an oversight role.

After all, they were both women who loved me.

The conquest of Nargust Prefecture, where Yagmoory Castle was located, had already been mostly completed by the units under the command of Little Kivik and Meissel Wouge.

At the same time, notifications to the capital had been delayed because of "complications." If that hadn't been the case, I wouldn't have been able to secure the time needed to complete Yagmoory Castle.

Kelara returned to Yagmoory Castle far ahead of schedule. She probably used a fast horse to get there.

"Kelara, I'm leaving this castle in your care for a while. Use it as you see fit."

Kelara politely offered her thanks. "I'm humbled by your trust in me. You can rest assured this castle won't fall while I draw breath."

"I doubt this place would fall even if you were the most incompetent commander on the continent. Your greatest task will probably be looking after Lumie."

"I will also take care of your wife wherever necessary."

I let out a dry laugh at how hard it was to get her to take a joke. But given that was also partly why I was leaving things in her care, I suppose the situation was my fault as well.

"The next time I return, it will likely be in triumph."

"I certainly have faith in that." Then Kelara approached me and quietly whispered into my ear, "I will notify you immediately if news arrives that His Majesty is raising troops."

"Got it. I'll leave that to you."

Right before I set off to the Great Isle Region, I took another look at Yagmoory Castle from the outside.

What stood before me was an enormous fortress, the likes of which had never been seen in this kingdom.

I doubted there was another castle in the kingdom with a moat so wide. Even the royal palace didn't have a moat of this scale.

"This castle won't fall to any enemy. If we struggle in the Great Isle Region, we can simply return here."

"We need to take a ship to get to the Great Isle Region, right…?" said Laviala. "I'm not very good with ships…"

As a forest-dwelling elf, Laviala seemed to have reservations about heading out to sea.

"If you have concerns, then go to sleep the moment you get aboard. The Sanado Channel is small enough we'll finish crossing it while you nap."

"It won't sink, will it…?"

Evidently, being rooted to the land the way the elves are makes them susceptible to seasickness.

"If it sinks, then we'll have another ship pick you up. So long as there's at least one ship afloat, you'll be fine. If they all sink, then swim your way to shore."

I set off from the western edge of Nargust Prefecture, traveling by boat upon the river, and brought my army to the port of Land's Beak in Yargurtz Prefecture. We would be meeting up with Little Kivik and Meissel Wouge's divisions here.

An armada made up of countless squadrons had already anchored here at Land's Beak. Several of the squadrons belonged to Soltis Nistonia. I had asked him ahead of time to gather them here in preparation for this campaign.

Soltis Nistonia himself wouldn't be directly participating in this campaign, but his younger brother, a man by the name of Ordana, commanded his ships.

I exchanged greetings with Ordana. Compared to Soltis, Ordana was the very image of a sailor, with a leathery, tanned complexion.

"My sailors have been put through their paces. We've been here for a while, so we've been able to learn the local tides and current. Rest easy, we'll have you there safely."

"You're exactly what I would imagine a pirate king would look like. Far more trustworthy on the high seas than any pale-faced merchant."

"Since I didn't have to inherit the clan, I was given the job of leading our clan's sailors. All of our lads say it'd be a damned embarrassment to lose to the lubbers of the Great Isle. If you'd like, we can skip going to the nearest port on the Great Isle and take you straight to the former king's headquarters."

"It's not a bad idea, but the former king's set up far inland. Better for now to slowly but steadily eat into his territory. Besides, most of the soldiers aren't used to long sea voyages."

The former king, Paffus VI, had "transferred the capital" to a city called Sopheli located between the domains of the two major lords of the Great Isle Region, the Counts of Talmud and Samuur.

It was probably the result of wanting to avoid offending either of the great lords. After all, the worst possible scenario for Paffus would be for the two lords to go to war with one another. There was no way that Paffus could retake the capital if he didn't have the entire strength of the Great Isle Region behind him.

Our warships set sail for the Sanado Channel.

The voyage itself was peaceful. It would have been difficult for it not to be, given that the channel was narrow enough that one could see the opposite shore.

We knew which of the Count of Talmud's forts were prepared to fight.

Aberthy Hanistra, the Count of Talmud, was a great lord who ruled the three northern prefectures of the Great Isle Region. He was a blue blood descended from an ancient line of military nobles. In addition, his clan was economically prosperous from generations of trade with foreign countries.

The reason the Count of Talmud wasn't able to unify the kingdom under his own banner was simply that the Great Isle Region was on the periphery, far from the royal capital.

There had been, if I recalled correctly, a lord of the family who had served in a role similar to that of regent, but a rebellion had occurred while he was away from his lands and he had hurriedly returned home. As a result, the clan had a tendency to prefer staying in its own territories.

Furthermore, the lords of the Great Isle Region had a great deal of pride in their local culture. From their point of view, the continent and the royal capital were the culturally backward backwaters. Many vassals had advised the lords to simply declare independence from the Kingdom of Therwil.

——Hrmph. I don't know if this Count of Talmud is your equivalent of an Otomo clan or Ouchi clan, but both were surviving shugo families. Neither was all that much to worry about, however.

Aboard ship, Oda Nobunaga seemed rather more animated than usual.

——The truth was that I was never able to step foot in Kyushu itself. My life ended before I could get that far, which is why I find this expedition rather exciting.

Well, this isn't Kyushu. Although my objective isn't too different.

Fortunately, the Great Isle Region was sunny during this time of the year. It was a perfect time to invade.

It's not that I'm afraid of storms. I am, however, afraid of our not being able to fight at our best.

——In my day, arquebusiers started from Tanegashima. Pity the enemy who has yet to see them firsthand.

There's no way you feel pity for them.

The enemy was going to try to slow us down with a series of small forts and try to defeat us in an open battle on the plains.

That was where I would show them what my arquebusiers could do.

My army safely made landfall on the Great Isle Region.

◇

There were certain norms to be observed in a war. I had sent a surrender ultimatum to the former king, Paffus VI, and Aberthy Hanistra, the Count of Talmud.

The enemy might be a rebel, but he was still royalty. It behooved me to act with a certain amount of respect.

Of course, there was no way the enemy would accept such an ultimatum.

The first person I met in the Great Isle Region was an enemy messenger who swore that they would fight off the hated invader. He went as far as demanding that we surrender to them instead.

"I will be fulfilling my duty as regent. Please pass on that message to the former king and the Counts of Talmud and Samuur."

I politely sent the messenger back on his way. There was no advantage to sullying my reputation here.

I left Ordana Nistonia in charge of protecting the armada, and we advanced into the Great Isle Region. We moved our troops toward Doorn and Central Doorn Prefectures.

"It's so humid here. The sweat's just pouring out of me."

During our march, Laviala wiped the sweat from her body. The climate was definitely a lot muggier here than where we were from.

"The heat is fine, but it'd be a serious problem if there's a disease outbreak or the like. We shouldn't let this campaign drag on."

"Either way, we don't have enough supplies to do a long-term siege. We don't know the terrain well. It'll be a problem if we can't quickly crush the enemy."

Laviala had a good grasp of the most important parts of this war.

True, we had come to fight in a place so distant that we couldn't return home without using ships.

If we were to suffer a large loss, we'd quickly end up being the hunted side. What would await us then would be a hellish scene of utter pandemonium.

Which was why we had two strategies available to us:

Slowly, cautiously take the lands closest to us and secure them.

Or aggressively attack the enemy and inflict enough damage on them that they couldn't regroup. At the very least, inflict enough damage that they couldn't pursue us.

With Hasse watching fearfully from the capital, I didn't have the breathing room the first strategy would require.

I needed to quickly crush the former king's faction and create enough time to return to Maust Castle.

"Fortunately, that chance will come on its own. No doubt it's inconvenient for them if I come at this multiple times. They'll bite if they think there's an opportunity to finish me off."

The Western Hanistra Plains were located just beyond the string of small forts.

The former king's faction intended to face us with an army of at least thirty thousand assembled by the Counts of Talmud and Samuur and the various minor lords of the Great Isle.

My army was about the same size. I could still add reinforcements if I wanted to, but given that I couldn't trust Hasse to my rear, it would be dangerous to bring too many of my troops to the frontline. Having a large amount of territory under my control meant I needed to deploy a corresponding number of soldiers to defend those lands.

And I was worried about the possibility of having a general I didn't know well and diluting my ability to effectively command my forces. We were the invaders on this island. I didn't want to clash with the enemy without having all my forces on the same page.

My soldiers progressively conquered each small fort and arrived upon the Western Hanistra Plains.

The enemy had already deployed on the opposite end of the plains.

We, of course, held a council of war. It was our first large field battle in some time. There were likely many who had never participated in a battle of this scale.

There were many who wanted to attack quickly and inflict a heavy blow on the enemy as swiftly as possible. Orcus, the captain of the Red Bears, was one of them, but even Leon, captain of the White Eagles, recommended a similar tactic.

I understood their desire to avoid staying too long in unfamiliar territory. That instinct itself was fine. I agreed that we didn't want to dally.

However…

——Don't rush in. Advancing without a clear plan for victory is recklessness, not bravery.

Oda Nobunaga, I completely agree. Perhaps that just meant I was getting that much closer to becoming a conqueror.

I knew that the enemy had a large number of longbow archers. If we moved first, we'd be at a disadvantage. We'd take heavy losses.

"Everyone, I ask that you entrust your lives to me. I swear I'll return them to you with interest. Your lives are my wealth. I'm not a man who would simply throw away his riches," I declared as I looked upon the faces of my generals. "My profession is an extremely special one called Oda Nobunaga. When I first learned of it, I was devastated. But in trusting my profession, I've risen this far."

I was sure that Oda Nobunaga's effects were in play now.

But I no longer needed them. I had become a man like Oda Nobunaga himself.

"However, the war isn't over yet. I need to win here as well. I need a total victory so that I can return to my homeland. Which is why I'll choose the best method to achieve it."

"I, Laviala, place my life into your hands, Lord Alsrod."

Laviala was the first to confidently declare her trust.

That roused the rest of the crowd.

Cries of "You have mine as well!" and "I entrust everything I am to your hands, Sir Regent!" followed.

It was a heavy responsibility, but I had no intention of buckling under that weight.

"Thank you. We will be victorious—worry not."

Then, while looking over the map, I slowly explained, "We'll shift our forces to make the enemy think we're withdrawing from this field." I traced my finger along the map. "Fortunately, no matter which direction we go in, we're in enemy territory. There's a city we can plunder in every direction. We'll make them believe we're trying to force them into a series of running battles. Then we'll have the enemy pursue us."

My finger then stopped after the right distance.

"Once we've withdrawn to a decent distance, we'll stop. This is when we make our counterattack. We'll wipe out the enemy vanguard."

I repeated myself to make certain they understood. "I'll say this again, we're wiping them out to a man. This isn't a figure of speech. We're going to kill every man who advances on us. We're invaders. We need to show them we're deadly serious."

I wasn't a softhearted man like Hasse.

In terms of good or evil, I was probably the latter.

But that didn't matter. If I could obtain the kingdom, I was fine with being a villain.

I smiled and continued, "I ask nothing more than for you all to frighten the enemy, to fill them with despair. Do your worst."

I was about two steps from unifying the kingdom.

If I won here, I would have one last step to go.

The first day of conflict ended with the two armies glaring at one another across the field. The next morning...

I moved my forces on to the next battlefield.

I chose a direction that made it appear as though we were going to withdraw from this field of battle and circle around to attack the strategic center of Aberthy Hanistra, the Count of Talmud.

With that the enemy, of course, set out in pursuit.

They couldn't possibly just sit and wait for us to retreat. To do so would invite mockery and disdain.

We confirmed the enemy's movements, then stopped at the appropriate distance. High-quality intelligence flowed in from the rappas through Yadoriggy. Once the enemy came this far, they were bound to charge into us.

"Arquebusiers, prepare to fire!"

We had three thousand arquebusiers on our side.

I'd cracked the whip on the dwarf Ortonba to finish readying them.

With this many, I had nothing to fear. All I had to do was wait for the enemy to approach to finish the trap.

Because of the large number of guns, they were divided among multiple commanders, but Ortonba was at the heart of those forces. As the guns' creator, he understood them best.

Ortonba stood with his arms crossed, gauging the distance from his enemy.

"All right, lads, you see that large oak tree? Fire when the enemy steps in front of it," Ortonba said.

"You heard the man. When they cross beyond that oak, fire by company! Immediately prepare your next volley once you fire! Kill them all!"

I barked out my orders, sending my words to the farthest flanks of my forces.

"Archers, focus on taking down whatever the guns miss. Don't let anyone say that the Great Isle Region has better archers! Given we won't be crossing here to fight very often, you won't have a chance to redeem yourself if you fail! Be damned sure you don't miss!"

"Aye!" came the answering shout from the troops.

The ground rumbled as the enemy approached.

I enjoyed that sound. It drove home the point that we were on the battlefield.

Then the enemy crossed the oak in question.

"Fire!"

If the enemy's approach was a rumble, ours was a crack of thunder. The sharp reports of the arquebusiers echoed across the battlefield.

Almost simultaneously, the enemy soldiers began dropping like flies.

But they were a vanguard charging in, shouting their defiance at death. This was hardly enough to make them falter.

That was fine. We needed them to keep coming.

"Second volley, fire when ready!"

Small pops of thunder rang out from all around.

The enemy once again fell in their tracks.

The gap wasn't just in our professions. The gap in technology was overwhelming the enemy.

Yes, that was enough. We'd done enough damage in the opening stage of the battle.

Enemy corpses had begun littering the field before our forces collided.

As this pattern repeated itself, the enemy's movements grew sluggish.

With those ordered to charge gone, the less steady forces to the rear started appearing along the front.

"Archers! Maintain your fire as well!"

Now it wasn't just the arquebusiers firing. Arrows rained down upon the enemy, too. More enemies fell. Their problem was that they had initiated the attack.

If one had long-range weapons, waiting provided an advantage on the battlefield. There were several examples in history of a large army being decimated by archers and forced to retreat.

The enemy also knew this, which was why they'd sent their archers to the front and tried to draw us into attacking them.

Or perhaps their plan had been to stretch out our formation and try to break us by hitting our exposed flanks.

But that was meaningless if our forces didn't advance. I was in no hurry. There were plenty of ways for us to take the territory.

It had been the enemy who had lost the waiting game. An alliance force tens of thousands strong consisting of soldiers drawn from multiple armies didn't have the option of waiting and not fighting.

The great lords supporting the former king had no choice but to follow me. It wasn't possible for clans with such a long history of ruling these lands to simply sit back and let us pillage their cities.

Which was why the battle had been over before it began. The side that could employ effective tactics would win.

Once the enemy had suffered catastrophic losses, Little Kivik's forces, Meissel Wouge's forces, and Dorbeau's Black Dogs attacked.

The core of the enemy's offensive had already collapsed. Now we clashed with them to gouge away more of their forces.

I could hear energetic shouts that proclaimed, "Another enemy general down!"

It was over. The enemy was just trying to figure out how to escape.

"That wasn't very difficult," said Laviala. I had kept her near me rather than send her up front.

"That was the intention. If I had just attacked normally, we would've had a fair number of losses. I couldn't guarantee your safety."

The side that couldn't afford to wait typically lost battles of this sort, and since we were in enemy territory, ordinarily we would be the ones who needed to force the issue, but my tactics had been focused on giving us that breathing room.

If I'm honest, I wanted to be the first one charging into battle. I wanted to be able to return home from the Great Isle Region as quickly as possible. But if I forced the issue and ended up getting routed, it would delay my return all the more.

"I won't die, Lord Alsrod," said Laviala. "I'll continue to serve by your side until you become king."

This was less the statement of a loyal vassal than it was an affectionate declaration from a consort.

"Yes. And it doesn't seem like it'll take much longer for that to happen."

The commanders on the offensive had started to return. I had warned them ahead of time not to go too far when attacking.

Getting caught too far forward raised the risk of my being eliminated in turn. It was enough for my purposes to make the enemy *feel* that they had suffered a massive rout.

We'd secured a great victory in the Battle of the Western Hanistra Plains.

◇

We raised a victorious cheer, then rested our soldiers in a post town.

It appeared that a great number of enemy generals, including the Count of Talmud's kin, had been killed in battle. The ones who'd had to lead from the front, given their position, had drawn the short straw in this fight.

Meanwhile, we waited for news at the post town.

That night, Yadoriggy appeared in my room dressed as a lady-in-waiting.

"Speak as you wish. I've a fair idea of what you're here to report."

Yadoriggy nodded faintly before she quickly delivered the news.

"His Majesty has declared you to be a traitor and has ordered you to be killed."

Hasse had finally chosen to fight me.

No. Hasse had been determined to do that to begin with. He had just been debating whether to send notice to the entire kingdom.

"Based on the timing, it sounds like he made the decision around the time I made preparations to invade the Great Isle Region."

"Yes. His Majesty has already mustered an army at the royal palace and is attempting to rally his troops."

"Well, it's something to be grateful for. It means the time for political maneuvers is over."

I meant that to some extent.

To conquer the Great Isle Region, then just pressure Hasse until he attacked me, was neither very like a conqueror nor very like a hero.

Fight the king and either win or lose. That was easier to understand, and one could say it was more suited to my personality.

Yadoriggy added another piece of news.

"Further, His Majesty has signed a peace agreement with the former king and has committed himself to an alliance with the purpose of defeating you, Sir Regent. He will be recognizing the Great Isle Region as the Kingdom of West Therwil."

"That's as expected."

If Paffus could kill me, he could once again become an undisputed king, at least in name. Once I was gone, he would probably go back to fighting over the western prefectures of the mainland with Hasse, but since Hasse didn't have the means or the ability to mount any real invasions of the Great Isle Region, it would return to a stalemate for the time being.

Paffus had a fair amount to gain if he could place himself as King of West Therwil during that time.

Of course, he had to drive me out of the Great Isle Region first.

"Understood. No surprises there. We'll continue on our present course."

Yadoriggy swiftly left the room. She wasn't one to linger after finishing a task.

——Seems we've finally lit a fire under you.

Oda Nobunaga sounded amused.

It's fine—it was a fire I was expecting to be lit eventually.

——You're in a race against time. If you don't take down this former king or whatever he is, you'll have nowhere to return to.

My castles are tough. Maust Castle was also designed to be highly defensible.

At the very least, I have no intention of letting a fool like Hasse and his hangers-on conquer it. My consorts will do wonderfully as acting lords and ensure I have a place to go home to.

Besides, you seem to be really enjoying this, Oda Nobunaga. I can tell without even seeing your face.

——Well, of course. Those who ought to become conquerors always have many enemies. And you have good justification to fight. The will of heaven has tilted in your favor. Fight to your heart's content—and win.

Certainly. You'll have a front-row seat at my conquest.

The next morning, I informed my generals of His Majesty's revolt.

Some were rattled by the news, but they were the minority. Most seemed to have expected this to happen eventually.

"It's an extremely lamentable development. I helped His Majesty long before he rose to the throne. His Majesty was the one who offered his sister as my bride. For His Majesty to declare me a traitor is still hard for me to believe."

While I said it was lamentable, I showed no signs of lamentation. There was no need for a conqueror to sulk.

"You need not be told, but as regent my role is to defeat all enemies in the name of unifying the Kingdom of Therwil. That is in no way a rebellion. No doubt his courtiers filled his ears with nonsense. His Majesty will no doubt eventually realize his mistake, but I cannot simply wait for this to happen while I'm in enemy territory."

I made a point of enunciating and projecting my voice as I made my next declaration.

"So as of today, Mad King Hasse I will be dethroned, and Lumie I will be crowned as the new queen regnant of the Kingdom of Therwil!"

Those words set my generals abuzz. That was also unavoidable.

I showed them the letter Lumie had entrusted to my care.

"I did not do this of my own volition. Her Majesty had already witnessed the troubling developments in the royal capital. And Her Majesty had made preparations to assume the throne as the new ruling monarch in case Hasse I were to lose his senses!"

This was a step I was able to take because Lumie had come all the way to Yagmoory Castle.

If my opponent was going to consider me an enemy of the monarch, then I would raise up a new monarch of my own.

There was no question that Lumie was a member of the royal family. There was nothing that would prevent her from assuming the throne.

When she had come to me alone, I had told her of this plan and gotten her approval.

"Her Majesty has issued a royal declaration that I am to continue in my role as regent and strike down Paffus and his allies in the name of the crown. I remain the regent of the kingdom, and we are no rebels. Fight to your heart's content!"

"We'll win for the queen!" Laviala shouted. "If we lose, Her Majesty the queen will be executed as well! We can't allow such an unjust thing to happen! Let's do whatever we need to do to win and return to Yagmoory Castle!"

Cries of "Hear her! Hear her!" greeted her statement.

Based on Laviala's expression, she hadn't planned this speech but had rather blurted it out from genuine righteous indignation. Given that it was rallying everyone in the room, her outburst wasn't a problem.

"The previous king—no, he isn't even the previous king. Paffus is based out of a small city named Sopheli. We'll conquer that city and bring stability to the Great Isle Region. It probably won't take much time. Give it your all!"

Morale was plenty high.

There wasn't a single person in this room who believed they had been cast out as a rebel. In the end, the one who held the army was the strongest.

Lumie was probably now sending out declarations that she was now the rightful monarch of every corner of the kingdom. That would be plenty if it canceled out Hasse's extermination order.

I had already secretly sent a peace envoy to Aberthy Hanistra, the Count of Talmud. The envoy would tell him to abandon Paffus and come to my side.

I'd also told the envoy I would give the Count of Talmud some land should he opt to join my side, and even if the Count of Samuur did not yield, I was sure Paffus's one-sided loss in the previous battle had shown the Count of Talmud that he had little hope of holding out long in his capital. He was probably worried that he wouldn't stand a chance if his own home castle was attacked now.

This all stemmed from Hasse's reluctance to render a decision.

The situation might have been different had Hasse been able to seal his alliance with Paffus before I won the Battle of the Western Hanistra Plains.

The Count of Talmud no longer had the strength to repel my attacks. He had few choices left.

But I had something I needed to do before dealing with the Count of Talmud.

Conquer the city of Sopheli.

◇

As Lumie I's regent, I brought my soldiers southward and headed for the city of Sopheli, where Paffus the Pretender was holed up.

I hurried my army along this time. I knew that there would be hardly be any interruptions on the way. Paffus himself had no military base of his own, while the Count of Talmud needed to concentrate his forces at his own capital because of his recent rout.

The castle at Sopheli was more of a manor built on a plain than a castle, and it was hardly a defensible location. Ultimately it was just a temporary "capital" for the former king.

That castle fell immediately. Rather, Paffus set fire to it and fled.

The question was where he would flee to.

Paffus bet on Salkhoz Samuur and headed southward.

He evidently didn't trust the Count of Talmud.

This settled it.

It didn't take long for a letter to arrive from Aberthy Hanistra, the Count of Talmud, swearing fealty to me.

"I wondered why you didn't quickly push south and finish off the former king's faction, but this was the reason, wasn't it?" Laviala said as she read the articles of surrender that Aberthy Hanistra, the Count of Talmud, had sent to me. "This effectively means that there's no one in the northern part of the Great Isle Region who can resist you, Lord Alsrod."

"That's right. It does take some time to bring in those who were willing to bend the knee."

It would always take several days for a lord to judge the situation, decide whom to side with, then hurriedly send a quick messenger. Which was why I'd stopped at Paffus's administrative capital of Sopheli. I wanted to at least secure the northern part of the Great Isle.

"Either way, I can't stay in the Great Isle Region for long. The lords who have sided with Hasse are in the midst of eyeing up both Maust Castle and Yagmoory Castle. Which is why I wanted to secure the Great Isle Region before I left."

I slowly colored in the map of the Great Isle Region spread out on the table in front of me.

I was coloring in the sections under my control. There were still a number of minor lords left, but they'd probably come to swear fealty when they found out the Count of Talmud had done so.

"Also, the next battle against Salkhoz Samuur is one we can't afford to lose. If we lose, the tables will be completely turned on us. Worse, we'll be stuck in the ass end of the Great Isle Region."

The Samuur clan had a long history, although they hadn't been secure in their position for long. In fact, up until about fifty years ago, the clan had been mired in a civil war between members of their family that had raged on and off for a century. That conflict had started even before the kingdom had fallen into the Hundred Years' Rebellion.

They had been able to survive in spite of this internal division primarily due to advantageous terrain. There were few forces that could invade all the way into the farthest reaches of the Great Isle Region. Indeed, the only ones capable of doing so were cadet branches of the Samuur clan itself. The crown had decided to ignore an internal conflict happening on the periphery of the Great Isle Region to focus on more important matters.

As a result of this history of ongoing civil war, the Samuur clan had developed into the most independent-minded of the regional cultures within the Kingdom of Therwil, and its cities were supposedly almost like foreign countries.

"It seems that because of their location, they've also been heavily influenced by cultures from other continents. They have units that wield a distinct pole-arm called a trident, while their elite units will fight to the last man even if their general is slain."

Laviala shuddered. "The elite units—you mean the Brotherhood of the Blood, yes? They're said to drink one another's blood to form a bond that won't ever be broken in this life..."

As a woodland elf, Laviala apparently was a bit creeped out by rituals that used human blood.

"The current lord, Salkhoz Samuur, is a gray-haired champion of a man rumored to be the son of a foreign princess. Rumor has it he's covered in battle scars from head to toe. This is a different kind of fight than we've had until now. It's dangerous to treat this like our usual battles."

"He's the type of opponent that's scarier the more you learn about him... The forests in this region are a lot darker and more sinister than the ones I know. They're only supposed to get thicker from here, right...? I don't even feel like we're fighting in the same country..."

But this was where my serious expression crumbled.

I didn't understand why, but I felt the whole situation to be irresistibly funny.

I burst out laughing. I couldn't keep my voice down.

"Um...Lord Alsrod, are you all right?"

"Oda Nobunaga, you didn't spend much time on the front lines in your later years, did you? Yes, that's probably the right way to do it. It was enough to send your vassals out to fight on the battlefield. A king shouldn't fight his own battles."

"Lord Alsrod, what's wrong?"

Sorry, Laviala. It's not like I'm possessed by an evil spirit or anything. It's just that I'm elated.

"But me, I want to keep riding across the battlefield. If it's at all possible, I want to cut down the last enemy with my blade and claim the country. That's much more interesting, isn't it?"

——Whether that's interesting or not is up to you. I certainly don't agree. It's too dangerous. When I was wounded when reinforcing Mitsuhide against Honganji's forces, my only thought was that I'd erred in my tactics.

Oda Nobunaga was saying that, but he wasn't seriously rejecting my point of view. I knew from our many years together.

——But it's true that I did think it was rather fun fighting at Honnoji. I felt like I'd tasted battle for the first time in a long while. I felt the same way when I charged at Imagawa on the hill at Dengaku Hazama.

See? Told you. You were, in the end, a warrior as well.

——Which reminds me, I'm told that my son Nobutada fought rather well at Nijo Castle. He was quite the skilled swordsman. I suppose that's why he didn't think to run. If he was as cowardly as Nobumasu, he would have been able to focus on fleeing, and it would have just delayed the Oda Conquest of Japan by a few years.

"A conqueror shouldn't think this or that about his children. I mean, sure, you love your children, but a conqueror is someone who lives to enjoy his life. Bringing peace to the country or unifying it are all just excuses."

——If you keep talking out loud to me, the elf girl will think you crazed.

"What does that matter, really? A conqueror who cares about what others think of him is the one who's odd. You can't become a conqueror that way. Also, Laviala would follow me whatever happens."

© Kaito Shibano

"Um...I don't quite know what's happening...but I'll follow you forever, Lord Alsrod... We'll even die together!"

"Well said."

I grabbed Laviala by the shoulders, then placed a long kiss upon her lips.

After the kiss, I pulled my face away and said to her, "Follow me by my side. I'll make you a witness to the moment we pacify the Great Isle Region."

"Of course! I'd be honored!"

So much had happened—so much had changed over the last decade or so...

But Laviala's spirited voice was no different from when she treated me as her little brother.

◇

It took little time for the majority of the lords to offer up letters of surrender and hostages after the Count of Talmud's surrender.

Now the stage was set.

I had already received a situation report from Kelara, who was defending Yagmoory Castle. Even though the castle was under attack by the enemy, the structure was so well fortified that it showed no sign of falling. That was definitely what I needed it to be.

I had already settled upon a perfect order of battle for attacking the Count of Samuur.

With the northern part of the Great Isle Region under my control, I now had infinite paths into the enemy's territory.

I had gathered the necessary information to choose the right paths to use.

What was most certain was that we would charge into the hardest, best-defended route with me as the supreme commander.

Because it was the best defended, it almost meant that the "capital" that Paffus the Pretender had fled into was just past it.

If he was going to flee, he should've fled all the way to Samuur Castle, the residence of the Count of Samuur, at the southern edge of the count's domain. But it seemed that Paffus was as proud as Hasse and felt that fleeing to the very corner of the kingdom was beneath him.

No doubt his reasoning was that because he was a king, it wouldn't be right for him to simply hide in a mere lord's castle.

I wouldn't judge that reasoning. If not for that sort of pride, I supposed he wouldn't be able to continue his resistance.

But it wasn't a bad thing that we could go after Paffus himself.

I proceeded south with my personal guard companies of the Red Bears, White Eagles, and Black Dogs by my side.

There were also the rapidly formed Blue Tigers.

The Blue Tigers were a new unit that had been put together solely with men from the Great Isle Region.

Newcomers were always in an awkward position, which was why I'd promised them they'd be recognized just as much as my existing vassals if they were to put up results in the upcoming battle. Of course, the personal guard units had a high fatality rate. The Blue Tigers were made up solely of those who were committed enough to accept that risk.

I knew that the Count of Samuur's elites, the Brotherhood of the Blood, were waiting along this route. I needed enough manpower to break through them.

After we summitted a relatively low peak, the land opened up to the south. Just beyond was where Paffus's "capital" lay.

The peak was defended by a little over three thousand of Samuur's forces.

We numbered a bit under five thousand. Too large an army would slow our advance. This was the most we could take.

We had superior numbers, but the enemy had the advantage of holding the high ground.

There wasn't any room for finesse or tricks. It was a question of whether we could break through their defenses with brute force.

Laviala, riding next to me on her horse, patted my back.

"Rest easy, Lord Alsrod. I will protect you no matter what happens."

"And I'll protect you. I need to be able to defend what's mine."

Laviala let out an exasperated-sounding sigh. "You know, Lord

Alsrod, you weren't quite this ambitious when you were younger. You wouldn't have claimed me as 'what's yours' even as a joke back then."

"It's because I got a strange profession when I became an adult. Forgive me for that."

Now we could see the enemy banners waving atop the peak.

I didn't need to say much to communicate my orders to my forces. The majority of them had fought alongside me for a long time. They all knew their roles.

"Orcus, Leon, Dorbeau—no need for precise orders here. I'm told the enemy won't stop fighting even if their commander disappears. You all just focus on killing the enemy in front of you."

Leon folded his hands together and cracked his knuckles.

"I'm going to charge straight through them and go take the former king's head. That'll do, yes?"

"Indeed. The former king is a rebel against the Kingdom of Therwil. Go slaughter him in the name of Lumie I."

Leon howled with laughter. "Very well! I'll definitely take his head! Then my name will live forever in the war histories!"

"Just remember, I'll also write down your name if you're killed in action," I added.

The Red Bears began laughing.

"We've come this far, we may as well live to see the triumph in the capital!"

"Yeah, go and admire the precious face of our new queen! All soldiers, charge! One kill per man!"

Our forces stormed in with a collective roar.

The enemy—the Brotherhood of the Blood—furiously waved their tridents. Just as the stories said, they were a unit assembled as a group of heroes to drive off the enemy.

"We've come too far to lose! Crush them!"

Special ability Conqueror's Presence activated.

Takes effect when recognized as a conqueror by many at once. All abilities are tripled from the usual.

Additionally, all who lay eyes on you experience either awe or fear.

Special ability Conqueror's Guidance activated.
Allies' trust and focus will double. Additionally, their offensive and defensive abilities improve by thirty percent.

With all this at my disposal, losing was out of the question.

Go and grasp a victory to offer our new queen.

Of course, I'll fight all out as well.

I swung the symbol of the regent, the Stroke of Justice, then charged into the enemy's midst.

"You can stand in front of me if you wish, but get out of the way if you're not prepared to die!"

Evidently there weren't any foes not willing to die.

A few were able to go a few strokes against me, but it all ended when their heads left their shoulders.

There wasn't a soul who could defeat me so long as Conqueror's Presence was active.

As the melee continued, I heard a cry of "I've taken the enemy general!" The one holding up his spear was one of our soldiers.

We had at least achieved our minimum objective.

"Don't let up! Kill anyone who attacks!"

The enemy didn't seem any closer to fleeing. They had a different air to them unlike anyone we had fought before. They were all willing to die for the Samuur clan.

This wasn't a region of the kingdom—it was an independent country of its own. While all the lords behaved like independent monarchs during the Hundred Years' Rebellion, the level of independence here was far greater than elsewhere.

Laviala rapidly fired arrow after arrow.

She shot down the nearby enemies and opened a path for me.

"Let's press onward, Lord Alsrod!"

Laviala looked utterly elated. True, battle brought terror, but there was a certain joy to it as well.

"All right! We're going to push our way through! We're going to eliminate those who stand against Therwil!"

Based on the progress of the battle, it looked like I could get to Paffus.

After we'd essentially wiped out the enemy, we regrouped, and I gathered my commanders.

"Casualties?"

"Seven Red Bears lost."

"Eight White Eagles missing. Fifteen wounded."

Captains Orcus and Leon reported their losses. Given that we had broken into an enemy formation where the enemy had the advantage, we had taken some hits. The newly recruited Blue Tigers had suffered the most.

But the operative word was *some*.

"Those who sacrificed their lives to create a new kingdom will be rewarded."

We'd defeated the enemy's famed elite forces with light casualties. Things were going well.

If that was the extent of our losses, we had no reason to stop. I was going to keep marching down the conqueror's path.

"It's time to take down Paffus! Do it without mercy! Once that's done, we take down Salkhoz Samuur, the Count of Samuur! Then we return to Yagmoory Castle, where Her Majesty awaits!"

The morale among the troops was the highest it had ever been. They seemed to sincerely believe they were the crown's army.

"I'd like to make sure we kill Paffus. Having Paffus die under his protection will deal an enormous blow to the Count of Samuur's authority."

Paffus had holed up in what had once been the manor of a lord of moderate influence. While it had a moat, it wasn't particularly wide. It wouldn't hold out for more than half an hour once my forces attacked.

"Leave this to us, please. It's our specialty," Dorbeau of the Black Dogs proposed to me. "If you proceed with a large force through the front, the cowardly enemy is certain to run. We'll approach the manor ahead of time and cut off their routes of escape."

"All right. Make it quick."

"As you command. If you could proceed slowly, perhaps while taking hostages from the nearby villages."

Apparently Dorbeau's plan worked, as by the time we arrived, Paffus had been forced to hole up in the manor.

There were a large number of enemy corpses sprawled nearby. Among them were some dressed more like merchants than like soldiers. No doubt they had tried to escape by disguising themselves.

"Women and merchants were trying to leave, so we killed them without question. At which point those in the back hurriedly returned to the manor. A man who matched Paffus's description and those who appeared to be his retainers were among them," Dorbeau explained to me. "It seems the man Paffus was going to resist, but not take up a blade himself."

I supposed he couldn't accept that his time was over, even as he faced death.

"Very well, then. Time to go with brute force. I'm sure they all want a shot at Paffus's head. Or have the Black Dogs already dealt with him?"

"No. We were afraid of how the other units would react," Dorbeau answered jokingly. It was true that he'd be resented by Orcus and Leon if it appeared he'd stolen a great achievement from under their noses.

"All right. Then I'll take part as well. It's a race to see who gets him first!"

We had no mercy left to give. We cordoned off the manor, laid down ladders with planks attached to them over the moat, and attacked. There wasn't much in the way of active resistance.

When we entered the manor, it triggered a memory.

It was of when I'd entered my brother's manor.

The circumstances had been far different. At least on the surface, I had been there to visit my ailing brother. In the end, an assassin had already been sent into the castle.

It wasn't that I would obtain greater rank from killing Paffus, but it would be closure of a sort.

The ones up front were the Red Bears. If we proceeded like this, the Red Bears would end things.

But for some reason, I was certain I'd be the one to put an end to this battle myself.

Inside the manor, I circled around toward the back of the house.

There was a distinguished personage being protected by his retainer in front of the stairs leading to the cellar.

It had to be Paffus.

"Am I safe in assuming that you are Paffus, who once served as King of Therwil?"

I cut down an enemy who lunged at me and headed in the direction of that group.

"Is there an escape route dug into the cellar? Or were you clinging to the hope that such a thing exists?"

"Could you be Alsrod Nayvil?" the retainer asked. Was the former king too proud to open his mouth and address me directly?

"Yes. I'm afraid it has been a long time since I ascended to that title despite my youth. It has been so long, there has been a change in monarchs."

From Hasse to Lumie, that is.

"You wicked scoundrel, to drive the king to this backwater! No doubt you're fated to burn in the fires of hell!"

It seemed the retainer at least had some nerve, shouting those words and waving a sword in my direction.

"With all respect, that's impossible. As for why—it is because I possess a veritable Demon King upon my person."

Both the retainer and Paffus looked confused.

"Evidently he's known as the Sixth Demon King. Since he hails from a foreign country, I'm afraid I don't know the details—but it's safe to say that this Demon King is not on the side that burns in hell, but rather the side doing the burning."

Oda Nobunaga cackled in my head.

——Yes, that's right! To think that a line I wrote as a joke in a declaration would end up so infamous!

* * *

"Damn you... You're possessed by something, aren't you...? Listen carefully—I'll give you the opportunity to serve the greater good. Take His Majesty here into your protection. That is what we consider justice in the Kingdom of Therwil."

Paffus, cowering behind the retainer, brought to mind my brother's final moments.

"You, the retainer. What's your name?"

"...Mould Buleur."

Ah, yes. There was a man of that name who had served the crown.

"Mould Buleur, I'll only say this once. Serve me."

"I cannot do something that goes agains—"

I cut down the retainer with my sword.

Paffus and I naturally locked gazes.

"Paffus, you aren't on the side of justice. You're merely obsolete."

I brandished my blade at him.

"It's not your fault alone, but the ruler must take responsibility for the suffering of his people."

Paffus turned his back to me and babbled something akin to a scream. It was the first time I'd heard his voice.

I slashed him diagonally across his back.

The man who had once been king died without taking any responsibility to the bitter end.

"This is where the Kingdom of Therwil ends."

With the death of the former king, Paffus VI, the war was nearing its conclusion.

I immediately sent an ultimatum demanding that Salkhoz Samuur surrender to me.

In it, I claimed that since he no longer had the need to serve a usurper to the throne, he should obey the current rightful monarch, Lumie I. Of course, I included the threat that if he refused to bend the knee, I would attack Samuur Castle with my full army and execute his entire clan.

Before I received an answer from Salkhoz Samuur, I placed all of the cities of Samuur Prefecture under my control. They had no choice but to obey when they were told we wouldn't sack their cities if they'd just produce hostages. There was no military force capable of resisting us.

My honest hope was that he would just go and admit that he'd lost. If he chose to fight to the very end, although we would win, it would take time to bring things under our control. That would mean we'd have to stay in the Great Isle Region for a while.

I had detailed reports about the state of Yagmoory Castle. While it wasn't at any risk of falling anytime soon, that wasn't necessarily impossible. And I was worried about Lumie's health. Diseases would sometimes spread while people were holed up in a castle.

Furthermore, I had learned that Hasse had put all his effort into laying siege to Maust Castle. While I also didn't think Maust would fall, many of my consorts were there. I wanted to go relieve them as soon as possible.

I had been planning for various scenarios, including the worst-case scenario, in which Salkhoz Samuur would declare Paffus's child the next monarch and stand against me.

In that case, I would leave most of the offensive to Aberthy Hanistra, the Count of Talmud. Talmud and Samuur had long been rivals. There was a good chance he would move for the opportunity to finish off Samuur. Seizing Samuur lands would be an enormous boon to Talmud.

While the Great Isle Region forces attacked Samuur, I would return to Yagmoory Castle.

After confirming the situation there, I would choose between relieving Maust Castle and invading the royal capital.

The lord of the Great Isle's southern region chose to swear fealty to me.

He swore to offer up three of his own children and his son's children as hostages for a total of ten hostages from his family.

The audience to confirm the arrangements was conducted in a city I was occupying.

The Salkhoz Samuur who appeared before me was an older man, his hair streaked with gray, but well-built and still fit enough that I could easily imagine him running across the battlefield. But what was most unusual about him was the fact that he was dressed in a priest's outfit.

"From this day onward, my son will inherit the title of Count of Samuur, and I shall devote myself to God."

Salkhoz Samuur looked thoroughly exhausted.

"When I couldn't protect our king, I was disgraced. If I remain the Count of Samuur, no one will follow me."

The frustration was evident on his features. For many years, the Counts of Samuur never had to bend the knee like this to anyone. No doubt Salkhoz had balanced the need to protect his clan and his pride before coming to his decision.

Oda Nobunaga likened this to a conquest of Kyushu, meaning the entire western half of the kingdom was in my hands.

"The crime of fighting for the false king ended with the false king's life. All that's required of you is to serve the proper monarch from now on."

"The proper monarch indeed."

Salkhoz Samuur gazed at my face as though assessing my worth. I knew in an instant that he wasn't obeying out of any newfound loyalty. But neither did he hold me in contempt.

"I ask that you make certain the proper monarch doesn't change. I'd like to stop being yanked around by those in the center."

"You have nothing to worry about. Lumie I, my wife, has the legitimacy to rule the kingdom. And more than anything else—"

I slowly and firmly shook his right hand with my own.

"—she has the strength. The strength to unify the kingdom. Hasse lacks that strength. That means no matter how saintly a man Hasse might be in his personal life, as a king he's the embodiment of evil."

Salkhoz Samuur stared at my face as though in fear.

He must have found my naked ambition unnerving.

"If Hasse were, by some miracle, to win, this kingdom wouldn't be at peace. I ask that you cooperate with me to wipe Hasse off the map for the sake of peace."

"Understood. If you are going to do it, then go as far as you need to."

And with that, I placed the Great Isle Region under my—no, under Lumie I's control.

◇

We boarded Ordana Nistonia's ships and departed the Great Isle Region.

Technically speaking, we hadn't ended all the conflicts in the Great Isle Region. There were still those causing trouble, such as those who attempted to resist my rule, those who were engaged in disputes with the Count of Talmud, and members of the Samuur clan who were dissatisfied with Salkhoz's surrender.

But those were problems that the Great Isle Region could solve on its own. My destination was Yagmoory Castle.

There were several revolts happening around the castle itself. You certainly couldn't describe the situation as calm. The lords had protected those lands throughout their families' histories, and for me to come in and wrap up the show would have rubbed them the wrong way.

But they were all small brush fires.

A minor lord rising up in anger would never be able to bring down Yagmoory Castle.

And there was no one who could serve as a leader for them.

There was a royal who had been assigned to serve as Hasse's stand-in as general, but he had made no progress against the impregnable fortress. It appeared he was just conducting a long-term siege for appearances' sake because he had given up finding a way into the castle itself.

If I was going to return to the castle, I wanted to return to a clean one.

I sent Yadoriggy ahead of us to deliver a message to Yagmoory Castle.

Three days later, a force commanded by Kelara sallied from the castle and attacked Hasse's stand-in.

Kelara was a far superior general to her opponent. With the gap in skill, there was really no need for her to defend. Oda Nobunaga commented as well: "Mitsuhide was skilled in history and courtly manners, but it was because he was extremely skilled as a military commander that I made him one of my warlords." He was praising the man who had killed him.

Meanwhile, I moved to conquer the royal general's base of operations. That meant Kelara would attack from the castle and I from his rear, catching him in a pincer attack.

We completely destroyed Hasse's army. We surrounded opponents who had little in the way of morale in the first place, so they fled almost immediately. That opened a straight path to the enemy general. A member of the Red Bears took down the general.

Orcus, the captain of the Red Bears, looked a bit bored as he came to report.

"Sheesh, it's almost frightening how well things've gone."

"Yes. I'm sure it was a much easier battle than what we've dealt with until now, but rest assured, I'll properly reward you for it."

I fixed my attire before I leisurely and triumphantly entered Yagmoory Castle.

Lumie waited for me at the end of the bridge that spanned the wide moat.

I knelt in front of Lumie and kissed her hand.

"Your Majesty, I have returned safely after eliminating the traitors that were in the Great Isle Region."

"Welcome back, Sir Regent." She then chuckled. "Or should I say, 'my dear'?"

◇

I conducted the meeting to plan our future actions in front of Her Majesty.

I stood before Lumie I, queen of Therwil, who sat upon her throne, while in front of me stood our vassals.

Most of those present were military officers, while the rest were at Maust Castle, making this a rather small meeting.

"Regent Alsrod Nayvil, you have done well on our behalf. It is thanks to you that we have purged the Great Isle Region of the evil that had taken root there."

Lumie smiled serenely, but the content of her statement was rather alarming. I wouldn't have ever imagined Lumie as a regnant monarch when she first married me. With the passing years, she had grown into a true heroine.

"I am truly honored to have played a part in rebuilding the Kingdom of Therwil. To think that will be remembered as the greatest accomplishment in the Nayvil clan's history fills me with immense joy."

Lumie and I continued our rather excessive display.

We were playing at being queen and vassal as a couple. However, so long as the others were present, this was no play. It was a matter that would be recorded in the annals of the kingdom.

"The western threats have been eliminated. All that remains is to defeat my brother."

Lumie momentarily looked pained. There would be no avoiding a direct clash with Hasse.

Lumie didn't completely despise her brother. She would much rather not be in a position where she would have to kill him. That was where our respective relationships with our brothers differed. I couldn't decide which of the two of us was better off.

"Your Majesty, we must be cautious as we proceed from here. That is because we must demonstrate to the common people that we are the proper reigning government of the kingdom. Please take a look at this map."

I turned and gestured with my hand.

A map was spread out over the table behind me.

"Currently, the land that we can say for certainty is under our control makes up approximately half of the kingdom. However, I believe now that I've returned to Yagmoory Castle, more will declare their support or want to declare their support for our side."

"Indeed. The Margrave of Machaal has been making progress in putting down our enemies to the north. I believe we can safely state that she controls the North."

It seemed that Talsha, the Margrave of Machaal, had been making her mark up in the Northlands. That had allowed me to shift my forces for my conquest of the Great Isle Region.

Had Talsha been on Hasse's side, the situation would have been significantly different. I would've had to worry about defending Maust Castle and its surrounding territories.

And in that case, I wouldn't have had the breathing room necessary to build Yagmoory Castle. There was no mistaking the fact that this castle's creation had increased Hasse's paranoia.

"Very well, then, how should we proceed?" I asked my vassals. Everyone present in front of us was not only my vassal but also a vassal of Lumie, the queen.

Laviala was the first to raise her hand.

"Let us immediately send forces to Maust Castle! Maust Castle is still surrounded by enemy forces! By securing Lord Alsrod's castle residence, we can demonstrate that we have the upper hand!"

Of course that would be the first opinion offered.

I nodded. "Yes, it's unacceptable to have my castle of residence besieged by the enemy. However, this is still a place for varied opinions. Any of you can propose alternatives. Any alternative at all."

The next to raise her hand was Kelara.

"If we combined the current forces gathered here in Yagmoory Castle with those we can raise with a levy, we should be able to conquer the royal capital. There are risks, but it would allow us to force the enemy to surrender in short order. I believe Maust Castle will be able to maintain its defenses for now."

I felt that this plan was one that tried to account for Lumie's feelings.

If we surrounded the royal capital and forced Hasse to submit, the war would end without us having to directly attack the royal capital. There would be fewer victims, and the royal capital would survive mostly intact.

All that we would need to do then would be imprison Hasse himself. The Kingdom of Therwil would then be reunified.

We just needed to have Hasse formally abdicate the throne and send him off into retirement.

When I asked which the assembled group preferred, the opinions were roughly split down the middle.

Each side had a point. The ones who argued it was already possible to force Hasse to submit were right, as were the ones who noted it would send a signal to the kingdom about our power if we first relieved Maust Castle.

——The key question is, what do you think?

Oda Nobunaga inquired.

——I have nothing more to say to you on the matter. It's for you to decide. After all, I died before I could get to this point! The only

thing left is for you to choose your own path to conquest. I'll be here to witness that to the very end.

Still, I'm sure you have a plan or two of your own. You usually say what you would do under these circumstances.

——I do, but I'm not going to tell them to you. Because I was interrupted by that fool Akechi Mitsuhide, I haven't experienced this for myself. I didn't even finish conquering Chugoku or Shikoku, never mind Kyushu. I don't have the right to tell you what to do.

It's a bit unsettling when you're this modest.

——Besides, regardless of what I say, you'll just go and do what you want anyway.

Well, that's true, yes. I've crossed bridges that you considered far too dangerous to cross. I've always been brash, from the day I was born.

——That is why you should do as you wish and craft your own vision of conquest. No matter the path you walk, the one you choose will be the right one. So long as there isn't a revolt, there's no one to stop you.

Indeed, the war itself was decided the moment that the enemy failed to take Yagmoory Castle. No doubt future historians will note that the construction of this castle with its impregnable defenses was one of the turning points in history.

Do as I please, mm?

Since I've gotten the approval of a conqueror, I suppose I'll be self-centered to the end, then.

"I think both of the proposals have their merits. I can't choose between them. Therefore"—I looked around the gathered group and continued—"we're going to liberate Maust Castle, then continue straight on to the royal capital."

Evidently, because I didn't elaborate sufficiently, there were those who didn't quite grasp what I'd said. It was true that it was less a plan and more a goal.

"If we were to advance upon the royal capital from here in Yagmoory Castle, it's fastest to just head eastward on the highway. To go to Maust Castle, we'd have to change course to head northward along the way. Which is why—"

I placed my hand upon Maust Castle on the map.

"—we will issue orders in the queen's name to all the lords of the kingdom. Gather at Maust Castle. With our large numbers, the enemy will probably collapse on their own. Their morale is probably low. Then we'll turn this army toward the royal capital. If there's anyone who stands in our way along the route, we'll crush them. We should have more than enough forces to accomplish this."

Then I turned to Lumie.

"We will have you accompany this army, Your Majesty. Simultaneously, we'd like you to hold a triumph in the royal capital. The monarch of Therwil ought to be in the royal capital."

Lumie's eyes sparkled as she looked at me.

"Yes! I would be happy to travel by your side! It would be rather sad to arrive at the capital once everything was already finished."

True, I suppose I'd been neglecting my wife for a while. That was because the war had been dragging on, of course, but that was a lousy excuse for being a lousy husband.

"In addition, I would like to decide my brother's fate directly. No doubt it would make coordinating such things difficult if the queen were here in the West."

"Yes. We would need you to render your judgment upon the matter, Your Majesty."

"Then I will begin by writing letters to the various regional lords to assemble at Maust. I believe I will take the opportunity to write them in my own hand. I spent more time practicing my handwriting at the convent than I care to remember. Thanks to that, however, my calligraphy is rather lovely."

I bowed formally to Lumie.

"Thank you for your consideration."

And then I added, "We're only a step away from reuniting the entire kingdom under the banner of the crown."

Over the last hundred years or so, the kingdom had allowed the various lords to do as they wished. During this period, the so-called Hundred Years' Rebellion, the kingdom had been divided into countless petty fiefdoms.

The kingdom was now going to be reunited into one whole nation. This unusual era of wars happening without the monarch's involvement was coming to an end.

"There will be some time until we mobilize our forces. Please rest your bodies until that time in order to witness the end of an age of strife with your own eyes."

Lumie's bearing was regal, and she looked every bit the queen regnant. She was, without a lie, the queen who held the kingdom together.

All that remained was to unify the kingdom under this queen.

As she'd promised, Lumie personally wrote letters to the various regional lords until she could write no more.

Each letter went into detail about the local circumstances, guaranteeing possession of a particular territory to lords who cooperated or offering to provide the territory of a hostile lord as compensation.

This was made possible by Kelara's precise knowledge of the realm's rulers. Kelara knew which clan valued which territories as their ancestral lands.

My primary concern before the campaign was ready was Maust Castle, but as there were even defections among the enemy lords, it seemed that my concerns were overblown.

Most seemed to have grasped that the kingdom was at a turning point.

It was about a month and a half after our arrival at Yagmoory, and we'd had enough rest after our battles on the Great Isle.

I set off with my entire army to Nayvil County in Fordoneria Prefecture to the west of Maust Castle.

I wanted to travel through my clan's homeland on my journey. Furthermore, I couldn't exactly assemble my forces near Maust, given the presence of the enemy. Nayvil County just happened to be the best location.

There was basically no resistance from the enemy. There was just too big a gap in numbers. And most of the western lords of the kingdom were already on my side.

By the time we arrived, there was already a sizable army in Nayvil County.

There was my longtime ally Soltis Nistonia.

Despite the distance to Nayvil, he had made the effort to be there.

Then there was Talsha Machaal, Margrave of Machaal.

Talsha's presence was practically a declaration that the northern parts of the kingdom had thrown their support behind Lumie I as the queen regnant.

"Seems you're doing well, Sir Regent."

Talsha was carrying a baby in her arms.

"Have you recovered from giving birth? I suppose your presence already answers that."

Perhaps it was because of her occupation of Takeda Shingen, but Talsha had a healthy complexion, as though itching to get onto the battlefield.

"Well, times like these don't allow for much rest, after all. Worry not. I have no intention of retiring until our child can inherit the Machaal clan."

"I sincerely appreciate your help. I'll do everything in my power to reward your hard work when peace comes."

"Then there is something I want first."

Talsha pressed her body against me.

"I have no doubt that this child of mine will grow up strong, but one never knows when a child may die. I want more seed—yours, if possible."

I was impressed with her candor. Rulers had no use for shyness. Having heirs was part of the job, after all.

"All right… I plan to stay in these lands today… I'll make time…"

"I'll squeeze every last drop out of you."

Talsha's eyes were serious.

With Maust's liberation in sight, I'd been trapped by quite the opponent…

The forces loyal to Lumie I assembled in Nayvil County and its surroundings numbered nearly sixty thousand.

Fifteen thousand had been assembled by Talsha from the North. Talsha's contribution was crucial, so it was contingent on me to do what I could for her.

I stopped at my clan's ancestral graveyard before we departed.

There I swore I'd do my utmost in fighting for Lumie I.

It was, of course, theater of a sort, but better to be safe than sorry. The history of a country's founding is told before the country's actual founding, after all.

I divided my army into three and advanced toward Maust Castle.

◇

Hasse's army had built simple fortifications around Maust Castle and taken to watching its defenders.

It's a standard tactic for laying siege to a castle. For a long siege, occupying temporary fortifications protected by a web of trenches and earthworks that can withstand sallies from the enemy is the right choice.

But that's true only when time is on your side—for example, when the besieged forces suffer from food shortages or the like.

Just surrounding a castle doesn't end anything in and of itself. To actually conquer the castle requires attacking and accepting the possibility of losses.

Hasse's army had barely done any of that, partly because Maust Castle's defenders had bravely fought them off. But despite the long siege, I hadn't received much in the way of battle reports.

Meaning there hadn't been much in the way of direct combat.

The lords mustered by Hasse had effectively been independent during the Hundred Years' Rebellion. None of them were inclined to lose their own troops by following a weak king's orders. They would still send out their forces when summoned, but those forces weren't going to commit heavily to the fighting. They weren't nearly as dangerous as their numbers suggested.

On the other hand, Maust Castle's defenders were fighting for their lives and resisted tooth and nail.

The difference in morale was crystal clear.

I prepared to go after the Hasse faction's fortifications from three directions, splitting the army into three divisions: one commanded by me, one commanded by Soltis Nistonia, and one commanded by Talsha Machaal.

Near me were all the units of my personal guard, and even closer by was Laviala, while Kelara was behind me.

"It's been a while since we've been back here, Lord Alsrod!"

"You seem excited, Laviala."

"The long journey was tiring. But I know this entire terrain by heart. It doesn't take you to know where to attack from."

That was true. The Hasse faction army were outsiders. We had the advantage.

"The fortification to the south of the castle is the greatest concentration of their forces. If you defeat them, the enemy force will likely scatter," Kelara said calmly.

"Of course. That's the plan."

"We already have some defectors. I've proceeded to make the necessary arrangements."

Kelara always had this sort of thing figured out.

I intended to use everything we'd acquired to this point.

After all, there would be no way to use it once the world was at peace.

The fort, located on a small hill, started billowing smoke.

It seemed one of our collaborators had set fire to it.

"I'm sure there's a fair number of lords around as well," I said. "Go claim yourself a general's head! Show them the strength of the regent's army!"

The vanguard of my army charged toward the enemy, instantly inciting a melee. Despite the fact that they were the defenders, Hasse's forces were immediately pushed back.

Then there was additional movement.

Maust Castle's garrison suddenly sallied forth. The soldiers defending the castle had switched to the offensive. It was the exact same tactic we'd used at Yagmoory Castle.

"Good. Now do your worst!"

The enemy soldiers who had been assigned to watch the castle were quickly massacred.

It was an overwhelming display of force. It made me think there was something more fundamentally different between my soldiers and Hasse's than just simple matters like skill.

History was on my side.

For some reason, I was certain of that.

Orcus of the Red Bears and Leon of the White Eagles approached, carrying the heads of enemy generals. More heads followed suit.

The enemy couldn't escape and had been annihilated. It seemed like the enemy had stayed there simply to be destroyed. It almost felt like they had been placed there to be crushed by my forces.

"I'm glad we made sure our goal wasn't just liberating Maust Castle, but taking the capital as well. Liberating the castle barely got you lot warmed up," I told Orcus and Leon.

It was an almost frighteningly overwhelming victory. Soltis Nistonia and Talsha Machaal's forces also easily routed their opponents. The most the enemy could do was try to flee toward the royal capital.

Just as the wind blows sawgrass in a single direction, I doubted anything would stop our momentum now.

The liberation of Maust Castle was accomplished with ease, and Lumie I's influence extended to the vast majority of the kingdom's territory.

The royal capital, given its location, was no longer the center of anything. It was, at most, a frontline base for Hasse's forces.

At this point, the battle between the two competing claimants to the throne had been decided.

——So this is how it turns out. Had I only lived another year or two, I could have seen the same thing myself.

* * *

Oda Nobunaga sounded intensely moved.

——See what I told you? I have no further advice to give. You've already won. There's no one who can defeat you now.

I fully understand what you want to say, but I'm not ready to let up my guard just yet. They could still catch me in my sleep, after all.

I doubt you could count the number of people who've fallen victim to sneak attacks over the past hundred years.

——Even if Akechi Mitsuhide is here, there won't be any betrayals.

Kelara had distinguished herself during this war.

Speaking of Kelara, I should ask her about the proper ceremony and forms to be observed when we entered the royal capital.

But for now, it was time to enter Maust Castle.

I still had to show my appreciation to my consorts and generals for holding out in the confines of the castle for so long.

My consorts Seraphina, Fleur, and Yuca all welcomed me as I crossed the bridge over the moat and entered the castle proper.

"What took you so long? If we'd starved to death, I would have haunted you for the rest of your days," Seraphina said with a laugh. But I caught a glimpse of tears in her eyes.

I doubted she'd felt any sadness during the siege. And I doubted she was overwhelmed with emotion at our reunion.

This was Seraphina, after all. She probably believed that history was changing before our eyes.

"If you came to me even after you died, I'd be a happy man."

I firmly embraced Seraphina.

The cheers from the soldiers added to the mood.

"All that's left is to take down the royal capital," she told me.

"That'll be over quickly. If anything, the work awaiting us afterward will be the difficult part."

◇

After we restored peace to Maust Castle by sweeping away Hasse's forces, Lumie issued a royal decree as queen of Therwil, ordering the defeat of the traitors to the crown.

Lumie now sat in the chair where I had sat as the castle's master. It served as a temporary throne.

"Thanks to your efforts, peace has been restored to over half of the kingdom. First, allow me to offer my sincere gratitude."

All of the crown's vassals, myself included, knelt in front of Lumie I.

No one here doubted Lumie's claim to the throne.

The fact that the royal line had been divided in two and the two sides had been fighting over the royal capital had worked out in our favor. If there had been greater stability in succession, no one would have taken the king's sister seriously when she declared herself the new queen regnant.

However, the crown had historically been worn by the one person capable of conquering the royal capital through military force. That was why it seemed perfectly natural to the kingdom at large for Lumie to act as sovereign and call for the defeat and ouster of Hasse.

"As queen, I shall issue my latest command. You are to defeat the pretender to the throne and his allies occupying the royal capital and restore our kingdom to its rightful form."

"I, Alsrod Nayvil, regent of the kingdom and representing your vassals, answer in their stead. We humbly accept your orders, and swear to pledge our sacred honor and lives to unify the kingdom!"

"Regent Alsrod Nayvil, rise."

At Lumie's words, I slowly stood to face her.

"I hereby appoint you supreme military commander for the purposes of securing the royal capital. Accept this sacred sword that was kept in the crown's temple as the symbol of your office."

I respectfully bowed and accepted the blade.

It was odd, if you thought about it. When I first made Hasse king, I hadn't considered marrying a royal at all. I had thought taking a wife from a family I intended to wipe out would eventually create resentment.

Hasse, too, surely made me marry Lumie to keep me in line and tie my fate to his.

Yet somehow, Lumie had become my greatest asset in creating a new kingdom.

"I have subjugated the royal capital once before," I replied. "It will be of no consequence. I've already made the necessary preparations."

"We look forward to your success. It is time to end the age of bloodshed."

It was ironic—the more blood I shed on the battlefield, the greater the territory under my control and the more peaceful the lands became.

I turned my back to Lumie and faced the vassals.

"All who can swear to obey me and fight to the last for Her Majesty's sake, stand. Those who stand will be forever remembered in history."

Of course no one remained sitting.

The lords who had gathered from the various regions stood up one by one.

They were all dressed differently. Some wore armor because it was a time of war, others the refined clothing of nobles, and yet others, because they were in the royal presence, the ceremonial garb of their rank.

Among the crowd were those who had been with me practically since birth, like Laviala; those like Meissel Wouge who had joined me as I expanded my influence; those who had come from the far-off Great Isle with a hundred soldiers in tow; and northern lords sworn to Talsha, who were dressed in their customary furs.

It was a complete hodgepodge of styles, but there were more than enough to take the capital.

"Lord Alsrod—no, Sir Regent. Have you a plan for this campaign?" Laviala asked me.

"It will be simple enough to capture the royal capital. But allowing the royal capital to be caught in the crossfire between armies is an unforgivable act unworthy of the crown of the Kingdom of Therwil. If fighting were to break out in the city itself, we would lose the ability to bring it under our control."

I continued, "Which is why we will slowly cordon off the royal capital from the outside, tightening our cordon as we proceed to make them give up their resistance. If they recognize that they have nowhere to flee, Hasse will undoubtedly realize he has no choice but to submit."

"What is the specific plan?"

I couldn't help but smile.

It would be an enormous encirclement the likes of which had never been seen in history.

"First, we will pass by the royal capital and take down the only region supporting Hasse's claim to the throne, the eastern prefectures. At that point, Hasse's authority will cease to exist outside of the royal capital."

Those assembled began to murmur as they digested my words.

Quite a few faces seemed surprised. Well, of course, what were they expecting? I guess they must have been expecting that we'd directly charge into the city, just without the typical sacking and looting.

"Lord Alsrod—Sir Regent. Wouldn't that take time?"

"It will. However, even if we advance from the West and take the royal capital, it's likely that Hasse the Pretender will simply flee east. It would be quite the chore if he were to escape into the mountains and continue his resistance. Which is why we'll make it impossible for him to flee. And—"

In truth, this was closer to my true motivation.

"—it's much tidier and prettier as a story to end the unification of the kingdom at the royal capital, wouldn't you agree?"

◇

I led the effort to organize our order of battle into a set of coherent units. Given that I had been granted supreme command, I was simply doing my job.

As the days progressed, more and more lords declared their intention to submit to our authority.

We were able to mobilize an army well over a hundred thousand strong. There was no way to gather that many into a single location, and doing so would be inefficient, so we chose to close in on the royal capital from multiple routes.

The actual war planning was conducted in a small council of war limited to my top advisers and great lords such as Talsha.

During that meeting, I decided to use a particular place as the center of my campaign.

"While this is technically a cathedral, it's also a proper fortress. It would make a great center for our operations."

My first objective was Orsent Cathedral, home to my sworn enemy, the Archbishop Cammit.

"Um...do you really think that man will peacefully obey us...?" Laviala asked worriedly, but that was understandable. Of all my enemies, he was the one who had caused me the greatest amount of trouble.

"All the more reason—even he knows he has no feasible way of resisting me."

That man was too smart to try to resist me.

I had imagined a scenario in which Hasse would surrender before we set out, but that didn't end up happening.

I didn't know if he still thought he could win or if he simply didn't know when to quit, but I was glad that it wasn't going to end in an anticlimactic fashion.

I set off from Fortwest Prefecture toward Orsent Cathedral with my army.

There were no forces to fight us along the way. Even if Hasse's forces intended to subdue us, they were probably planning to engage us somewhere near the royal capital. Rather than hole up in some fort on the front lines and try to bleed us, they would probably much rather fall back and wait for a chance to fight us on the field.

Archbishop Cammit and I were reunited for the first time in ages in a city a little over an hour away from Orsent Cathedral. We dismissed our retainers and chose to have a one-on-one summit.

"We intend to cooperate with the wishes of Her Majesty, Lumie I."

Archbishop Cammit looked far older than when I'd last seen him. In fairness, it had been over five years since we'd last clashed blades. It could simply be that I still looked much younger than I ought to thanks to my profession.

"There's no one else listening. You don't need to pretend to be humble and welcoming. You can say whatever you want to me, and honestly, that would make things run a bit more smoothly."

"The fact that I couldn't defeat you in our past battles is my greatest failure," the archbishop said in resignation. "After that, there was no one left who could restrain you. Had I known it would turn out this way, I would have stayed put and joined in the alliance of Ayles Caltis and Brando Naaham."

——That ended up happening to me. If not for Honganji, I would have unified the country far earlier.

Oda Nobunaga evidently had some lingering resentments. He's less anti-religion than he is anti-Honganji.

"It's not your fault. It just so happened that I was stronger than the typical lord who came into the capital. Based on history, you were well justified in thinking you had enough to defeat me. What are your demands?"

The archbishop shook his head, as though exasperated.

"We have no choice but to follow your new regime. If you were to declare that you were going to burn down the cathedral, I would resist with all my might, but if you were that foolish, you would have died a long time ago."

"Very well. I'll do what I can to make sure you don't come out of this too badly. You have my word."

I offered my hand to the archbishop.

"I would have never imagined shaking your hand like this..."

The archbishop's hand was covered in wrinkles and oddly yellow.

"Are you ill?"

"Well, I'll survive long enough to watch the kingdom be united. Worry not."

Perhaps it was time for the Great Men of the Old Era to quietly exit stage left.

◇

After making Orsent Cathedral our rearward base, my army then skipped past the royal capital and invaded the East.

Those who planned to resist had stayed in the region anticipating our attack, but they stood no chance against us.

Because this region had been limited to, at most, small skirmishes between lords, the castles and forts weren't designed to be as defensible as in other regions. The enemy might have reinforced these fortifications, but they were still weak enough that we could simply open them through brute force.

The pacification of the eastern prefectures took only a month and a half.

All that remained was the royal capital.

The forces under my command slowly began to tighten the net around it.

I strengthened the patrols watching the highways. There was the possibility that Hasse would attempt to escape. Hasse's survival wasn't a great concern, but we needed to witness the moment he completely lost all pretense of being king.

Leaving a relic of the old era like Hasse to linger on in our new era would be a stain upon Lumie I's new order. Besides, if Hasse managed to remain hidden somewhere, the war itself wouldn't end.

Oda Nobunaga agreed with this. Royals were a convenient tool for those who planned to revolt. Akechi Mitsuhide, the man who had slain Oda Nobunaga, had apparently intended to restore the deposed shogun's title.

Even if Hasse himself was incompetent, his value as a tool remained unchanged. Which was why we needed to make sure he was neutralized as a threat.

I could slowly see the end approaching.

That night, I spent a quiet evening with Seraphina.

After the liberation of Maust Castle, I had been too busy to find time to spend with her alone.

"You're rather modestly dressed for a man who's about to become king."

Seraphina smiled teasingly after she looked appraisingly over my outfit. Her attitude hadn't changed much since she first married me.

"We're still at war. The fancy, ostentatious garb can wait for later. At least the wine I've prepared is nice."

I poured wine into Seraphina's glass, then into mine.

"You're sure it isn't poisoned?" she asked.

"I've already had a tester drink it."

"My dream will soon come true..."

Seraphina's face was reflected in her wine. She seemed to be gazing intently at her own reflection.

She was smiling, but it was an expression that included a complicated set of emotions.

"I've put you through a lot over the years, Seraphina."

I had wiped out the Caltis clan for defying me, thereby robbing Seraphina of a place to return home to.

"There can only be one man left standing at the end. It just happens that my clan wasn't chosen to be that last one standing."

Despite her words, Seraphina's eyes were moist with tears.

"Father really did senselessly throw everything away with a stupid blunder at the end. At the very, very end, he sacrificed everything, not just himself, and for nothing. What a foolish man..."

She then looked off into distance and said, "But your daughter has now ended up the consort of a king. I think I can at least build a small shrine to you, Father."

"Yes, once the kingdom is at peace, build as many monuments as you want to him."

Seraphina stood up from her chair and sat back down on my lap.

I gently stroked her hair, but stayed still otherwise.

"Seraphina, you and I are still young. Our lives from here on out are probably going to be longer than the years we've lived so far. So let's be sure to be even happier over the next few decades."

Seraphina tightly clasped my hand and squeezed.

"Yes. That's a promise."

◇

We slowly, slowly closed the net around the royal capital as though we were strangling the city with a silken rope.

The goal was to create just enough of a food shortage within the royal capital. It would eat away at morale, and more than anything, if it became clear that he wasn't able to protect or feed the royal capital's people, it would make Hasse's position all the weaker.

A monarch's primary duty was to protect their people. Even in an age when the kingdom was split into countless mini-kingdoms, the fact that Hasse couldn't save the people of the royal capital was more than enough to show he was unfit to be king.

With that said, it would be a reputational nightmare if we had a mass starvation on our hands. Which was why we were allowing ordinary citizens to leave the city. We did maintain a strict watch on the refugees to make sure that Hasse and his allies didn't escape.

I had sent multiple ultimatums in Lumie's name demanding Hasse's surrender. The eastern lords whom Hasse had pinned his hopes on had all surrendered or been eliminated. There was no faction left that supported Hasse. The tiny forces around him couldn't change the outcome.

We then finally built forward castles near the palace and began observing the enemy.

Lumie sent in a final ultimatum, noting that she would have no choice but to resort to an all-out assault if he didn't end his resistance.

Whether we ended up doing it or not, it was still a threat.

Still, Hasse maintained his silence. It was less that he was stubborn and more that he didn't want to face reality. His dream of being considered the king who had revived the Kingdom of Therwil was about to end in the worst way imaginable.

But in contrast to Hasse, who remained silent, those involved with the crown were fleeing the royal capital.

I couldn't imagine making use of them once we'd taken control, but killing them would be counterproductive, so we let them live.

Then, on the fifth day of our complete encirclement of the city, a single bureaucrat from the royal capital came seeking an audience.

It was the dragonewt Yanhaan.

I took advantage of the opportunity and met with Yanhaan in a hastily prepared tea room.

"How long has it been since we last met like this?" Yanhaan asked with her usual leisurely attitude, which made one almost believe everything was normal at the royal capital and nothing had changed.

"I noticed you'd stayed in the royal capital. I suppose technically you're not a vassal of the regent, but a servant of the crown..."

Most of the bureaucrats who had a strong relationship with me had left the city. Some had left the moment Hasse had declared me a traitor.

That was perfectly understandable. Had they stayed, they could have been accused of being spies, and even without that possibility, they could have been at risk in other ways.

"I can't conduct my business if I'm not in the royal capital. Besides..." Yanhaan smiled, though she hid her smile behind her hand. "Besides, I am here today to negotiate the terms of surrender. I am here as Hasse's envoy."

"I see. Seems Hasse is smart enough to at least take that step."

I caught glimpses of Hasse's desperate desire to end things peacefully behind Yanhaan's serene expression.

"Everything I am about to say is Hasse's words, so don't blame me for bringing them to you."

Given that preamble, I guessed that Hasse hadn't let go of his delusions even at this late stage.

"He'll forgive my rebellion, so he wants me to withdraw my forces, mm? Seems he believes himself to be king and can't be convinced otherwise."

"Well, it is the basics of negotiation to start at the furthest extreeemes. So what do you intend to do?"

"Please inform him that Her Majesty is fully considering killing the previous king if he continues his illegal occupation of the royal capital. We could easily send in assassins, after all."

Yanhaan continued to smile serenely, not even so much as batting an eye.

"Understood. I will tell him those exact words as a messenger. However, I believe Hasse simply wishes to secure his personal safety. If you can make that clear, I believe things will progress rather more quickly."

Before I could reply, Yanhaan pressed herself closer to me.

"I have a scheme of my own."

It wasn't a bad scheme at all. I was glad Yanhaan had come out here. She had given me something Hasse's courtiers never could have.

"Very well, let's go with that. I'll inform Her Majesty."

"Yes. Thank you for your help."

◇

The next day, a messenger appeared from Hasse's camp acknowledging their surrender. It was a young man who had been promoted because he had been one of Hasse's favorites.

Hasse was going to formally abdicate the throne to Lumie I, and then he would live quietly in retirement at an estate provided to him as a former king—those were the terms of his surrender.

Simultaneously, Hasse would formally conduct an abdication ceremony in which he formally handed the crown to Lumie. With that, the civil war would have peacefully drawn to a close.

Because it would unify the country, Lumie had no reason to turn it down.

The Hundred Years' Rebellion was about to end. It was the dawn of a new age.

* * *

In the days leading up to the abdication ceremony, Lumie and I purified our bodies. This wasn't part of any particular tradition, just something that Lumie had proposed.

Her ascension to the throne would be completely different from that of those who had come before. Lumie said that she wanted to approach it with an appropriate amount of responsibility and commitment.

"I'm sorry for making you go through this with me. Are you sure you're not cold?" Lumie asked, draped in a white cloth. I donned an identical cloth.

"This sort of hardship is nothing compared to the bitterness I had to deal with when I was a child."

I wanted to embrace the shivering Lumie, but I felt that would defeat the purpose of our purification ritual, and so I kept my hands to myself.

◇

Early that morning, the southern gate of the royal capital was opened slowly from the inside. The sun shone onto the moat, and the water of the moat glittered from the sun's rays.

As we, Lumie I's Royal Army, lined up in front of the gate, we could see the central gate of the royal capital before us.

We were about to proceed inside those gates.

Inside the gates, the soldiers who had followed Hasse were bowing—no, they were hanging their heads.

While their equipment wasn't particularly dirty given the lack of actual fighting, they appeared worn down and defeated.

We, the Royal Army, on the other hand, marched proudly into the city. This, too, was part of our job. We bore the authority of the queen upon our shoulders. It behooved us to behave in a manner worthy of that authority.

My armor was festooned with both the Nayvil clan crest and the crest of the royal family. I had returned to the royal capital not as the lord of the Nayvil clan, but as Lumie I's husband and as regent of the Kingdom of Therwil.

Immediately next to me was Lumie. Even though she wasn't a military officer, she wore a stern expression on her face as queen. Of course, the expression alone wasn't enough to completely hide her natural gentleness. Lumie was playing her role as monarch to perfection.

"Not to worry. Even if there are those who might take aim with bow and arrow, the rappas have already dealt with them," I whispered softly to Lumie. I could see that she was tense.

"Such a thing hadn't crossed my mind." Lumie managed a thin smile. "I felt the weight of what it means to carry a kingdom upon one's shoulders and was simply steeling myself to that responsibility."

"Lumie, how many of your line have been monarchs of this kingdom?"

"I will be the twenty-fifth. The kingdom was established three hundred and twenty-eight years ago. However, in the last hundred years, the reign of each king became dramatically shorter."

Yes, since the Hundred Years' Rebellion had started.

To think that something that had lasted that long would change today. Even I began feeling a little nervous.

As we passed by Hasse's soldiers, the citizens who had come to watch our procession lined the streets.

There were those who were cheerfully and thoughtlessly crying, "Long live Queen Lumie!" and "Long live the regent!" while there were others who watched nervously because they couldn't read how the future would play out.

If Hasse were to remain in control of the royal capital, words praising Lumie I were dangerous to say. A wise person would keep their mouth shut for the time being.

That, and the people of the capital seemed to instinctively realize that something big was about to happen.

There had been changes in kings before now, but the atmosphere was completely different this time.

After all, there were no forces that could resist the new queen.

The division in the kingdom was about to end with the complete surrender of the previous king.

Eventually, we arrived at the royal capital's largest intersection.

We were joined here by soldiers who had come in through other entrances—specifically, the western and eastern gates.

The western gate was represented by Talsha Machaal, while the eastern gate was represented by Soltis Nistonia. Talsha's child was of my seed, while Soltis's daughter Yuca was one of my concubines, so one could say I'd set things up to be dominated by my in-laws.

Soltis had tried to turn down the role, stating that he wasn't a lord worthy enough of that honor, but I had him accept at my insistence on the importance of the occasion. Given that he had the title of count, this shouldn't be a problem.

The three rows of soldiers that came together in the center then crossed the bridge that led to the royal palace's central gate.

It was at that moment that the bloodless surrender of the royal palace was accomplished.

To have acquired the royal palace without killing a single soul was an achievement to be celebrated.

We set out to reach the throne room, where we would be conducting an audience.

With that said, Hasse had already abdicated the throne. I had forced him to accept that condition. Hasse was no longer king, merely the person in possession of the crown.

Hasse looked like he had shrunk since the last time I saw him. He wasn't old enough to be ill, so it was probably stress from recent events. I also saw streaks of gray in his hair. In his unsteady hands was the crown. The fact that he was holding it made the crown look oddly cheap and insubstantial.

Standing behind Hasse were the last of his "loyal vassals."

Some were glaring at Lumie or me. I admit I didn't feel anything from their stares. I had known that living as I did would buy plenty of resentment. I'd been hated enough in my life that I could be reborn ten times and still have lifetimes of animosity to spare.

Mixed in among the loyal vassals and courtiers were some bureaucrats like Yanhaan with close ties to me. They, too, looked solemn, but it was easy enough to tell the difference between them and Hasse's underlings.

The main star of this occasion wasn't me, but Lumie, the queen.

However, I was still supposed to serve in an introductory role. I immediately stepped in front of Lumie.

"I ask that you now return the royal crown to Her Majesty," I said to Hasse with a cold expression. I had no reason to show any further emotion.

"Brother, were you the one who planned to install my sister as queen?" Hasse asked dejectedly.

"You were the one who declared me a traitor. You're no doubt aware that my wife, Her Majesty, was furious with your accusation."

This wasn't the place to throw my emotions at him. All of that had already ended.

But Hasse didn't even understand that.

"Please, hand the royal crown to Her Majesty."

I shifted a step to the right. Lumie and Hasse's eyes met.

Lumie then held out her hands in front of her.

"Please, hand me the symbol of the office of the monarch."

Hasse briefly gazed up at the heavens, but then he slowly began walking forward.

His shoes clacked against the stone floor, each step ringing sharply.

Then, when he approached within three jargs or so of Lumie...

"Halt, former king!"

...one of the retainers leaped forward—

—and shoved Hasse to the floor.

The room buzzed as a murmur rippled through the crowd.

Before any of Hasse's loyal vassals could say a word, the retainer who had shoved him spoke up.

"O former king, with what intent did you hide this dagger?"

An unsheathed dagger peeked out from under Hasse's formal attire.

Lumie couldn't help but cover her mouth with her hand. It was as though she was too shocked to speak.

The Lumie faction soldiers who had been by my flank immediately stepped forward to restrain Hasse. They also confiscated his dagger.

"Wait! This isn't my dagger! I truly don't know what it was doing here! I'm innocent!" Hasse shouted.

Well, of course.

His words were, in fact, the unvarnished truth.

I had planted the dagger on him. I'd already paid off Hasse's people. Or, more accurately, there had been plenty of my people left in the royal capital.

I had decided upon the plan when Yanhaan was sent to negotiate with me.

Hasse had appeared to believe that my lover Yanhaan would help broker a peaceful end to the standoff, but the opposite was true.

I was able to end things in a way convenient for me.

I had worried that some would attack us at the sudden revelation, but no one did such a thing. There were no warriors in this room loyal to Hasse.

No matter how many bureaucrats supported him, I could slaughter all of them by myself.

I stepped in front of the restrained Hasse and stared down at his half-crouched form.

"What a crushing disappointment this is," I said. "Just when everything was about to end peacefully, you were planning to murder your own sister to satisfy your own petty hatred?"

"No, no, no! I don't know anything about—"

I drowned out Hasse's denials with my voice.

"Why do you think Her Majesty, Lumie I, pushed back the attack upon the royal capital for so long? That was because she wanted to reduce the possibility of harming you, her brother. It was possible for us to attack the royal capital directly from Maust Castle and kill you in the process. Yet, she ordered us not to do so."

I continued my long condemnation of the man, all the while looking down at Hasse in utter contempt.

I could do this only because I truly felt that Hasse was worthy of that disdain.

"You are a sinner."

I slowly picked up the royal crown that lay on the floor.

"For now, we will imprison you. The price for your treachery will be extracted later. Take him away."

The soldiers restraining Hasse then forced him to his feet and led him out.

The room remained abuzz, but no one had the nerve to object.

"It's become quite the situation, Your Majesty. What shall we do about the ceremony?" I asked Lumie.

We had already discussed how she'd answer.

"While I am indeed shocked, I would like to continue the ceremony for the sake of rebuilding our kingdom. Regent, as the next-highest-ranking man in this room, you will serve in the former king's stead."

"As you command, Your Majesty."

I then gazed fixedly at the crown for the first time. It still had all its gold and silver detailing, since it had been preserved solely for use in ceremonial functions.

So this was what I had spent so long fighting for. That said, this crown symbolized the king of Therwil, so I supposed it might not be the exact same thing as what I'd been striving for.

When I formed a kingdom of my own, I'd have to create new traditions.

I lifted the crown with both hands and placed it upon Lumie's slightly bowed head.

At that moment, Lumie formally became the queen regnant of the Kingdom of Therwil.

"Congratulations, Your Majesty."

It was supposed to be an act, but I found myself on the verge of tears.

I had finally unified this kingdom—I, the second son of a backwater noble.

——You, above all, have earned those congratulations.

I heard a voice commending me in my head.

——You've finally done it. You've arrived here sooner than I would have expected. That's all due to my help.

Yes—I have no intention of denying that.

Without Oda Nobunaga, I would have died protecting my fortress.

I would have perished without even leaving my name to posterity.

In a sense, I had died that day at Fort Nagraad.

From that day on was my second life. And in that second life, I had accomplished all this.

"Thank you for everything, my dearest."

Lumie had tears in her eyes. Because she was so overcome with emotion, she slipped up and addressed me as "dearest" in public.

I was sure she was conflicted because she had ended up dooming her brother in this way. But despite that, Lumie had chosen to participate in this plan.

In all honesty, I wanted to embrace Lumie right then and there.

I thought that would convey so much more than even a million words ever could.

But that wasn't an option. We weren't here as husband and wife.

"There are still many things we must do, Your Majesty. I look forward to our contributions together."

"Yes. No doubt I will cause you some distress, Sir Regent, but I nonetheless ask that you please continue to support me."

That day, for the first time in a hundred years, the conflicts and wars in the kingdom stopped.

No matter what happens, I don't think I'll ever forget that day.

The only thing that was left for me now was to formally become king myself.

Nonetheless, I thought I should wait a while for that.

I'd already conquered the kingdom. From Oda Nobunaga's point of view, I was already the conqueror of the land.

Under the reign of Lumie I, I eliminated any threats over a period of two years.

I took my time in doing so, but it was more routine work than anything else. After all, there wasn't anyone left in the kingdom who could challenge me.

Of course, that didn't mean it wasn't a busy time. There were plenty of decisions I had to make.

"This isn't something to take lightly," Kelara clearly insisted.

Laviala immediately stood up and shot back, "No! We should move it to Maust! After all, Lord Alsrod's residence is not the royal capital but Maust! We should make Maust the royal capital and this the subcapital!"

The debate continued about where to place the new royal capital.

"Lady Laviala, moving the capital would cause chaos," said Kelara. "Creating new enemies is not a prudent idea."

"All of the regional lords have sworn their fealty to Lord Alsrod and Queen Lumie. It won't make much difference where we put the capital. Many of the merchants have already moved to Maust anyway!"

They both had a point. Lumie and I were sitting side by side and chuckling as we watched the proceedings.

"What do you think, Your Majesty?" I asked.

"Well...," Lumie began. "Seraphina, what do you think?"

"I believe either is fine. More importantly, I feel the regent should be treated as the coruler and become king," Seraphina offered with a teasing mien.

"Seraphina, let's discuss that another time," I said.

"I don't have any opinions about the capital," Seraphina added. "My dream is to be the wife of a king. Fulfilling that dream is what matters most to me."

She was nothing if not consistent.

"Then next—Fleur, what do you think we should do about the capital?"

As my official wife, Lumie asked each of my concubines her opinion in turn.

Fleur bowed before standing. She had softened compared to her formerly combative self, but she still held her own in matters concerning politics. She didn't seem like a regent's wife.

"The current capital will not be able to handle any additional city planning. We need more space. We should move the capital to Maust."

Laviala looked vindicated at the words.

"Next—Yanhaan, what is your opinion as a merchant?"

"Merchants will naturally move to where the profit is. With that in mind, there are many people hoping for a new market in Maust, while there are those who are prepared to put down roots in the current capital. Go on and do as you please."

After finishing her statement, Yanhaan sat down and helped herself to the tea that had been brewed for everyone. A rather relaxed attitude, considering she was in the royal presence.

"Thank you. Margrave Talsha Machaal, what are your thoughts?"

"Maust is closer to my territories. The people of the Northlands will welcome a shift in the capital."

She hardly showed the proper respect due to Lumie, the queen, but we'd invited her knowing that was likely to be the case.

With that, sentiment seemed to shift toward moving the capital.

"And Yuca, your thoughts?"

Yuca glanced around at the others, then rather meekly answered, "I'll support the majority, who prefer Maust..."

In a way, that was a wise choice.

"Thank you for your opinions, everyone," I said. "I'd like Her Majesty to make the final decision, however."

I glanced briefly toward Lumie.

Lumie returned the glance, then smiled, turning to the table in front of her.

"I would like to settle upon moving the capital to Maust. The former royal capital will then be called South Capital."

The profession within me once again said something that made no sense.

——South Capital, mm? I suppose that makes it akin to Nara, which was also near the capital.

If there was precedent in Oda Nobunaga's world, I supposed it was fine to change the capital.

After enough time for people to settle in after the capital was moved to Maust—

Surrounded by our retainers, Lumie appointed me coruler.

In other words, I finally became king. The king of Therwil, to be precise.

"From now on, I ask for your support not simply as my husband, but as a fellow royal."

Lumie then placed her crown upon my head.

"As you wish. I will protect you until the day I die," I swore as I kissed her hand.

The following year, as she prepared to have our second child, Lumie abdicated the throne and left me as the sole monarch.

No doubt later historians would debate whether that day or the day Lumie made me coruler was the founding date of the new dynasty.

It didn't matter either way.

The fact was that I became king.

© Kaito Shibano

* * *

A few days after my coronation, I visited Seraphina's room at night.

Laviala and Altia were already there.

"Good evening, Your Majesty," Altia greeted me jokingly.

"Quit it, will you? I come here to get away from all that."

"But there's no point in becoming a king if you're not going to act like one," Seraphina joked as she prepared tea for her guests.

"Lord Alsrod, you've finally done it. I'm so extremely happy!"

Laviala embraced me without regard to who was watching, so I gently patted her head. But I couldn't help but think she was embracing me as an older sister at that moment.

"Still, there's still an important thing to consider," Seraphina said as she poured tea into each cup in turn.

"What are you talking about?"

"If Lumie's next child is a boy and inherits the throne, then this dynasty might just end up being treated like a continuation of the old one."

Ah, the next king.

True, the name of the dynasty might change if the next king was my eldest son, from Seraphina, rather than a son from Lumie. If there ended up being a succession war, that'd be a serious problem.

I couldn't help but laugh.

"Just what do you find so funny?" Seraphina demanded.

"Well, I'm just glad I'll have plenty of work to keep me from getting bored."

A peaceful kingdom was best, but a boring one was a problem. No doubt my kind wasn't suited for a peaceful age.

"In any case, I'd also like to build a new temple."

"Brother, you're taking this far too lightly," Altia chided me.

You know, the entire reason you've maintained your youth is thanks to the man who's going to be worshipped in that temple.

"I'm going to build a temple to the god Oda Nobunaga, who has served as my profession. It'll be somewhat odd looking, but I do have a blueprint."

That's because he won't shut up about making it look like Azuchi Castle.

Lumie safely gave birth to our second child around the time construction on the Temple of Oda Nobunaga started. The child was a boy.

It looked like there might be some complications about succession, but that was just fine. I would tackle that problem head-on. After all, Alsrod I of Therwil's Nayvil Dynasty needs conflict to thrive.

END

Afterword

Long time no see! It's Kisetsu Morita.

A Mysterious Job Called Oda Nobunaga has reached its conclusion with the unification of the kingdom.

The novels are now at an end, but it appears the series will soon appear in a new format.

That is, the comic adaptation is beginning soon!

It'll be serialized in Gangan GA, the same magazine that carries the comic adaptation of my other novel series, *I've Been Killing Slimes for 300 Years and Maxed Out My Level.*

The comic version of *Oda Nobunaga* will be drawn by Riku Nishi.

I've already seen the rough drafts of the first and second chapters. Alsrod looks very cool, and Laviala is so adorable. I hope you'll cheer them on as they move toward unifying the country.

With the start of the comic adaptation, there was some talk of continuing the novels, but since the series was clearly a tale of Alsrod unifying the kingdom, I felt any additional material would be unnecessary filler and thus decided to end the main saga here.

It would be odd to keep writing on and on about the political history of Alsrod's new country…

Personally, I read a lot of books related to political history, so I wouldn't mind writing about the intrigues and internal conflicts that occur at the beginning of a new dynasty. Lately I've been reading about the political authority of the Ashikaga shoguns during the Warring States period.

But by that point, this story would clearly stop being a war saga and turn into a tale of messy palace intrigues...so I'll close things here with Alsrod creating his new kingdom.

I'd like to end with some acknowledgments. First, thank you to Kaito Shibano for the beautiful illustrations and character drawings from beginning to end.

In doing a war epic, I've ended up crafting an actual harem this time around, but the accompanying illustrations have really been a feast for the eyes!

And finally, thank you so much to all the readers who've kept up with this series down to the last volume!

I hope you'll enjoy the comic adaptation starting up in Gangan GA!

Respectfully yours,

Kisetsu Morita